CLEAVE

Nikki Gemmell was born in Wollongong, Australia, and now lives in London. She has worked as an actress and a journalist. Her first novel, *Shiver*, an Australian bestseller, was published in 1997.

Other books by the author

SHIVER

Nikki Gemmell

CLEAVE

PICADOR

First published 1998 by Random House Australia Pty Ltd

First published in Great Britain 1999 by Picador
This edition published 2000 by Picador
an imprint of Macmillan Publishers Ltd
25 Eccleston Place, London SW1W 9NF
Basingstoke and Oxford
Associated companies throughout the world
www.macmillan.co.uk

ISBN 0 330 37291 2

1 3 5 7 9 8 6 4 2

A CIP catalogue record for this book is available from the British Library.

Typeset by SetSystems Ltd, Saffron Walden, Essex
Printed and bound in Great Britain by
Mackays of Chatham plc, Chatham, Kent

For Clare Alexander

Raise the stone, and there thou shalt find me, cleave
the wood and there I am.

Oxyrynchus Papyri

If I do not remember thee, let my tongue cleave to the
roof of my mouth.

Prayer Book 137:1

Contents

Prologue

This is an account of six months in the life of Snip Freeman, a woman who turned her back on a man who was drowning. She was a painter with a waitressing problem, a wanderer. The sheets of her swag were thin and had too many sleeps ingrained in them. She wasn't anchored, she touched the earth lightly, she'd visit a place and find a man and a studio and a scrap of a job until the zing of uncertainty pulled her on.

The story begins with a cheque. The envelope that carried it was bruised with grubbiness and worn thin from too many hands. The envelope took two months to find her. The amount of the cheque was substantial and the typewritten instructions were blunt: hunt him down. Seduced by the cash but clogged by doubt, she stopped. She stopped tumbling into the oblivion of sleep or the joy of a singing painting or the trembling sweetness of a very slow fuck. Then on a warm spring night of a full butter moon Snip folded the cheque and slipped the sliver of paper down the front of her pants, she packed up her swag and rolled up her paints and moved on.

This is also the account of a man who used to lie with his head in the saddle of her back, to try to pin her down.

CHAPTER ONE

The Journey Begins

'My hair feels like cotton wool.' The gears are dropped and the car is stopped just before the bit-place underground town five hundred kilometres from anywhere.

'Out ya get.'

The young man walks to the boot of his Valiant Regal and hauls out a straining cardboard port that is held together by one rusted clasp. He kneels. The case springs open gratefully at his touch and he hovers by the empty roadside over the tangible bits of his life. He dips his hands in the mess of Bible and screwdrivers and caplamp and golfing mug and photos and shaving brush and singlets and Dr Spock manual and Masonic tie, until they stop at a pair of mean-looking, black-handled dressmaking scissors that he's remembered to take from the tangle of his wife's pink and padded sewing box in his last act of taking, twenty-four hours ago, from the love of his life.

'C'mon, out ya get,' he says to the little head propped

on elbows watching greedily from the wound-down car window and smartly snapping bubblegum. She gets out. She stands obediently before him. He crouches down to her, turns her around and holds out a dust-clotted, knot-clogged matt of hair, thick as his little finger, and snips it off.

Snip snip snip.

Seared into her is that careful, clean sound of resolution as the scissors close on each stick-tangle of hair.

Snip snip.

Until there are no more.

Her head feels like it's letting the air in.

She puts her hand up to the tufts and he puts his hand over hers and runs them over her scalp, like a basketballer feeling a ball before a game.

'There you go my little man, no-one's ever gonna find you now.'

ANOTHER JOURNEY BEGINS

Sydney to Alice Springs. One country girl, one city-boy, one Holden ute.

The city stop-start vanishes into a six-lane freeway and a biblical sky. *La Traviata*'s turned up. Snip yanks down the window and holds high her hand, hitting the breeze. The car is the cabin confessional that's to be the two strangers' close quarters for the next four thousand kilometres. The where-they're-at in the other-half stakes is quickly, cleanly established. He's called Dave. He's twenty-six. He's just out of a seen-from-afar-at-a-bar situation that never really connected. She's thirty and she's just had the recent farewell of the boyfriend of two months that she never loved, or maybe did but didn't know.

'You'd know, Snip, you'd know.'

'Hmmm.'

She smiles and stretches, four days to go.

Snip holds her face to the slap of the wind. She sees speeding green and a clutter of New South Wales signs. The land's so huddled, it's all town upon town and hill rolling on to hill. This is the country? Where's the space? She's a desert girl, sand is her dirt.

The city-boy is a talker and he tells Snip it's a hell truck and he loves it and he asks her how long has she had it.

'Look at the mileage.'

He looks, says crikey and sits up straight. Smooths down the kick of his fringe. Asks her why he's driving such a virgin car. Snip trails her hand out the window and the wind snatches her apple core. She stares back down the barrel of the road and says she came into a bit of money and it's a long story and she leaves it at that, hoping it's enough and knowing it's not.

Small talk is not her way. Her words often come out bitten and jagged and stopped up and wrong, so more often than not she leaves them inside. Snip will not be discussing the origins of the cheque. For ten days she's been brooding about it like a hen in the corner of a coop, waiting and not moving and blinking a black eye.

Dave says coming into a bit of money doesn't explain why he's driving her car and Snip tells him, stumbling and still not looking at him, that she's not too good in city traffic.

'It's country now.'

She holds her breath for three seconds and then lets it slide out. She draws her head inside and tells Dave, low and slow, that she's no good with gears and she's always driven automatics and that he's going to have to teach her how to drive a manual along the way. She holds her breath once again.

A grin cracks his face like a watermelon split.

'Don't you reckon you should've put all that in your ad?'

'I, I didn't want to scare you away. And I didn't want to end up with a driving instructor.'

Dave speeds up the car, scrabbles for the stereo knob and snaps off Joan Sutherland expiring. His questions gallop: why did she have to get out of the city so fast and how much money did she come into and how did she get it and where the hell is she from? Snip tells him again it's a long story and she turns her face back to the speeding green. He says they've got a lot of time to kill. She blunts it by saying she's buggered.

'So should I be scared?'

'Yes.'

Dave laughs and drives faster. Snip examines the puppy energy in his hand as it roams the new buttons and levers of the car, triggering the wipers and water and windows and horn. She laughs at him. He does too. She keeps examining him. The kink of his wrist as it rests on the rim of the steering wheel, the curl of a smile in the corner of his mouth. There's a looseness in him, it's the ease of someone who's been loved very much. He's like a rock that's been hit by the sun for too long and has collected its warmth and shines with it. He's not Snip's type. She's too set in her ways, too crabby and ungenerous and tactless and gruff. She can see the scenario ahead of them: her driving taut at the wheel and shutting him out as soon as she knows what to do with the clutch. She's not his type. She looks at the startling length in his city-boy fingers. Her hands beside his are thick-corded and practical and mannish and blunt.

Dubbo, the designated dot on the map to be slept in, is swept through in almost darkness. They push on to the next town and the next and then suddenly there's the drag of tiredness. The decision to stop. A consensus – the next dot: 'Nevertire'.

'Who'd call a town Nevertire?'

Snip doesn't answer. She's good at that.

'Hey? Who'd call a town that?'

DEMURE IN PYJAMAS

The pub owner is Ron. Tatts cram his arms. The ink is so dense that from a distance it looks like his skin has been horrifically burnt. Ron's hand stretches out strongly from behind the bar, searching out names.

'Snip, eh?'

'Don't ask.'

Her eyes slip from his and she turns, not wanting talk. Dave asks for a room. The bar hushes. Ron asks what sort and there's the loaded reply into the silence, 'Twin beds', 'Uh huh', and the room slides back to chat. Dave is bar-talked into pool with the lone local woman and Snip soon retreats to their room and Dave is quickly back too. They decide to unpack the back of the ute, not trusting the town, and the floorspace around them is swiftly rubbled with canvases and boxes and suitcases and swags. The door of their room doesn't lock and the lone chair is tilted under the doorhandle like in some lousy western: them against the world. Big yellow stripes are painted on the walls and each stripe is the thickness of a paintbrush and crooked. Dave and Snip laugh at their wobbly wallpaper, the audacity of it. They lie demure in pyjamas in saggy school campbeds and Dave asks her why she's called Snip and she says it's an old family nickname and leaves it at that. He's waited eight hours after meeting her to ask, it's a record, but she doesn't tell him that. They read a little, and tire, and turn.

There's the sudden suck of a snore.

Snip doesn't mind. She cocks her head and stares at him asleep, neat on his back. Envies the swiftness of his falling, his childlike obedience and trust. He's wearing a T-shirt, cleanly white and crisply ironed.

She's definitely not his type.

DAY TWO: THE SUSAN SONTAG MAXIM

Pingping pingping pingping . . .

The digital watch on Dave's wrist wakes Snip at a quarter-to-six and she likes it – it's country energy, work energy, her energy. The crumpled clean shirt he takes from his suitcase smells of her childhood.

There's a walloped-down bacon and eggs breakfast at a faded cafe. Butter is pooled golden on thin white toast, it's decadent, the way grandmothers do it. There's a scraping of Vegemite.

'Where are you off to?' asks the waitress, cigarette-lean and once sexy.

'Alice,' Dave says, handing over their money at the till.

'Alice. God, that place. It's full of Aboriginals, lousy with them. We've got enough of them out here, down by the creek. Vegemite village, we call it.'

They take the change with curt politeness and move quickly out.

'I was liking her till then,' says Dave. Snip says nothing. Her lips are rolled in, bloodless and tight.

She takes the keys from Dave's fingers and there's a shiver of something as the two of them touch. She strides away from it. Ahead of them both is her tackling of the clutch. Snip gets into the driver's seat and pushes the car strongly into the frontier space. Dave is concentrating and keen at her ear and his hand is firm over hers on the gearstick.

'Change, move up, clutch, clutch, listen to it, listen to it, that's it, you've got it!'

The ground flattens around them and the sky expands before them and the air is crisp and thin and vigorous and it makes Snip want to slice through it very fast. The woman from the pitstop is still sour in her head.

'The landing sky,' Dave muses. Snip smiles at him. She relaxes and puts the foot down on the accelerator and drives it.

There's a toll of animals as the streetlights and postboxes and fences drop away. There are death whiffs. Signs: Dismal Creek, Skull Gap, Dead Man's Hill. There's a lizard still on the bitumen with its head to the sun – *thud*, the head's gone.

'Damn.'

There's Dave's chatter about his job as a historical archaeologist, chatter about scrabbling through dirt and peeling off wallpaper and pulling away bricks in convict quarters and barracks and mansions and stables and sheds. His talk of the histories in houses, of respecting the layers. His talk of his childhood of private schools and piano tutors and his mates, his talk of his mother and his cricket run-rate. And his father, with only one arm.

'Ten years ago he was driving with his elbow out the window and this truck came along and sideswiped him. Dad stopped and jumped out and ran up to the truckie and asked him if he was all right, and then he looked down at himself – he didn't have an arm. You know what he's been called ever since?'

'What?'

'Breezy.'

The cabin fills with laughter. Snip keeps volleying questions and deflects when Dave lobs them back.

'I don't remember no childhood.'

She leaves it at that. He laughs, says come on and backhands her soft on the shoulder. She throws another question back and his talk kicks up again. Snip finds men are easy like that, they're always snatching the bait. A collector, that's what she is, an archivist carefully cataloguing talk. She transfers sentence scraps and sketches into the blank pages of her journal at the fag-end of most nights. Curiosity and questions are her shield, she's the listener, the master deflector who's prickly with long slabs of talk. Especially when the subject's herself.

Dave's chatter is rich. On an old girlfriend: 'The only thing we had in common was that we loved each other. When we didn't have that, we had nothing.' On relationships: 'There are probably only two couples I know who have good ones. My parents, for one. It's so amazingly rare, don't you think?' Snip murmurs and nods and says little and collects, liking a lot what she hears. Dave's good talent. And he doesn't need much of a prompt.

Somewhere in the stretch of the late afternoon there's a pub stop with the locals here and there around the big square counter plumping out the room. The locals all silent, staring, as one, ahead. There's the deep cool hush like a long cool drink as if there's no use wasting energy on all that bangbustle of talk, as if anything worth talking about has been exhausted long ago.

Snip and Dave sit outside with their bums on the gutter. They consume their thin milkbar sandwiches and hurt-cold milkshakes from silver cylinders. The food is childhood-cheap. Dave tells Snip about the 'fire-engines', the raspberry sodas he'd have side by side with his father following his tennis lessons every Tuesday afternoon at his father's club. Dave tells Snip about the Milo and white-bread sandwiches his mother ordered the housekeeper to make for him every day at primary school, because he loved them so much. Dave tells Snip about his school asking him to be a priest in his matriculation year, but he loved girls too much.

They laugh.

Dave looks at Snip.

He bins his ball of a sandwich bag.

Snip looks at Dave's hands.

She imagines them at a dig, his fingers sifting through dirt, its silky waterfalls washing over them and she feels a tugging coming over her, a crumbling, and all she thinks of in that moment is the Susan Sontag maxim on love at first sight, that it's a feeling always to be honoured and obeyed.

Snip doesn't have the courage to do a single thing. She knows that fear of humiliation is the enemy of risk but she's been bitten once too often, and too deep.

She stands.

She doesn't look at Dave.

She feels clotted by awkwardness. She hopes he doesn't speak because whatever she says back to him will be jagged and wrong and she hopes he doesn't look because she'll blush. She can feel it, the fierce pull like a hand inside her stomach. The wet.

Snip strides away from him.

For the last four days she has been drunk on the compulsion of getting into the desert, of following the carefully hatched plan: learning to drive the car, dumping the passenger in Alice Springs, stocking up on fuel and then driving deeper on, beyond road signs and bitumen and fuel stops and grog. She has to see Bud, she has to dig him out of his desert lair, and falling for a shiny happy chatterbox of a city boy is a grubbying of the plan and is not what she needs at that moment.

And is definitely not what Bud needs.

Snip walks to the car and gets into the driver's seat and drums her fingers on the roof. She looks back at Dave, unsuspecting. His nose is bent to one side as if the wind has pushed it crooked. She smiles at that. And his face that's all light. She couldn't paint it. She's used to shadows and shy eyes and hiding behind hands. She needs a handle to hold on to, something hidden that will allow her to work her way in. Dave's face is too open. He's not closed over like so many of the youths she seeks out in the towns she ends up in – youths who are children and then suddenly shut-away men. Snip only paints men. Her journals are crammed with sketches of them. Fragments of noses, an eye, a pierced nipple. A jut of a hipbone, a tatt, a cracked tooth.

It's all wrong. Dave's face is wide and open to the sun and his tallness blares middle-class good health. He's too glowing for someone like Snip. She's thin and bitten from too much life on the run. She hates the eyes always at her and she shies away from them, under her long thick red hair with a straightness that's cut blunt. She hides under men's trousers and blue singlets and white shirts, under duffle-coats and mothy jumpers and clumpy workers' boots and farmers' hats.

Dave is yarning to an old man in the doorway of the pub. A hand is on his hip and the point of an elbow is on the wall, propping him loose. He's soaking up the old man's talk.

Snip honks the horn. She's a lone wolf too set in her ways and it seems so long ago that she was young. Snip made up her mind several years back that she'd never live with a man. She wouldn't wish herself on anyone. She used to think people grew out of their insecurities and fears but she's learnt that's not so, that those faults become concentrated, more insistent as you go.

Snip's a serial sleeper. A man told her once that she's the type of woman men never leave. They don't. She leaves them. She gives them the feeling that any minute she'll be off, so while they're with her they're obsessed. She learnt that one quick. No-one knows her too well, no-one gets that close. She clamps down if they threaten to and hauls herself out. Men satisfy the zing between her thighs, the sudden, savage hunger for a hard quick prick and she arches her back under the weight of them and puts their fingers insistently on her clit. And when it's over, she's off. No number. No forwarding address. A new town, another rupture. Her one constant: anonymity.

Snip's addicted to all that. She always feels strongest when she's by herself, she always paints best when she's alone, with no man and no sex to soften and distract her. Her canvases are muscular and ferocious and enormous and bleak. Some scream the width of small rooms. There's the bewildered comment, again and again, from the men who've looked at them: 'Crikey.' (Or 'Fuck.')

Dave shakes the old man's hand and steps chuckling into the car. Snip roars it to a start with the tips of her toes, the seat slammed forward as far as it will go. She doesn't look at him.

'What's this?' Dave asks, lifting out Snip's journal that's jutting from a bag jammed between the car seats.

'None of your business,' she says, swerving the car and grabbing the book, and there's a strength in her snatch like the force in a sneeze.

Dave stares. Says nothing. She looks at him. He

grins, she does too. And rolls her eyes at herself and jams the journal back.

AWARE, THEN

Onward. To a twilight roadhouse, for the toilet.

PATRONS ONLY TURN OFF LIGHT CLOSE
DOOR WHEN FINISHED

Drinks are bought to justify the flush, and the eyes of the late-teens boy behind the bar fix on the bits that make up Dave – his hat, belt buckle, crucifix, boots. Snip recognizes the city-hungry stare.

The two of them squat outside against the pub wall in the shutting-down sunset, aware, and Snip volleys into the silence a question: why on earth did Dave answer her ad? He begins to say something and stops. Siphons his words, Snip can tell. He says he was intrigued by the wording: 'Girl plus ute, Sydney to Alice, share the lot, now.' He says he's got friends in Alice, old uni mates, and he's never ventured into the Centre. He says he was between contracts and had a fortnight to spare and he left a note on the kitchen table – 'I'll be home in two weeks' – and kind of walked out the door and didn't look back.

And then he says very low that he also answered the ad because he had to, because he's twenty-six and he's swamped by the attention of his parents and grandparents and mates and bosses and uncles and aunts – their expectations, their love, their push. And Snip thinks of the prodigal son who turns his back on everything he knows, has to, because he has no clearly lit way to the fierce truth of himself. The son who's been swaddled with love and needs to split from it to grow into a man.

She had to start doing all that when she was seven. She's a long way from being there yet.

They push on into darkness with Dave's talk of his ranger mate deeply embedded in the national park, his talk of the letter that the ranger wrote six years ago to the girl he loved from afar, and never sent.

'Oh,' Snip says. 'Missed lives.'

STRANGERS TOGETHER

Onward. To the next town and the next and at the town with many 'o's that neither Dave nor Snip know how to pronounce they slow and swing the bonnet to the buildings, and stop.

The hot stilled car ticks and clicks. They sit very still and their heads fall back in their seats. The car's ticking stops and slowly, slowly they haul themselves out.

There's no room at the first pub and the second is sixty bucks.

'Only twin beds I'm afraid.'

'That's okay,' times two, hurried.

Their plans to unpack the back of the ute are overheard by the barmaid. The voice comes thin and almost fierce from behind the counter.

'This is an honest town.'

A vinegary back leads them to a tall room. As the door shuts behind them their booted bodies drop on to thinned pink chenille and the mattress springs whinge. Dave and Snip contemplate the faraway ceiling. They turn and stare and grin and he says suddenly into busy silence how he wishes he could take her out for a drink, see her in the real world, know her.

'Maybe, Dave, you, you wouldn't notice me in the real world.'

'Oh, I dunno about that.'

As they drift to sleep there is the squeak of the floorboards and the drone of talk, the clink of glass and the swell of laughter of the Orroroo motorcross meeting in the room across from them.

Snip's hand slips between her legs. Just two more days and then she'll shake herself clean and move on. It's the best thing for both of them, she knows. 'The neophiliac' her mother dubbed her once, because she's so ferociously addicted to the new. It's a need that pushes

Snip from place to place every four or six months. She's addicted to a life of fragments, of doing things her own way, of shedding skins. She's fierce with the routine of it, the swift bailing out.

At three-thirty Dave and Snip wake strangely together in their side-by-side single beds, married-couple close. Dave murmurs something about Mr and Mrs Freeman, Snip's surname which the lady behind the bar has checked them in under, and he muses over it and chuckles in the matey darkness.

'Mr and Mrs Freeman. I like it.'

Snip smiles. Marriage and commitment and kids – she's not qualified for all that.

He's definitely not her type.

DAY THREE: DRIVE ON QUIET

A barely there morning. A mean-thin trickle of water from the shower nozzle. A breakfast of cornflakes no choice and white bread, no choice and Vegemite, no choice and Bushell's tea and instant coffee. A deserted dining room and a sideboard crammed with misted wedding photos and golden plastic football trophies. Dave talking loudly into the emptiness of how he wants to be a cool dad, Dave talking of Vegemite and celery sandwiches and the spark of his eighty-nine-year-old grandmother, Dave talking of her ageing blue cattle-dog and sudden grey hairs and mates.

He asks Snip again about her childhood and she replies, short with him, the words coming out wrong, that her mother believed if you wanted a child to do well then you ignored it, and that's what her mother did.

'Did you do well?'

'Fuck off.'

Snip's rusty with manners. She knows that generosity and kindness and graciousness and warmth are connected with love and well-being but for her all of that's been crusted over. A long time ago she used to bash people with her love, trying to force her way in, and when that didn't work she began the long process of shutting herself down.

'I think you did well, I can just tell,' Dave says as they walk to the car.

Her softening grin. She did do well, but she's not telling him that.

One night to go.

Onward. They pull away over the Flinders Ranges and laugh that they've entered Europe as they wind among the cram of hills and then drop into the cleavages of valleys. They drive on to lowlands, swampy still, and to Port Augusta eerie in the early morning. They drive quickly through it to saltpan country, and stop the car and get out and runrunrunasfastastheycan into a silvery, moon-plain vastness and whoop across the bleached bowl, wind-whipped, and stop, and gulp air, and stare at a faraway train as it wends its way silently. She wants to kiss him. Dave stares for a second too long, and they break the gaze quickly – walk separately to the car.

Drive on quiet.

There's a storm ahead, a steel-grey shower curtain is drawn almost the length of the sky before them and they slow with the flint smell strong upon them and the plummeting chill. They come to a stop and step out once again, gulping the smell and the sight of the dropping sky. Dave looks at Snip, she wants to kiss him. She's wet, but she can't read him and so they drive on with Dave at the wheel. There are the first angry spots and then the rain is furious and Snip yanks down the window and puts out her head like a dog, she holds her face out to the sting and the hurt.

HAPPY CHRISTMAS

To scrubbed sunshine and Coober Pedy. An underground town, a bit place not bothering with gutters or tarmac or the insistent beauty of the land it's in. There's a fat white dog stiff with laziness on the verandah of the pub. The spraypaint is bright graffiti-blue on its short-haired back:

NO FOOD

It says in big letters.

'The tourists. They're all feeding him. He's growing too fat.'

The flat-as-land voice is from the man beside the dog. The speaker leans like a plank against the wall, retreating behind the ball of his stomach. His hat is too small on his head. Snip drops down to the dog and pulls at his ear and the animal snatches at her hand in play. She laughs, draws away and stands. Dave goes to offer the dog the rest of his pie but thinks better of it and throws it in a 44-gallon bin. Snip backhands him on the bum. He stares as if he's been stung. She pulls a face and walks on.

'You know, you walk as if your fists are clenched, but they're not,' Dave says to her, laughing at her.

'Bugger off.'

'You're just smarting because you want to rescue that dog.'

She turns.

'Mate, I'm not the type of person to be trusted with looking after anything. Okay?'

He's starting to grate. There's a spat of a haggle over

whose turn it is to pay at the petrol pump and then they return to the pub for a quick camera click at the dog's back – 'Sorry mate.' Snip goes inside to the ladies' loos, she's wet and frustrated and needs time to herself. She rushes off her pants and flits her finger over her clit, circles it, savages it and slips two fingers deep inside her until she sweetly, deliciously comes, her face crammed hard against the cold of the cubicle door. She stays squatted on the tiled floor for a very long time, with her bare legs spread wide, then mops herself up and walks out through the crush of eyes in the bar. The ute's nose is pulled up hard against the pub door. Snip trails her hand over the bonnet without looking into the cabin, without looking into Dave's stare because she knows that's what he'd want. She gets into the driver's seat and revs too heavily and roars off past the white heaped mine mounds and the Aztec houses pocking the quarries and then they're out, leaving behind straggly shouts from some local kids and taking with them a sickening heat, desert-dry.

Early afternoon. The carcass of a calf is melted like ice-cream on the dirt by the road. A kamikaze bird thuds into the windscreen.

Churning silence.

The outside heat is pressing in and somewhere as Snip is driving Dave is pouring water from a bottle into his hands and trickling it in silence over her forehead and it's slipping down her chin, snail-cold between her breasts and rolling to her belly and he does this again and pours it into her outstretched hand as she keeps her eyes on the road and she slowly rubs her neck and stretches her arms and her back at the wheel, and in silence puts out her hand for more.

Then glances at the tray of the ute in the rear-view mirror. At a head poking out from under the tarp in the far left-hand corner. A white dog, gulping at the onrush of wind. Smiling insanely and joyously. NO FOOD painted on its back, Snip just knows, even though she can't see it. She swerves the car in shock.

'Jesus Christ!'

The dog stumbles and turns to her. Barks swiftly once, in reprimand.

'Happy Christmas, Snip. It's three months early but what the heck.'

Snip's laughter bounces over her anger. She hasn't had a Christmas present for four or five years. She doesn't tell Dave that.

'How – why – I *told* you . . .'

Going to say something but stopping. Gulping, mouth dry with where to begin.

'How, how on earth did you convince the old man?'

'Oh, with far too much money. He can go and live splendidly in Monte Carlo now. You mad bugger, you've bankrupted me. You'll have to take care of me for the rest of your life.'

Snip's laughter quietens into little eruptions of giggles that won't stop, like hiccoughs.

'The main reason I did it, Snip, was because I thought that a spraypainted dog had a bloody grim life ahead of him. And you, I feel, are the person to take him to worlds where no animal has ever ventured before. You've got a ute. It needs a dog. It's as simple as that.'

Dave gets hit over the head with the empty water bottle. The bubbling giggling continues.

FURIOUS HANDS WORK

A night ahead to be camped in. A roadhouse supply stop. There are sausages in plastic next to frozen kangaroo tails sorry with hair. There's white bread, precisely sliced, stiff with age. There are three tins of Pal.

To a dry riverbed. Snip's unsure about the delicacies of driving on soft sand but Dave assures her it's easy, he's done it before, he'll show her how. They turn from the highway on to dirt and to sand, drive further and fur— sink. Rev.

Stop.

Rev. Rev again.

Stop.

'Shit.' Dave, very still and very hunched at the wheel. 'Well then, that's that.'

They climb out. There's no shovel. No Food cocks an ear and looks enquiringly at them, from one to the other. Snip holds up the back of her hands to Dave. Grins. She's liking him too much now to get angry. They dig. No Food jumps from the tray and sits at a distance from them, watching warily. Dave's long-fingered and soft hands and Snip's sun-grooved and squat ones work furiously side by side; there's sweat and stones and sand and grunts and laughter and scratches and blood. And then they rev one, two, and they push on the tailgate and again one two and stop, and then flop, their energy scuttled. No Food inches closer to them on his haunches and stops when he catches them looking. Light slides. The car is fifty metres from the bitumen and they push themselves on to the empty highway and kick stones and throw sticks and challenge the yelling silence as they wander the expanse, Dave on one side, Snip on the other, No Food warily in the middle with allegiances to neither. And then gleaming ahead, chrome-shiny and red as an ad on a roadhouse wall, there's a road-train rig pulled over. Dave and Snip run to a truckie with a snowy white T-shirt and tight shorts and long socks and evening chops sizzling obediently on his mini-gas cooker and water in his silver billy rolling briskly beside it, but his CB can't do the trick and he'd never get his rig into the dirt and the dark is crowding upon them.

'It's okay.'

'It's all right.'

'We'll manage.'

Dave and Snip talk over each other and to the truckie and to their tiredness. They're not sure when the next cars will come, or if they'll stop, or if the owners will help out.

They'll go back to the creekbed and set up camp by the ute, they'll tackle it all in the morning.

WHAT SNIP DOES

The three of them eat burnt-sausage sandwiches with crumbling bread and spilling sauce and charcoaled onion and they're good and they have another. Between mouthfuls Dave and Snip grin in the firelight and swiftly settle into silence and then into their swags that are laid out side by side on soft sand. Like two kids on their bellies in front of a lounge-room TV they watch the lightning inside clouds in the wings of the sky. A silent orchestra here, now there, now back together, and somewhere from the tension, wire-taut, Dave says I think this has been the best day of my life, and he brushes Snip's hand, brotherly perhaps but she doesn't know, doesn't respond, and he rubs at her shoulder and again she doesn't respond, not knowing if it's a signal or what, and then silently he draws across the flap of his swag and she cannot read his goodnight and she sees a lifetime ahead of her dissecting the missed moment, the itch of what could have been and she tells herself you reap what you sow, *it has to be done*, and as she says goodnight she reaches across and strokes softly, once, his wrist and he rubs strongly back, his fingers learning her wrist and her arm and then he leans across, his lips and his tongue to hers.

Done.

'I've almost forgotten how to do this, it's been so long,' he says in the middle of it and she laughs softly in her loosening and loves him for that.

INTO THE CLOSE BLACK

Suddenly in the dark, wind and lightning and gusting cold are speeding upon them. There's a panicked, efficient dash to the car, a grabbing up of flung boots and bra and bits and pieces of whatever they can find in flashes of light that are bone-white. Snip shouts for No Food and realizes then she doesn't know his real name. There's no response.

'It's okay Snip, leave him, he'll find his own way,' yells Dave and together they pull away the tarp on the ute tray and spread the swags side by side snug inside and everything else is shoved into the cabin or jammed underneath and the covering is secured. And just before they slither inside their low oblong cave of tarp and car tray they stand together at the back of the ute, Dave's arm around Snip's shoulder, and they stare in silence at the cloud crowd and the wind-wild trees and they feel strong together, like a couple from a sparer age who've been irrevocably bonded through epic, wringing problems.

'This is something to tell the grandchildren,' he says, as they crawl into the close black. They hold each other while the rain tumbles upon them, Dave wet, his back, then Snip wet, her face, and in the rain gaps they poke their heads outside and sit and stare at the showy lightning, their drive-in in the sky, then sink again into the dark closeness and she eats the rain and the sweat and the dirt off his skin.

Love, infatuation, lust – for Snip whatever it is it's something ferocious and swamping and too soon. But she relishes the great warmth pluming through her, the strange zooming high.

Sleep is snatched, barely, in a just-dawn.

DAY FOUR: A COUPLE QUICK

They wake to a day already stale. There's sullen light and a strong kiss. Snip yells for No Food but there's no answer and at the back of her chest there's a flutter of panic. They walk on to the highway mud-spitted and sex-crusted, Dave with his shirt off, Snip with her hair knot-wild. The inside of her thighs still trembling in soft spasms from the night before. In five minutes there's a man in a four-wheel drive.

'I'm late as it is . . . weeeell, let me have a quick look.'

And he's a professional towing man who pulls coaches out of Top End wet season bogs with a tow-rope big, blue and new. His hands betray he's very proud of that rope. The ute slips swiftly from the sand, demure, and Dave and Snip laugh and wave their rescuer good-bye with their arms around each other, a couple quick. Then just as they rev the car No Food appears at a low swift run and Snip laughs and cuts the engine and gets out and lowers the backflap. She slaps the tray twice with the flat of her hand and the dog tries to jump in twice but falls back.

'You bugger. You're too fat,' she says grinning.

She picks him up clumsily and pushes him wriggling and scrabbling on to the tray. He thanks her by licking her swiftly once on the cheek and then crams his body into the corner, impatient to be off. She grins again. She's stuck with him now, she can tell. A dog is the last thing she needs. Or Bud needs.

They drive on with Dave's hand strong over Snip's on the gearstick and then his fingers are slipping between her thighs and she's arcing the small of her back in the seat and the car veers wildly to the right and they laugh and pull over and get out and kiss into the side of the car in the spare highway world of not another soul for a very long time.

Snip walks back to the driver's seat with a smile spreading through her. It's a complication, it wasn't meant to happen and she's liking it all too much. She thinks of the crust of a long-dry dam, melting under rain into a silky softness.

Maybe Bud can wait.

To Uluru because Dave's never seen it. It's a detour of four hundred kilometres but Snip doesn't mind because it's a lengthening of their journey together. They stop for fuel at the turn-off and an old Aboriginal man in a cast-off ranger's shirt leans into the ute and tells them of Sydney in few words. His shiny hand draws the arch of the coathanger and sails of the Opera House in the air.

'Yeah Sydney,' Snip laughs, sketching the coathanger back. 'Big Smoke. Been there, done that.'

They drive on in sun and then rain and then sun and then before them is the breathing rock, brushed by racing clouds. As they skirt its immensity they see waterfalls tumbling off it and five minutes later trickles and then they're going going gone until there are just vast streaks silvered by the sun.

To the Olgas – Kata Tjuta – and Dave walks ahead

and Snip flops to a rock, belly-down, sleepy in the sun and plumped with the grace of love and sweetness and relief and he comes back soon and drops down to her and rests his head in the dip of her back. She turns to bury her face into his thigh and soaks him up and they wish there weren't tourists.

Snip feels tall in her walk from the rock.

Bud can definitely wait.

ANEMONE

Onward. There's the destination pull as they near the lights of Alice Springs but they agree with few words to have another highway stop and then another for the roar of bush silence and the bush smell and a kiss. And at the last stop, staring into the late-sun hills, Dave stands behind Snip and tells her, stumbling and not sure how, that he'll take her out for dinner some time next week, but his friends in Alice are at the top of his list and she must remember that it is why he has come, to see them.

Like a sea anemone Snip draws the shutters and they sail into Alice, to civilization, with a silence, rich, between them.

Snip drives past the house where she's staying. She points it out to Dave with a flit of a hand and scrap of a sentence, her voice cobwebbed with tiredness and hardly coming out. She drives on to his hotel and pulls up outside. Dave goes to kiss her. Snip's cheek slides to his lips. She smiles quickly but tight with no teeth. She tells him she's sodden with weariness and because she can't bear to hear any more about friends and lists and why he's really here she revs up the car and leaves it at that.

'Well, I'll see you when I see you then,' Dave says. He gets out fast and doesn't look back. No Food stares and barks at him as he walks, laden, away.

Snip realizes in that moment she never said thank you for the gift of him.

It's not her way. She revs the car and jerks it into movement, her feet heavy and wrong on the pedals.

NIGHT FOUR: SKINNED

That night, late, Snip smarts from it still. She's hardly able to speak to Kate, her linguist mate. They've known each other for eleven years, they met on a coach trip to Alice. They were two east-coast girls starting new lives, sitting next to each other at the back of a crowded bus with a faulty air-conditioning system dripping on both of them. Each had a one-way ticket into the desert and a pair of Blundstone boots and soaring expectations. Kate stayed put in Alice, Snip meant to but didn't.

Kate's backyard now holds Snip's small studio, her besser-brick base. She pays for the space with sketches and paintings and gifts from her country-town expeditions. Snip's returned unannounced and triumphant from trips in the past with the curved jawbone of a horse or a hat from the 1940s or a metal 'K' from an old cinema sign or the feather from a wing of a wedge-tailed eagle.

This time she doesn't even unpack the car. No Food stays resolutely under it, refusing to explore the suburbia he's been placed in. Kate knows as soon as she sees Snip that something is wrong. Snip won't say what.

She excuses herself early from dinner and Kate holds Snip's head in her hands and bends it down low and kisses the top of it in concern. Kate's new lover, Annie, watches. Says nothing. Kate has just bleached her curly brown hair blonde and the curls hang limp, as if they're in shock. Snip holds out some strands and tells her to wear a hat.

'Bloody hell Snip Freeman, you're always so blunt.'

'I got it from you.'

They grin. The first day of the first time Snip stayed with her she swallowed a fly. She was told, abruptly, it was good for her. A spiky friendship became deep.

Kate hands Snip a saucer of honey ants dipped in chocolate as she goes. Tells her she'll bleach her hair tomorrow morning if she wants it. No thanks matey, Snip says, forcing out a laugh, you keep your experiments confined to food.

The screen door slaps behind her, taunting a gathering headache. The sweetness of the ant bellies explodes in her mouth. The night is soaked in the smell of eucalypt. She kicks away at No Food, who's crawled from the sanctuary of the car at the sight of her. Snip walks into her studio with the soft golden texture of the bellies, like warm runny honey, still with her. She props the door wide using a sliver of an axe head as a jamb, letting the night rush into the room's sour air. Her room is stale with half-finished canvases and screwed-up pages and dust. Daddy-long-legs collect in high corners. Their webs scour the small windows like the bottom of a pot. Paint-crusted fruit tins and margarine tubs are crammed next to upturned garbage-can-lid palettes and rows of grubby, grey paint-tubes like toy soldiers resting. Along one windowsill is a line of spines of the journals that catalogue her life. Their covers are painted the colour of the desert that she fiercely loves, the colour of old blood.

Snip stares at it all with the smell of trapped oils wrapped around her. She sighs. She's back, to a place she never graces with the name home. It's a stopping place from where she launches her next venture in any direction and to which she returns every six months or eight or ten. She potters and rests and reads and paints the Aboriginal way, with the canvas on the ground, until the itch to move on murmurs through her again and builds to a screech and she rolls up her swag and packs up her paints and takes off.

Snip calls out to No Food, regretting the kick. He doesn't come. She feels tears teasing the back of her eyelids, wanting out, and she knows from experience that if she lets them begin they won't stop. She drags the start of one away, grinding the hot wet of it hard into her cheekbone. Snip goes outside to No Food, coaxing him to her, rubbing her cheek and her eyes into the fur of his neck and jamming the threatening wet. The dog licks her cheek, once, with a slap of his tongue and she smiles at the forgiving sweetness in him and suddenly the tears come and come.

And then the unfinished canvases are attacked, three at once, with the ouzo bottle and Coke cans and coffee mug beside her and *La Traviata* turned up. Tonight, the paintings won't sing. Far beyond midnight Snip walks outside into the slap of the night and squats and pisses in the dirt by her door.

By four a.m. the colours are muddying. Snip falls into her swag. A clot of colours has accumulated in the webs between her fingers and on her knuckles and nails, in streaks across her cheeks and on her eyelids and hair. She's too tired to clean herself up with the turps, she has to get sleep. Snip's not been good with sleep lately, it hasn't been a tonic. Panic has been eating too much into her nights too often. She forces herself to lie down. She's got a long drive tomorrow, eight hours into the desert, to Bud. Her mind gnaws at worry, at her Grand Canyon loneliness, at the shadow of a person she sometimes fears she's become.

A scrap of a sleep.

WHAT SHE LEAVES

Snip's gone early the next morning. Kate has instructions.

'Tell the rich boy, the city bastard, when he calls, if he calls, that Snip Freeman has moved on.'

To the next town or the next. Kate and Annie won't be saying. They don't know.

Oh, missed lives.

RUNNING

At around the time that Dave is knocking on Kate's door Snip is running from the Three Well roadhouse where three local lads have decided to take No Food for a run behind their car.

Because she wouldn't let them buy her a drink.

Because she wouldn't tell them where she was headed.

Because one of them told her she had a city pansy of a dog who needed some exercise.

Because in the end she wouldn't turn her face and look at them, she wouldn't acknowledge them as they spoke.

Because she was scared. And she didn't want any fuss, she just wanted to be left alone. She smelt too much beer on their skin and she doesn't trust drunk men. Because she couldn't anticipate their next move.

Ten minutes after the three white men walked from the cool of the bar a fermenting dread kicked in Snip's stomach and she walked swiftly out and then ran weeping and screaming in panic when No Food yelped and strangled a bark as the rope around his neck was tightened by the roar of the men's jeep taking off, and gathering speed.

A flurry of dust and the squeal of a yelp.

Then nothing.

Settling dust.

Snip finds No Food a kilometre down the road, a broken bit of rope hangs forlorn from his collar, his left shoulder scraped savagely and his front paw pads ground off.

CHAPTER TWO

Dust Slapped

Snip wakes from a fat sleep to the noise of a scrum of dogs tearing one another apart. There's a protracted squeal amid a flurry of barks that rises to a sharp crescendo and then bluntly nothing.

Snip is in a room eight hours' drive from Alice Springs, a room with bulletproof glass in the windows and door. Outside is a post. YOU BIG RED HOLE is scrawled strongly upon it. Snip rolls on to her back and stretches and puts her hand between her legs.

Heat banks up at the windows, pressing at them, wanting inside. Snip puts out her hand to No Food, lying, at last, quiet by her side. His stomach still heaves, rattling with the pain. She wills his paw pads to stop weeping and grow back, she wills the skin on his raw haunch to close over. There's no change.

And the light has gone from his eyes.

Snip is slapped and streaked by red dust in this place, the tips of her fingers are valleyed as if all fluid has been drained from them, her long hair is weighted with smoke and dirt and wind, there are compacted crescents of dust under her nails, vivid accumulations between her fingers and toes, and in the palm of each hand a river map of ochre lines.

She's stinky in this place, sweaty and smoky. She's manless and motherless in this place. She's been ordered to come here.

The land where the light hurts is beyond the bulletproof glass and beyond the bulletproof glass, touching lightly the earth of the Tanami Desert, is a scattering of prefab houses and tin shacks. Four hundred or so Aboriginal people from the Walpiri tribe live on mattresses and blankets and bedframes around those houses. Thirty or so non-Aboriginal people live firmly within them, within barbed wire and mesh and bulletproof glass.

'Within the walls of a house you cannot see far,' says Queenie Nungala Mosquito, a person of this place. It's six hundred and fifty kilometres from Alice Springs. The only way to reach it is by travelling along a highway of sand.

DAMAGE

The land where the light hurts is pushing changes on to Snip's body. As the days pass the hairs in her nose are growing longer and fine furrows are appearing on the skin of her hands. A hide is thickening on the underside of her feet, a hide sliced with deep chasms on the side. Her walk is slowing, with a bowleggedness as if there's a rock between her legs. Her feet are leading, her back is following. It's stopping energy, she's been told, it's the Yapa way – the Aboriginal way – that way.

And in the oven-baked light, her eyes are narrowing to a line.

No Food's stomach still heaves. He barely raises his head from the floor for a feed, barely eats, barely licks Snip now. She rubs meat on his gums and feels his hot, sour breath on her hands. His paws are scabbing over but still he won't stand. People of this place tell her he'd be better off dead, that it's not right for a dog to survive like that.

Snip has been here six days or maybe eight or maybe twelve, she doesn't really know. It's just like the teenage Yapa kids of the community when they're asked their age – they say fourteen or maybe sixteen or seventeen, they don't really know.

And in the times before falling into sleep Snip takes

out the memory of Dave like a box of chocolates hidden under her bed. She unwraps the clothes from his body. She curls her torso around the warmth of his sleeping back. She imagines taking his earlobe between her lips and sucking again at the softness, her tongue playful with his loop of gold. He's under her skin and he won't let her go. In failed love, her mother had whispered to her once, lie the seeds of madness. It's in her journal, ten years back, the warning. If she could run a razor along her veins and pour Dave out of her, Snip would. He murmers and sings and calls through her blood.

And it was only four days, and she doesn't know why, and she doesn't recognize the pull. She can't paint with the mind-clot of Dave. And the anger over his gift of the dog. And her helplessness. She can't fix No Food, she can't seek revenge, she can't go back to that road-house place. Because she knows that's what those three men are waiting for.

Snip feels damaged in this place.

LATER LATER

'You take me hunting, Napaljarri? In your big car?'

Snip's called Napaljarri and she's a woman of value in this place, because she's a woman with a bush-bashing car.

'Napaljarri?'

The sharp shout skids across the dust of the street.

'Yehwah, I take you hunting.'

Snip yells back to the humpy. 'Later later.'

Later this afternoon or tomorrow or the next one again, it's the Yapa way that way. Just like later later she'll see Bud because that's why she's back in this place. Later later is the rhythm of this place.

The last time Snip was in the community, a year ago, she was frozen out. She took some Yapa ladies out hunting with Kate. The minibus they were driving in got stuck. Snip and Kate and the Yapa women got out and the Yapa women looked at the white women and nothing was said.

Snip got down on her knees by a tyre.

Kate grabbed at the shovel, viciously, in a huff.

The two of them started digging, cross that it was the white women, once again, doing the work.

They dug the bus out.

As they all drove back a silence that was deeply wrong settled on the white women. They got back into the community and the Yapa women didn't smile as they said goodbye to them, they averted their eyes. It was three days before Kate and Snip were told the reason they weren't helped: because the white women were digging into the surface, they were breaking the soil, of another tribe's land. Another transgression, among many other transgressions, that neither white woman had any idea of.

Kate's mortification was so swamping she'd never been back to this place. 'I'll never understand,' she said. 'Their lives and their beliefs are too complex and secret for me, I'm sick of crashing like a bull into all that. I don't mean to, but I do.'

Snip has returned to hunt Bud down. She's returned to a gentle, warm welcome from the women of this place.

'Napaljarri, my daughter,' said Queenie Nungala Mosquito in welcome on the day Snip came back, hitting her on the cheek with the softness of a whisper. As always, Snip is astonished at the generosity and the capacity for forgiveness in the people of this place.

LETTING STOP

No Food is to stay firmly indoors in the place that Snip is houseminding. She doesn't risk him among the dogs and the heat and the dust of outside. On his blanket by the door his stomach strains and his tongue still lolls. Snip refuses the rifle proffered her by Kevin, a keen-eyed neighbour.

'He'll come to. I just know it.'

Ferociously willing it.

When Snip wakes early in the morning, to get away from No Food's listless paws and rasp, she goes outside and walks by mattress huddles and blankets and sleeping people and watching dogs. She walks by bush-bashed Falcons and utes. Past the boarded-up community hall with the sign HARD ROCK CAFE skewed across its mouth. The missionary house, skull-hole gapped where windows and doors should be. By a car-crammed mechanic's compound with petrol pumps out the front, snug in their coats of mesh. The art centre that is hand-stamped and paint-dotted to head height. The health clinic, windowless, the store, windowless, the church, windowless. She walks by wrong trees planted by missionaries and as the desert laps at the edges of people she walks by flaccid silver bellies of cask wine, bleached-to-silver beer cans, a gutted television, and a graveyard of cars that has somewhere in there the Valiant Regal that first brought her to this place twenty-three years ago and then stopped.

Snip walks beyond all that to a place where she knows there's nothing but bush sapped of colour, stretching ahead of her to the sky.

She pulls off her pants and squats and pisses strong and hot like a horse. Foamy rivulets run in unruly streams beneath her and she widens the gap between her feet and widens the gap again. The smell of wet hitting dirt replicates in a tiny way the storm smell of the roadtrip and plunges her back to the nagging memory of

Dave. To his earlobe and his loop of gold and his crooked nose and his sifter's hands and the softness of his neck as she held her face to it.

The fizz of piss splashes Snip's boots in the thick of the thinking and she curses the sky with a very loud 'Fuck'. Works her feet into the sand, wiggles her boots clean as she thinks furiously. Maybe he's with her so much because he was the one who did the leaving. She's not used to that.

A thin blade of a leaf is Snip's toilet paper. She flicks herself dry. Stands and drops her skirt and plumes dust over the spreading damp as ants rush to worry the rim. She walks to a river gum and runs her hand across its shiny skin that's broad as a person's back and slides into a sit with her own back leaning against it and stares for a very long time at the great stretch of blue arching above and around her, at the shin-bone beauty of a lone ghost gum against a reddened hill, and she lets the spreading slowness push through her, she lets a stopping wash over her like a cool bath after a sticky-hot day, she lets a stopping like a tonic flood through her. She's come to this place not only to find Bud but to lose roads paved with bitumen and skies of thick cloud and now, after six days or maybe eight or maybe twelve, they're nearly gone. The last swag stop and job interview and order pad are almost wiped out.

In readiness for Bud Snip's head has to be rested and

clear. She rolls the instructions in her head like wine in her mouth – *hunt him down*. The words hold a fury or a playfulness and she doesn't know which.

She's here to find out.

Snip closes her eyes and the shapes of gum-leaves murmuring above her glow yellow and red in her lids, and for now Bud can wait. He's out of town, in Alice or Darwin or the Kimberley she's been told, and it's not known why or when he'll be back. Snip knows it won't be easy when she finally gets to him. Under the sky and the tree a sense of stillness seeps through her and it has the sweet coolness of soft mud and she lets it stay, for a long time, because she knows it's a rareness to be savoured.

BLOT

The wind has life in this place, telling moods. When there's sorry business, when someone has died, the wind has been known to skip through the houses and cause the humpies to heave, it scatters all tracks and all traces as it sweeps the spirit to the land. Snip has been told this, she's seen it, and she knows the wind must be for her too.

Sweeping away all the tracks, beginning a new way.

But her nights are stained by scrawny sleeps. The time before sleep is grimed with thinking too much about loving too plumply. Snip wants to shut her mind down into rest but she can't. She's thinking too much about a love so rare and so wrong. It's like black-market money in this place, with nowhere safe and right to deposit it. And she feels as if her strength and composure are being fractured by it.

Snip remembers Kate's story about her sister, who tore out the last three pages of every one of her boyfriend's books.

Manic city way that way.

And she couldn't do it to books.

She doesn't even know Dave's address, she doesn't know much about him at all. Just scraps: the names of a few Sydney suburbs, a childhood tennis club, a profession. Knows of an armless father, a housewife mother, a sparky grandmother. Favourite things: a woman's temple, her hipbones, the curve of her ankle, her cum. Hitchcock and Kieslowski, Nina Simone and Nick Cave, Bach, El Greco, Rothko and Knewarrye. Le Corbusier. Gaudi. Steinbeck. Ondaatje. Ireland, Broome and Havana. Curiosity. Honesty. Driving. The sea. Hates crumpets and porridge, tomatoes and dates. Loves Italian wines. Usually falls asleep in theatre. Flirted with filmmaking. Draws fragments of buildings with flair. Keeps a visual journal of odd letterboxes and beautiful fence posts and rooftops and old doors. Always carries a camera. Likes soccer but not rugby, swimming but not jogging. Hadn't slept with anyone before her for two and a half years, 'because it's hard to find someone, Snip, it's really hard'. Longs to get out of Sydney, to change his life. Has an untroubled, open face that crumples into a frown in sleep, and she doesn't know why.

No hard facts. Snip wonders where he is now and if he's with someone and how she could get in touch with him if she wanted to. She wonders how she can gouge him out from under her skin, how she can drain from her veins the nag of him.

Uncertainty is blotting the cleanness of her running and it never has before.

She recognizes she needs fixing.

TURNING FIERCE

There's a crush of dry twigs and leaves behind Snip. She rises fast from her spot under the tree. She turns, defensive and annoyed and fierce.

'Hey sister girl. It's only me.'

Shelly-Anne. Snip's known her for just on eight years, as a long-distance best mate. Snip had a hunch, ten minutes into their very first conversation, that a friendship with this singular, city-refugee would last. Shelly-Anne who always has a piece of floor for Snip's swag when she visits the community and a brew of chai tea with powdered milk. Shelly-Anne who tells Snip with a smile that the one way a woman can proclaim her independence and strength is to do something that will make her parents weep. Shelly-Anne whose name with the sea in it the Aboriginal people can't quite pronounce, so they call her Sharon. Even though she's been in the community for more than eight years, priming the canvases and mixing the paints and dealing with the buyers who grab at the dotted dreamings that are hung by galleries all over the world. Snip's been minding Shelly-Anne's house while she's been away in town, Alice.

'For business. And my boy. And pesto sauce at Woolworths and cappuccino, proper way, and newspapers and movies and sleep. Big one, while my boy is at work. He's got a lovely house, darling. There's a big quiet in that one, it's so serene. And no half-dead dog by the door. What on earth is all that about? Since when have you ever been the slightest bit motherly, or domestic?'

Snip laughs softly and sits down again and reaches out a hand.

'It's a long story, Shell.'

'I think I've got time.'

Snip laughs again.

'It's great to see you, matey.'

She hasn't seen Shelly-Anne for a year. Snip pulls her down to her like a lover and holds her and then says nothing for a while, just puts her head on her shoulder and breathes in the calm that's soaked through her. Shelly-Anne is a woman doing exactly what she wants to do. There are no compromises, she's learnt over many years to say no. That's why she's in this Aboriginal community in the desert and not in the suburb by the sea where she's from. Shelly-Anne is the only woman Snip knows who has that serenity deep through her.

'How, how did you track me down to here, Shell?'

'Darling, I always know I'm gonna find you somewhere nearby the car graveyard. It's the one thing you and Bud have in common, you can't keep away from those bloody old wrecks. He's always hovering around them, tinkering with them and pulling them apart.'

'I better find another spot then.'

Shelly-Anne hits out at Snip as she throws back her head and laughs to the sky.

She was assaulted outside her house several months ago. A young man stepped from the dark after her evening walk and grabbed her breast, but she didn't see his face. The trackers got on to it but nothing was said or found. After that Shelly-Anne spent several weeks de-kidding the house, telling them to go, and then the graffiti began on the posts by the door and the human stools in the underbelly of her house on stilts. But she doesn't smell them anymore and neither does Snip, and

Shelly-Anne won't go, she doesn't want to, and the artists and the old people of the community won't let her.

'Besides, I've got my first grey hairs. I'm an old one now, respected. No more bossing around, no more white slave.' And Shelly-Anne whistles for Reece, her pet Afghan, line-thin and silky and skittish and wrong in the bush.

WRONG

Sitting on a whingeing wire mat of a bedframe outside, old Queenie tells Snip the things that are wrong in this place:

> women wearing jeans
> arriving without food
> going bush without water
> saying the name of a person who has died
> white people without permits
> using lots of fuel for a campfire
> not offering a lift
> women with too many top buttons of their shirt
>   undone
> grog
> calling someone back who is gone.

'They have their own journey now. Let 'em go, Napaljarri, let 'em go.'

WAITING

'Have you seen Bud yet?'

'*No* Shelly-Anne, I, I haven't.'

'Then why are you here?'

Snip's smile is tight, without teeth. 'To see him.'

'You know he's back from his trip, don't you? He must know you're here. He waited by the church for an hour this morning, after mass.'

'I know. I, I watched.'

His shoulders hunched, his elbows on his knees, his hands loosely clasped. The stare at the hills to the side of him, the kick away at a cringe of a dog. Snip watched the stand and the toss of the keys in the air, the overhand snatch, the swift anger in it. She wanted to rush to him and hug him in that moment, to tell him she's here and it's okay. She didn't move.

Telling herself it's for the best, that it's making him work, that she's always giving in. Telling herself that he can wait, it's giving him a bit of his own back.

'You know what you are, girl? An allumeuse.'

'A what?'

'It's a new word I've just discovered. I read about it

at Woolies while I was waiting at the checkout. It was something about Jackie Kennedy. It means a match-woman, a woman who sets things on fire.'

Shelly-Anne pulls softly at Snip's hair, slips it behind her ears, clears her face and then pinches her chin firmly with one hand.

'So Pippy, I'm waiting. Why are you here? I'm gonna dig it out of you somehow.'

'Shell—'

And Snip jerks away from her. Her eyes narrow at the land. She walks away without a word, knotted inside.

But as she walks through the community and then far into the bush the light at six-thirty in the evening weaves its magic and Snip unfolds and relaxes, feeling again like she's home in the land. Nowhere else feels like this for her, she's never long enough in a place for it to seep through her and hold on to her. She's always afraid that if she stays in a town for too long it'll grow over her, clamping her down. So as soon as she loses the new eyes she gives notice at the cafe or bar she's been working at, she leaves the brief message on the new man's answering machine and she rolls her canvases and barrels her paints and moves out with the exhilaration bubbling through her that comes every time from scrubbing her life clean. It's like surfacing to gulps of air after diving too deep and holding her breath for too long. She's addicted to it, the sweet hit of it.

But Snip only fleetingly comes back to this place that feels like a home, the land that's a tonic to replenish her spirit. Bud's too much in it.

CALLED

Snip's skin name, Napaljarri, was decided for her by the people of this place twenty-three years ago when she first came here. She was seven and she left soon after. Then one day when she grew up she returned, and she loved it so much she's been coming back over the years ever since, every eight months or twelve months or ten.

Everyone of this place has a skin name. A European one too. Gideon, Zacharia, Noah – the missionary way. But now the missionaries are gone and some of the children have names from TV – Elvis, Sylvester, Scully, Bart. Or vivid hybrids – Gregwyn, Cindywyn.

'What your name?'

It's the anthem of demand from a young kid Snip hasn't seen before.

'Snip.'

'What your *real* name?'

'Napaljarri. What's yours?'

'Caleb Bly.'

'Caleb *what*?'

'Bly.'

'Oh, *Fly*.'

'Yeah.'

The stockman's naming, and the stockman's cruel joke, from way back. There was the name Hitler in the community once, and Prince of Wales, and Tonto. Snip's journals catalogue the names over the years. The adults fall away quick – there's lots of sorry business in this place. Queenie is there in the very first journal, drawn with a high crown on her head, teaching seven-year-old Snip a new language and way. Still doing it, telling her the names Yapa people give too. 'Waterbeds' for the Alice Springs police because they go up and down, up and down the town mall; 'green bush' for the leafy Alice Springs jail; 'cooka' for meat; 'little green suitcases' for cardboard casks of Coolibah wine; 'head-crack' for hangover.

Queenie's six children were taken from her long ago by the government and the missionaries, and she rubs her tissue-paper soft cheek against Snip's and speaks of 'heartcrack' too.

She never saw her children again, except Chocolate, the one who found her way back.

A WARNING

Snip hates the flap of a skirt around her legs but in this place she wears a skirt because she's expected to, because she's been told that in this place the thigh is one of the most erotic parts of a woman.

The little boys slip their hands inside her shirt and push aside the cloth and pat her breast matter-of-factly. They tell her the name in Walpiri and point to their nipple and hers; 'Little,' they say, and then, 'Big.'

'Breast is nothing in this place,' Shelly-Anne tells her. And asks Snip, if she had one wish, what she would want more than anything in the world. Snip says bugger off, she doesn't know and she leaves it at that, embarrassed at her weakness over Dave and embarrassed that she fell so hard and so quick. And that he left her. Shelly-Anne laughs, says Snip's lying and not saying and grabs her head tight in the brace of her hands. She looks her in the eyes and tells her she's going to squeeze her thinking out of her. Kisses her instead. Ruffles Snip's hair like a mother and tells her there's an old Russian proverb – 'Be careful what you struggle for, you will probably get it.'

Snip walks outside by herself, shaking herself clean from the questions. She wraps her arms around her waist and thinks again of wrapping her body around the foetal curve of Dave's back, her hand threading under his arm and across his chest and the sweet softness of flesh to flesh. She's sodden too much with the thinking.

'We fit,' he had murmured on the brink of sleep. 'We fit,' she had whispered back.

Snip's never felt that fit before, the spiritual recognition, the knowing. The spark from the start, the sharp flint of it. She's never felt so disempowered by memory. She feels mind-addled and sex-maddened and she can't walk away from it.

Snip thinks of Bud. His waiting for her on the bench by the church, the edges of his old hat curled like the petals of a rose too long in a vase. Then his standing and returning to his strange lone house that's down a disappearing track, over the hills in a place she's never seen. It's a lair Snip's never been invited to.

Bud can wait just a bit longer. It's the pattern of their coming together: holding off and assessing and waiting for the other to make the first move, and then the sidling up and the rushing headlong in.

SCRUB

Old Queenie, soon after the missionaries left, relinquished her Christianity. She sits close beside Snip on the wire mattress mat and tells of how she went back to her people's way by one day going to the riverbed and stripping down and rubbing sand all over herself.

Bud is early to the church, every third Sunday of the month. A band of red dust is ingrained across the extremity of his white-shirted stomach. Bud is fierce with his God in his tarnished whites in the desert. Twenty-odd years ago he helped build the windowless brick church in the thick of the January heat. The building is closed off to the land and its family is sparse. It's the pitstop every four weeks for the travelling preacher, with no building like it for six hundred kilometres and nothing in it to smash.

Queenie goes hunting on Sundays. So does Snip, when she's not watching Bud. Queenie tells her of a time a long way back, when she was nearly nothing, when church-going whitefellas, with the blessings of the blind eyes of the priests, went on shooting parties rounding up her people.

Killing the men.

Raping the women.

And for sport burying the children in the ground, and kicking off their heads.

NEARLY NOTHING

The women stab the ground with crowbars like they're punting on an English river. Their feet are bare upon the desert burs. They wear petticoats under their skirts even though it's sixteen years since the missionaries were among them and decreed that they must.

The women are hunting for lizard, big one, goanna.

Old women and children and Snip fan across a hundred metres or so, walking and digging and walking and digging and stopping, drinking bore water from old orange-juice bottles and then walking and digging and stopping, and eventually turning from the hills they've been moving towards.

'Goanna go, old one that one, goanna go,' says Queenie, sighing and murmuring and muttering talk.

They walk to a stop, to a campfire and a billy and a sit by the truck. The children draw patterns in the dust and upend plastic bottles on the branches of small bushes. The women change their pituri, their bush tobacco that they cradle on the inside of their lips in thick caterpillar wads, and then when the billy is boiled they hand across to the children flabby slabs of white bread stained sodden by milky tea.

'Long time ago, when I was nearly nothing, my father grew weak from pouring so much sugar in his tea,' says Queenie.

YAPA WAY

Snip is beginning again to talk Yapa way. Dropping 'and' and 'the', economical way. Saying little one, skinny one, cheeky one. Remembering that fire can be cheeky, and noisy dog can be cheeky, and tea that spills, and kids. Remembering ringamanu is telephone and sweepamanu is broom. Remembering the year is spelt the graffiti way – 8T7, 9T4. Yapa is 'Aboriginal person'; weyapa is a lament, 'poor you'.

Queenie tells her when the dead are buried, it's called planting them. Queenie tells her the kids in the community are coming up strong.

Queenie tells her that she will look after her. That Napaljarri needs looking after, feeding up. That Bud won't ever do it, proper way.

PRACTISING

Caleb sits on Snip's lap and looms to her and smacks his little pursed lips against her mouth and springs back and he does it again and again, as if he's seen it on television, as if he's practising.

Shelly-Anne tells Snip she's heard the Aboriginal people say that whitefellas 'do it like dogs' – about the way they'll fuck anyone. That they think whitefellas have no culture, spirituality, and are backward for that. Snip eyes up some of the young men in the community, their sexy leanness, their encroaching fierceness. She wonders and Shelly-Anne reads her stare and hits softly at it, telling her not to.

'There'd be big sorry darling, big one, it's not worth it. Out here white men can do it with Aboriginal women, it's tolerated. But for a white woman in the community, it can't happen. She'd be hounded from the place and that's about the worst thing that can happen – exile. That's just the way it is, Pippy.'

Shelly-Anne grins, wry. She's got her Aboriginal man in Alice. He runs the indigenous television station and Shelly-Anne's in Alice a lot.

BIG SORRY

The community is scattering, the place is emptying. There's a payback coming, a big one. There was a murder in Alice a couple of weekends ago.

Three men are brought into the community in the back of a ute. They're kept on the oval for almost the whole day, with the heat and the tension and the dust. And then the grandmothers and aunties strip off their shirts and move in, they get stuck into the trio with nulla nullas and sticks. Then there are the men of the dead man's family, there's the beating and the spearing to the bone, hard into the thigh from a metre away, and the strong line of blood like ink down the legs. Three bodies thudding to the ground. The grandmothers and the aunties all beating themselves, the wailing and the blood, everyone bloody and the health clinic on standby. And there are the whitefellas rimming the oval, waiting for the moment to move in and not wanting to too soon.

Snip watches and not watches behind bulletproof glass in Shelly-Anne's tall house on stilts. It's the only high house in the community. Her hands are light and dry and trembling as she pours herself another gin and tonic. And another.

This world is as close to a home, and a family, as she gets.

CARESS

There are sudden hot patches in the waterhole. It's like swimming in child's piss. There's the scum of cattle shit in still corners. Snip watches for brown snakes, their arrow heads skimming the water's surface, and she never quite relaxes into the water's caress.

She could ring every historical archaeological firm in Sydney to find Dave. He'd be back in his city world now. You reap what you sow, she knows. Or she could just leave it.

Around her are sleek brown bodies of kids in the water, slippery and shiny and wet in the sun.

She'll leave it. He's probably moved on to someone else, anyway.

She goes home and curls her body around No Food, lying on his blanket by her door, his stomach still heaving and his scraped skin still weeping.

BELONGING TO

'You married?' says Roseanne, the young girl with old and scaly hands who is playing and playing with Snip's long lanky hair that copies the colour of the dirt; she's pushing it behind her ears and then pulling it over her face and threading her fingers through it and smelling it.

'No, I'm not married.'

'Baby?'

'No!'

'You skinny one.'

'Yehwah, maybe.'

'You belong to Bud out bush?'

'Yehwah, I belong to Bud.'

Belgian chocolates Shelly-Anne has given them explode like soft clouds in their mouths. Roseanne asks if Snip has any lipstick. She doesn't. She smiles. That's one of the things Dave said he loved about her: a woman with no lipstick. Roseanne asks Snip if she has any sunglasses. She does. Roseanne puts them on and stares straight at the sun and Snip covers the girl's eyes with her hands in concern. They both laugh.

What nags still are: his fingers at her cheeks, her nipples, her thighs. His tongue flicking at her clit and deep in her. And being still with him on the side of the road, cheek to cheek, like horses quiet in a field.

Snip's branded by memory.

BUNDLE UP TIGHT

Snip watches the women bundle up the kids who are to ride in the back of the ute, back to the community from the hunting trip. She watches the women enclose the children in blankets, folding and tucking the fabric like they're wrapping gifts. They hold the bundles tight to them as they sit crosslegged in the tray of the ute, wedged among crowbars and billies and the toolbox and tyre, ready for the lurch and bump along bush tracks, ready for the wind and the cold as the night drops upon them. The old man who's come with them, who says nothing and who stays by the ute all the time, is to sit in the front with Snip.

Just before they hit the lights of the community there's a perentie stretched almost the length of the road ahead of them. Snip swerves violently and as the big lizard accelerates away she remembers the people in the back and her heart thuds and she stops to check everyone's all right and apologizes. They're yelling and thumping the roof and jumping out and running into the bush – not because she swerved, but because she missed the lizard.

'Better squash goanna than no goanna,' chuckles the old man, and Snip – eventually – chuckles too.

She drives on, quiet, to a community bunkering into

dusk. She lets someone off at a flickering TV set on two old flour tins under first stars and a bedframe with a mattress of clothes, and she lets a group off at a cracked basketball court with a spindly light and another to a campfire and another, and it seems that the lights of the fires and the TVs are sucking hungrily the very dark from their tight, warm radius. And when Snip's the only one left in the car she drives on quiet to Shelly-Anne's tall house that groans and cracks in the heat and there, on the front steps, is Bud.

'Well, are you going to give me a kiss?'

Snip climbs slowly out of the truck. 'I'm not sure.'

'We all come back one by one.'

In reply she coughs clear the dust of the drive.

'You've got your mother's cough.'

'Well, Dad, thank goodness I didn't end up with yours.'

They chuckle.

'I hate being called Dad.'

'I know.'

'You shouldn't be trying to find me, Snip. Some people aren't meant to be found.'

'I know.'

Grin meets grin.

Hunt him down.

They're her grandmother's instructions. Snip doesn't know where to begin.

AIR THICK WITH THE SEA

The house where Snip grew up didn't let in the sky.

It was Snip's grandfather's gift to the three women in his life after he was crushed flat by a collapsed coal seam three kilometres underground. A two-tonne rock fell on top of his continuous miner, buckling the cabin roof and killing six men.

The house sat high on a blustery coast, at a place where coal washes left stripes like watermarks on cliffs that dropped down to the sea, where coal dust spilled across roads and coated windows and stained the blond sand of the beaches. It was a mine manager's house, clinging to a cliff above the Pacific. A large deco bungalow of solid walls and mean windows, bunkered against the wind-whip and salt-scour about it. A house that never celebrated the land it was on. A family home firmly shut to the world. And that family became Snip, her grandmother and her mother.

The air around the house was thick with the sea.

In the rich man's house that didn't let in the sky Snip was taught to urinate standing up, because her mother was so incensed with the way the world treated women. Snip was often fed soft foods like yoghurt and ice-cream and chocolate spread on white bread, because her mother had read in a magazine that slippery food makes you forget and sticky food makes you remember. Snip was taught to forget ever being a boy. She was taught to make a salad sing and her bed as crisp as a nurse, because her grandmother told her she had to be prepared for the time when she'd be 'on the market', and the day when she might not have the means, as they now did, to afford an ironing lady and a gardener and a cleaner twice a week.

Her grandmother would rap sharply on Snip's bedroom door at six-thirty a.m. and tell her to get washed and brushed and dressed. Not like the Flahertys, she'd say, they love their gowns, they're still in them at ten o'clock and their place shows it, it's always messy. They love their gowns and they never have enough energy she'd say, whereas the Freemans, we have to get dressed. Her grandmother would curl Snip's wilfully straight hair and paint her fingernails and prod the small of her back. Would tell her to be a lady, to sit up straight, to round her vowels and stop her slumping.

'N*othing* not no*think*.'

'Yes, not yeah.'

'*Phillipa*, not Snip. That's not a name. It's a nothing.'

And she was taught by both women from the age of eight to forget to remember her father. The man who'd chopped off all her hair and had chosen her nickname and had one day abandoned the three women in the house on the cliff.

She was referred to steadfastly as Phillipa in the household of women. Until the Friday when Bud had been gone for exactly two years, when Helen was far away at an international conference and her grandmother was down the road collecting five-cent coins behind the sweep of her forearm in a game of poker at her sister's. It was playlunch. She calculated she had until the end of the lunchtime bell. She walked out of the back schoolyard gate and up the hill to the house on the cliff. She walked past the letterbox with her grandmother's neat sign, ADVERTISING MATERIAL PLEASE. She walked around the side of the house and went into the garden shed and took out the spade and started digging a hole in the hard soil around the clothesline in the backyard. To turn it upside down. To speak to the aliens. And to speak to Bud.

Her mother came home early.

The fury in her fingers dug into her daughter's shoulders and seared into her memory as she dragged her, slapping and screaming, into the house.

'I'll *never* contain you. I'll never understand the hold he has over you.'

And from then on, in the household of women, she was called Snip.

And the slippery food stopped.

And the absent parent was tacitly acknowledged as the idolized parent.

And Helen gave up.

Snip was sent to a convent school which discouraged the polishing of shoes too highly, for fear that the shine would reflect glimpses of bright white panties. A school which encouraged its girls to layer the surface of their bathwater with talcum powder, to guard against the possibility of them gazing with pleasure upon their developing bodies.

She didn't assimilate. She buried herself in books and dreams and sketching and solitude and excelled in her studies. Her consistent topping of her classes was like a scream to be noticed. All her achievements a shout for recognition, for attention from Helen and Bud. In her final year Phillipa was dux of her school. She could choose to study medicine or law, she had the pick of universities. And she finally had the undivided attention of both her parents. Helen wanted law; Bud, medicine, spelled out in the first letter he ever wrote to her. He told her she was the first of the family to make it to university. No Freeman he knew of before her had completed high school, let alone gone on to tertiary education. Bud himself had left school at fourteen to work in the pit. 'It's what you did in my day,' he wrote.

Snip told both her parents she was going to follow her heart. That the profession she had chosen was painting, and they had no control over that.

Then she strode on to a bus headed for Alice Springs.

AN ORDER

When the instructions arrived to hunt her father down, Snip's immediate reaction was to sit very still. It stopped her soaking up the faces and the vistas of Collector, the new town she was in. Her mind was a clot of thinking, a trying to understand.

Thirty thousand dollars is to be left to Phillipa. A portion of that money is to be used to hunt her father down. And to buy herself a utility.

Snip's grandmother had been dead from dementia for two months when the cheque finally found its way to her granddaughter. The one line of flimsy, clumsy demands shrieked through the tight suburban solicitor's instructions and Snip was stopped by the oddness of her grandmother's wish.

And the bloody-minded wispiness in her words. And the playfulness in the request to buy herself a ute, of all things. Snip always smiled thinking of that. Her grandmother hated Snip's old bomb of a car, with its ripped seats and slashed dashboard and rust. Her grandmother was furious when she lost her licence at the age of seventy-two because of failing eyesight – she was effectively stranded in the house on the cliff. Snip became her chauffeur on her infrequent visits to the hearing-aid specialist, hairdresser, boutique and bank. And every time Snip visited, her grandmother railed against the tinniness of her granddaughter's city sedan, telling her a woman needed a reliable car more than she needed a good man.

The ute was a whim. The rest of the will's bequest was the problem. What did 'hunt him down' mean? Snip knew where her father lived. And what was she meant to do with him when she finally got to him? She felt the money would be tainted if she took it without following through with the spirit of the request, but she couldn't grasp the weight of it, she didn't understand. She knew the story, more or less.

Snip had a feeling it was just one of her grandmother's jokes. A bit of fun from a woman who stayed up all hours each night, watching old black-and-white 'fill-ums'. Her grandmother hardly slept, fortified by continual cups of tea and a phalanx of pills. She devoured her fill-ums at night and in the daytime her Hollywood biographies and gossip mags. One day she ordered Snip to stretch the skin on her face and stickytape it close to her hairline, because she'd read somewhere that Dietrich did it. She declared that if she ever won the lottery and became filthy rich she'd use Dom Perignon every day to wash down her pills, because that's what they did in Bel Air. 'It helps the circulation, you know.'

The mysterious request in the will was all too ridiculously Hollywood. Snip's first inclination was to let it all lie, to just take the money and run. The cheque would buy her a blissfully long stretch of painting time, with no distractions and exhaustion from waitressing. Her grandmother had been getting gaps in her brain, Snip had seen it towards the end, the splintering and forgetting and rambling. Her last birthday card to Snip was blank and when she was told she said, 'Well, that's the end of me then, isn't it,' laughing it off long and loud. So maybe the will's instructions were a flippancy, a joke. Snip felt that her father could stay buried where he was because he'd done nothing wrong except leave them all once, long ago. Lots of fathers did that.

But Snip's conscience told her to look more closely into the request. She couldn't paint and couldn't sleep with the thinking, the trying to work it out. There were too many gaps and too much she didn't know, too much she was never told. There had to be more to it. Maybe her grandmother wanted Snip to track down her father so she could enjoy a family when she herself was gone. Her grandmother had been the closest to a traditional white family life that Snip had ever got. One thing Snip knew was that her grandmother had had a soft spot for Bud when he married her daughter.

Snip's mother was the key.

GOING HOME

The decision comes suddenly and swift and it's like a great weight has lifted from Snip when it's made. In Collector, on the night of a full moon, she packs up her swag and her paintings, her catalogues of men against pale bush and busy skies and grasses the colour of the sheep that are on them. She drives from a stretched landscape that looks as if a milky film has been washed over it, a palette of pale blues and silvers and bleached greens and greys. She drives up the Hume Highway fiercely, without stopping, in her old automatic with its accelerator pedal flapping wildly and sticking too much to the sole of her foot.

It's time to get a new car. Snip has the money now.

She drives north and then turns east off the highway. When tiredness drops over her she pulls up and sleeps fitfully in a hotel room where a rooster begins crowing at one a.m. and doesn't stop until four. She wakes in a grubby first light and drives towards a stretch of the ocean through a valley with good bones, a valley that was cow-ad green and idyllic once, a valley now pimpled with coal heaps. She has to slow, impatient, behind squat, grumbly trucks dribbling coal dust around corners. She drives past a field with flaps of corrugated iron that litter the ground like birds' wings, she drives past an old clawed bathtub used as a trough, she drives past a girl on a tall horse and instinctively slows, remembering what Bud had told her once: always give way to horses, that's the rule of the country.

Snip had been that girl, once. She drives impatient through her country and has no reverence for the land.

She turns a corner in the dip of a valley and slows the car to a crawl past a small sandstone church, weighted with ivy. Headstones cluster around the building and crowd it in. Every grave has bright flowers on it, shouting the vividness of the community spirit. Snip isn't fooled: every flower is plastic. Her mother had paid for the plastic on one of the graves not long ago. The funeral had been sparsely peopled and brief and Snip had fled swiftly from it, having no idea at the time of the mystery that lay beyond it in the form of the letter and cheque. Typical Nan, never letting her go completely, always looking out for her. Feeding her up, tucking her into bed, following her out the door, shouting instructions after her.

Snip speeds out of the dip and climbs to the sky and suddenly wide before her, as the rise flattens, is the ocean, the Pacific. It's flat and calm and so joyously blue it twists at her heart.

Snip drives slow to the house on the high cliff, on a bluff to the north of the Wollongong coast.

HELEN

Helen wants to hold on to the meanness of the house and Snip isn't sure why. Helen's discipline is light, her passion is monumentality and width and height. She's an architectural lighting designer who brings skyscrapers and streets and bridges and monuments to life, at night, with light. Her international break came when she relit the Sydney Harbour Bridge so that the arched span of the steel seemed to hover between the stone stanchions, seemed to be made weightless by light. She's now based in London.

As Helen hauled herself out of her marriage, as she clawed her way through university and on to Sydney and beyond it, her mother was always in the wings distracting the child. In the cliff house of frugal windows, which Helen rarely returned to. The house which has been left to Helen and which she now, resolutely, refuses to sell.

'I feel that my history is soaked into this house. It's a part of me, I just couldn't let it go,' she had said to Snip in a letter.

Snip steps through the front door, still clogged by the thinking.

The house smells of old rain pooled on carpet somewhere in a far corner. Her mother doesn't come out.

Snip finds her in her childhood bedroom, opening the windows to the rush-in of breeze. She watches for a moment without speaking. Helen's body is cluttered with clothing: a short kimono jacket over pencil pants and a vivid Aboriginal print shirt and a beret and a mell of necklaces. And buried among it all is the plain gold band on her left hand that's from Emery, her second husband, an American architect. They don't sleep together, Snip knows that. It's a marriage of mateship, Helen told her once. I like it that way she had said, don't go into it, don't pry.

Helen's sensuality is in the tumbly curl of her hair and her talky energy and the jumbly vividness of her clothes. It's as if she's cramming into her later life a joy with choice, with colour and vivacity and energy and light that she never had as a child in the grim coalmining village she grew up in, a spartan place where the windows and brickwork and pillowslips and sheets were always smudged black. Snip smiles at her mother's back, curving now with age. Her high shoes are kicked off, making her small.

'Mum.'

Helen turns. She holds out her arms in the swell of the curtain cloth. Snip can't catch her face. Helen steps from the billowing, laughing, and they come together in a hug. Helen asks her where on earth she's been.

'Around. You know, the usual. I always come back.'

'I just wish it was a bit more often.'

'Yeah, yeah, you can't talk.'

They both laugh. It's the way Snip always starts their reunions, rushing herself into love with her mother, throwing her joy at her. Before it turns.

Mother and daughter move from room to room and from window to window with Helen flinging them all wide. She's never still, she's never doing nothing. Snip follows her mother as she strips sheets from the beds, as she flings open cupboards and sorts through chipped teacups and plates and throws down old towels from high shelves.

'I didn't get a chance to even start any of this after the funeral. That Paris commission dragged me straight back home and I had to wait until everything was tied up before I could even think about getting back.'

Helen chatters on in galloping, nervous talk about the pollution in London and the latest tube strike and Emery's retirement and redecorating her flat. Helen's loudness is always in sharp contrast to her daughter's watching. It's as if her chatter has bitten Snip into a fierce, competing silence. But this time there's something else behind the accelerated pace. She's shutting something out, Snip can tell.

'I got a letter from Nan's solicitor, Mum. There was a cheque.'

There's a sudden silence, a souring. Helen doesn't look at Snip.

'And there were some instructions, to, to hunt Dad down or something. It was all very melodramatic and strange.'

'Yes, I know about it.'

'You know?'

'Ron McCormack, the solicitor, told me. It *is* very melodramatic.'

Helen turns to Snip, her face a blank canvas her daughter cannot read. And she tells Snip, casually laughing, too casually laughing, not to worry about what her grandmother was going on about, to just take the money and go on a trip overseas, or stop being a waitress or study art in New York for a while. Snip still hasn't made up her mind what she's going to do but she doesn't tell Helen that. As her mother says that her grandmother went a bit potty towards the end, and tries to laugh it all off, Snip suspects that perhaps the request in the will wasn't just a joke. She hovers around her mother's soft panic and plays with it, to see where it will lead or what slip it may yield.

'I'm thinking of buying a ute in Sydney and driving it back to Alice.'

'That dusty old place. Snip, I don't know what the hell you see in it.'

The reply comes too quick. And Helen never uses 'hell' like that.

'I'm going there because of Bud.'

'Oh Snip, *when* are you going to grow out of it?'

'What's going on, Mum? I don't get it.'

'It's got nothing to do with you. I really wish you'd drop it.'

'I want to find out.'

A heavy sigh. 'It's between me and Bud and your grandmother, just stay out of it. It all happened a very long time ago. No-one's inviting you into this.'

And Helen walks past Snip with her hands hovering in front of her shoulders, her fingers clawed frozen in anger. As if they've been dipped in blood, as if she doesn't want them dripping and staining.

The front door slams shut.

The smell of Helen is all that's left of her. Snip rolls her lips tight together, clogging the beginning of frustrated tears. It's the point they so often and so swiftly end up on: the put-down phone or the walk-out that snaps the conversation shut. Again and again it's the unclean retreat, the simmering silences, the stew.

Not this time. Snip strides out after Helen. The weather has turned. She hadn't noticed it inside.

No-one gets under her skin like her mother does, no-one hits on half-truths like her. Each one of them knows the other's mental jugular and goes straight for it, in arguments as fierce as fights in the school playground. Neither of them has grown out of it.

PUNCH

'We forget catastrophes, the worst that has happened to us. All right?' says Helen hard and swift, holding her face to the punch of the wind. 'We filter the remembering. For God's sake, Snip, you have to move on. It's a survival instinct. You were just a little girl, you wouldn't have coped.'

Helen grips the white railing at the top of the cliff as the furious wind tugs at her, flipping and cracking her thin kimono jacket like a whip. Snip tells her to come for a walk with her, it's too blowy where they are, to walk down to the beach and the shelter of the pine trees that rim it. Tells her they need to talk rationally, as two adults, that it's ridiculous the way they always seem to end up. Helen goes to say something dismissive and curt but stops herself, and reluctantly agrees.

On the path down to the beach Helen tells Snip that her grandmother turned into a kind of living frown at the very end. That Snip wouldn't know because she wasn't really there, and when she was her grandmother put on a show. She tells Snip she will never talk about Bud and she could throttle her grandmother for raising it, but it's typical, the mischievous way she's done it in her will, and Helen has no control over it.

Snip buys vanilla ice-creams for them both at the roadside van and they sit on a wooden bench facing the sea to eat them. As Helen finishes hers off she says to Snip that the truth is often awkward and unfinished and not beautiful and she tosses her head back at the house on the hill. She tells Snip to get away from it all, to experience the world. And then she turns to her daughter and looks her straight in the eyes and softens and pleads with her not to follow it through, to let it all lie for God's sake.

For her sake.

Snip doesn't have the heart in that moment to say she's finding it difficult to obey. She says nothing. She swallows Helen's plea. She gives nothing away. She has her mother in her power and she's never been in that situation before. They stand. Snip tells her she's going back up to the house. Helen doesn't follow. Snip says see you up there then, and walks away from her.

'I don't know what you see in that dusty old place in the desert, Snip. It's a weakness in you, the way you always run back. It's not being able to cope.'

The viciousness in Helen's flung words makes up her mind, her mother has given Snip the push that she's needed. She will use the money to hunt her father down. It's how Snip's operated so much during her life. Chasing the exact opposite of what her mother desires for her, slipping from expectations, thumbing her nose at her, refusing her wants.

Snip climbs the hill to the house with the wind strong on her back.

HER COUNTRY

Snip drives to Sydney the long way, through the coal-mining district that is dying. She drives over one-lane wooden bridges that clank under the slap of the tyres. She drives past sagging grey houses abandoned like tree stumps in fields. She drives past falling fences and junk-pocked paddocks and haysheds of streaked and rusted corrugated iron that lean dramatically from the push of the wind. She drives past rows of mailboxes at the top of steep roads, boxes that are empty, left behind by families that moved from the valley one by one as the coalmining in the district stopped.

Bud hasn't set foot in this country for twenty-three years, the country he came to as a child and grew up in. His family's country, and he's fiercely exiled himself from it. And Snip doesn't really know why.

She pulls up by the only milkbar in the main street of town. There are sagging check curtains in the windows and lamingtons squashed into a plastic tray, and at the back of the shop brightly coloured videos whose rows wallpaper the length of the wall. They're the only objects in the room that seem to have any energy left in them. Snip stares at them and smiles, thinking of her grandmother, who became addicted to videos after the television channels replaced the old black-and-white films that ran overnight with reruns of soap operas and music shows. Her favourite videos were of her daughter and granddaughter, made with their home camera. 'Walkie-talkie photos,' she called them. And as Snip stands in the dusty old shop with its forlorn shelves and faded colours, she tries to remember other examples of her grandmother's private family language. The scratcher, for steel wool, is the only other word she can recall.

Of course she has to obey her grandmother's wish. There could only be love behind it. Of course she must dig up the past.

Snip buys a lamington. She stands outside the shop and the cake crumbles with staleness in her hand as she bites into it. She reads the bleached texta sign in the shop window that sums the district up: 'Local lad, 23 years old. Work wanted. Will do almost anything.'

She knows she won't come back to this place for a very long time, if ever. And that if it were up to her she'd get rid of the house on the cliff. She's not sure when she'll see Helen again. Or how she'll tackle Bud.

She jettisons the lamington into a bin and drives, determined, up and out of the valley.

Snip leaves her car at a train station nudging the bush on the very edge of Sydney, not wanting the clot of traffic, not wanting lane changes and reverse parks and tetchy honks. She looks up the phone book and catches a train to the closest suburb with a Holden car dealership. Persuades the dealer to catch a cab with her back to her car. He checks it over. She trades it in. They go back to the car yard and she picks out a ute. She offers him fifty bucks to drive her, in her new manual car, into the centre of the city. He says bloody women and grins and drives her for free.

At a red light, Snip stares at a white plastic grocery bag flipping and fluttering in the breeze around the stalled traffic like a happy ghost. She lifts her arms behind her head and stretches her neck and smiles. She's not sure what's ahead but she's ready for it. The neophiliac, hungry for the next hit.

Snip checks into a five-star hotel curving around the water's edge at The Rocks. She orders room service and runs a bubble bath and pockets the shampoo. She places an ad for a passenger for a roadtrip to Alice in a local street mag and begins sketches for a new painting of the sea while she waits for the calls.

Dave is the first. There's an ease in his voice, an

openness that stops her still. Snip tells him to be at the hotel at ten the next morning for an introductory coffee. She adds that he's probably got the gig because for some reason, and she doesn't know why, she thinks she trusts him.

He chuckles and says, Hey, are you sure about that?

FLIT

A Tuesday night. Helen is away, at some place that was never specified.

Snip has come back early from her grandmother's high house on the cliff. She is put to bed by Bud. She is woken deep in the night.

A sleepy seven-year-old with cat yawns and daddy snuggles is slung over Bud's shoulder. Is bundled into the Valiant Regal, still cocooned in the blanket from her bed. There's the panicked gentleness in her father's hands as he places her floppy head on the pillow by the driver's seat in his last act of taking from the love of his life. There's his talk cantering continually through the taking, 'Come on darling, don't cry on me, it'll be fun, ssshh, Daddy's here, ssshh, ssshh,' and there's his reversing of the Valiant into the carport post and the crunch of the bash and the swearing and the not stopping to check in the speeding away from it all.

Bud burns the petrol like a demented man, not knowing if the lights in the rear-view mirror are the cops coming to take him or his daughter away. He pushes the car swiftly through the daylight, from stars to stars and from pub to pub. And each night the faces in the bars turn and stare and stop their talk when the two of them walk hand in hand through the door and Bud asks for a room – a twin, please, mate – and the publicans' wives stare knowingly at them and bend down to Snip and fuss and brush bits of her hair from her face. Some of them pull a scrunch of a handkerchief from the ends of their sleeves and wet the cloth quick with their tongue and rub the wetness hard across her cheek and she squirms from it and turns and buries her eyes in Bud's thigh.

On high barstools Snip and Bud sit side by side, his beer close to her pink lemonade with its striped paper straw, and they click glasses and drink and say little and move on. To more roads. To more mean thin walls of hotel rooms. To more sagging beds. To snores and grunts and hacks and spits from various roadworkers' and miners' and truckies' rooms running the length of creaky corridors. In barely-there mornings it's always a cold, sleepy scramble to the Valiant and the swing out to the lonely bitumen, to more bridges and hills and servos and signs. There are roos swerving from the road and kissing the tail end of the car. There are back roads and the jolt of corrugations, rattling Snip awake. The slap of tyres on cattle-grids. Heat. Feeling sick. Heaving and spluttering and coughing up milk gone solid until one day Bud gets so tired of stopping the car he tells her to do it out the window for Christ's sake and she does, streaking it in great lumpy lines across the length of the car, choking with the crying, and him yelling Jesus Christ and slamming on the brakes and stalking out and looking at what she's done.

Bud crouching, still, beside the road.

His head in his hands. Not speaking. Not looking at her. Not saying why.

Thinning road signs. No more fences. No more pubs.

Then one day Bud drops the gears to a stop in the just-rained-upon start of the desert. Both breathe deep. The smell of it cuts like menthol across the grime of the drive and Bud gets out of the car and rummages in his suitcase by the side of the road and finds the scissors and snips off her hair and turns her into a boy.

Driving on. Bud swerving to avoid a roo carcass in the middle of the road. Its eyes fresh-pecked holes, the reddest blood Snip has ever seen, and she leans far out the window and stares back in the flap of the wind, stares at the crow as it flies, slowly, from it. She doesn't have any idea what's ahead. And she knows, for the very first time in her seven-year-old life, that her father doesn't know either.

She has absolute faith in him, nonetheless.

CHAPTER THREE

What Fathers Do

Snip turns on the tap to brush her teeth for dinner. She's in Shelly-Anne's crisp bathroom. There's the smell of shit in the water. Shit smell is trapped in her toothbrush as she brings it to her mouth and shit smell settles on her wet eyelashes and hair and hands as she splashes her face.

In the room beyond her there's quick white talk. Shit smell will be on the people in there too, for they have all been in this community for a very long time. Even Shelly-Anne, whose scrubbed house this is, will smell faintly of shit. Shelly-Anne who hangs a plastic ball of floral scent from the rear-vision mirror of her four-wheel-drive troop carrier. It jigglejiggles on satin ribbon over the dirt corrugations of the roads and sometimes smacks smartly against the windscreen, but never breaks.

The quick white talk in the room beyond rises and drops to laughter like a wave flopping on to sand. Snip has to stride into it, she can't put it off any longer. It's a community of rare visitors and bare nightlife and she knows it'll be an evening bustling with yarns, she knows the white people of this place will grab her with stories and won't let go, as if their rich record somehow justifies their being in this place that isn't theirs.

Shelly-Anne has told her that if she stays too long in the land where the light hurts she'll lose the art of white person's talk, she'll lose the urban way. Shelly-Anne tells her the speech patterns of the people of this place are hers now, and it's too hard to revert when she's in white people's company. She says she's at a loss to communicate when she goes down south. That she can't speak with the prying faces unless they know something of her world away from the world, unless they know of its people and politics.

Snip has been in this place for twenty-one days and she feels like she's totally lost the art of talk, dinner-party talk, she feels as if the wind and dust and sun and stars have blown it cleanly out of her.

She stares in the mirror at the stubborn rim of reddened dust that's settled where her forehead meets her hair. It was make-up, once, that nestled there. Bud's in the room beyond. He hates her wearing make-up. And throughout the years has always wanted her hair short.

Snip turns off the tap, wrenching it tight. She grips the smooth basin sides and her knuckles push up like little alpine mountains in the smooth stretch of flesh. She flicks up the toilet seat. In the scrubbed, deeply stained bowl a scum of dead insects floats – they've drowned in the ecstasy of finding liquid in the desert. Snip drops her pants. Her shit is watery with nerves. She flushes the toilet, opens the door, strides down the hall, positions a smile and steps across the threshold.

Hunt him down.

BIG DRINKERS ALL

There's a scraping of plastic chairs. A ragged greeting of raised glasses. A table crowned with a gaggle of beer and wine and spirit bottles. It's a community that's designated dry – signs by the cattle-grids that ring it intone thousand-dollar fines for anyone caught with grog in their hand or their car. Snip knows the scene. The white people have their alcohol permits, they stock up in Alice, consume nightly and dispose of the empties in anonymous boxes so the Yapa won't realize what they're doing. They take their boxes in car boots back to Alice and they're big drinkers all of them.

Except Bud.

'He's someone you'd think would bury himself in drink. You know, the type of person that'd drink to forget to remember. But instead, he buries himself in

God,' Shelly-Anne had said to Snip on the day she came into the community from Alice.

KNOWING

Bud runs the abattoir at the New Bore outstation twenty k from the community. He extracts pieces of scrap from cars in the metal graveyard five k from the community. He rarely steps into the community, except to go to church, and has never told anyone where he's come from or what his life was before he arrived in the coughing Valiant Regal, twenty-three years ago, and stopped.

Snip knows he came as a child to this country fifty-odd years back, from a place on the other side of the world where the sky is so low it almost touches the rooftops. She knows he has coaldust ingrained in black lines like thin leeches on his knees from sliding down coalheaps as a kid. She knows he's called Bud because his brother christened him 'Little Budder', when he was born.

'Well, is it good to see your daughter, Bud? She's coming up strong!' Shelly-Anne says at the table head.

'My daughter? I didn't know I had one,' says Bud, staring at Snip.

She sits opposite him, saying nothing. Lifts her eyes to his eyelashes that as long as she can remember have been so distinctive, his special mark. One set is deeply black and the other is longer and completely white-grey and it gives him a compelling, unsettling look. The three other people at the table hold their talk, watching them both.

Bud sits with his hat on. It's holed and deeply stained where the rim meets his head. Snip was with Bud when he bought it, twenty-three years ago. She remembers squealing at the time and christening it 'the verandah', because it dipped so big and slanty around him. Bud had dropped down to her and vowed on the day he bought it that he'd never take it off when his daughter was with him. And he never did. He went to church in it, shopped in it, drove in it, swam in it, even told her he showered in it. Snip always tried to catch him out and never could.

She'd forgotten all that until now.

'If you're not here to see your daughter, you old bugger, what are you here for, hey? What's the grand occasion?'

'Business, Shell.'

'Oh?'

'Car business.' And Bud turns to Snip and asks where has she been, which is always his way of saying hello.

'Around.'

'Are you still making pictures?'

'I'm always making pictures.'

'When are you going to get a real job?'

'This *is* my real job, Bud. You know that.'

They always have this conversation, always beginning with Bud teasing and Snip justifying.

'I do know that.'

'It's really important to me, what I'm doing. I'm getting shows. And it's why I'm moving around so much. I'm gathering fresh material.'

Richard, beside Snip, snorts a laugh. Richard the schoolteacher who began writing to her after they met on a previous visit. Richard who would send dense black script wishing she'd live in the community for good. Dense black script about cleaning his government-issue fibro house that was dotted with human stools, about enjoying it Ajaxed. Then dense black script about the young Yapa students who left a trail of blood from the back of the ute to his fridge, which was stuffed with roo tails and meat chunks from hunting trips, then month after month of writing wishing she'd come back. Signing off with love every time, even though Snip barely knew him.

Richard's letters always took several weeks to track her down. She never wrote back. Last Christmas, Snip realized, the dense black script had stopped. She missed it.

In the oblique, lecturing way that Bud has, cutting across conversations and steering his own path, he tells Snip not to think of going back and studying any more of that art business. He says she doesn't need any of that classroom stuff, that she can pick up what she needs from a library. His deep, slow voice commands the conversation, stopping the rest of them as they turn their heads to him. Bud looks at Snip and no-one else. He tells her his best mate from childhood is now a millionaire and he never got past primary. That his mate was asked on his last day at school to name two days in the week beginning with 'T' and he answered today and tomorrow. That his mate didn't have any need for education, he got where he was through hard work and discipline and a good woman behind him.

'So that explains why you're here, Bud,' says Richard. They all laugh, except Bud. Snip stops herself when she looks back at him.

'Richard's found God. All he says now is Jesus Christ. Especially when he comes home from school and his fridge is full of roo tails. Jesus Christ he says all the time, Jesus bloody Christ,' says Shelly-Anne.

A WOMAN OF VALUE

Richard leans back in his chair and looks at Snip. He fingers his wineglass stem and smirks. 'Why have you got your hands around your face all the time, Snip? Have you got arthritis in your elbows or something?'

The young men at the table laugh. Snip pulls her hand from her mouth and blushes. Richard sees it and shuts down his smirk.

'How did you get here this time, Snip?'

'I drove.'

'Whitefella way – on your own?'

'No, Richard. I got adventurous. I picked up this bloke in the city.'

'City-slickers,' says Bud, butting in. 'Don't trust 'em.'

'Yeah, he was a bit of a bastard.'

'That's good.'

'Why do you say that?' Snip frowns at her father. 'Bud?'

''Cause he rang.'

'He *rang*?'

'Some bloody barmaid in Alice who should've known better said I was your father and gave him the number at the abattoir. He was looking for you, his words were all tangled up, and when he knew he'd got your old man, he was going on about how he thought you two had been married out there by the air or some stupid thing and I thought he was a right wally and told him so.'

'Good,' Snip says.

And Richard is talking of exhaustion because every night he's organizing football or a disco or a basketball match to keep the kids from sniffing the petrol that's killing them and Richard is talking of blue tongue, too much blue tongue, and Richard is talking of leaving and maybe going to the city and asking Snip about the traffic and reverse parking and is it impossible down there and she's telling them about her new ute and how it takes diesel and there's approval at that and she's toasted as a woman of value now, a woman with a bush car, and she's thinking of his hand over hers as they shifted to second gear and third and fourth and fifth and she flings back her head and finishes her wine and crosses her legs and arches her back at the table, she's thinking of pushing the car strong into an expanding sky and his fingers burrowing deep between her thighs and she's laughing as she says the hitchhiker had to teach her how to drive the bloody thing, she'd never driven a manual before, it took her twelve years to do it, no hang on, ten.

'Those bludgers are good for something, then,' says Bud.

Annoyed, Snip grabs at Richard's lighter. She wants to tell him that people who don't succeed in some way, who are frustrated or failures, are often the ones who are quickest to judge but she stops herself short and flicks at the lighter again and again, grating her thumb 'til it hurts over the flint, snapping it shorter and sharper.

'The girl who steals fire! I'd forgotten that,' Bud says. He grins and tips his hat to her. 'My little fire stealer. You've always done that.'

Snip sits very still and holds the flame under her chin until the glow turns to hurt.

MEN'S BUSINESS

'There were these Yapa guys and they got a flat, and they didn't have a jack,' Kevin says, beer froth like milk on his upper lip. 'There was this big yellow government grader by the road and they hotwired it, they lifted the arse end of the car up by the scoop and changed the tyre just beautiful, and the magistrate let 'em off, a big fucking grin on his face, and the coppers and the council were all fucking fuming.'

'I want one of them jacks,' Bud says.

Kevin turns to Snip. He grins loony-wide and circles his fingers in the air around his ear, the Yapa way, a hunting signal, meaning 'mad one', and he asks her why she bothers to come back to see Bud, why on earth she's here. 'Why aren't you off living it up with that big fancy mama of yours? Where is she, New York?'

'London.'

'Running as far away as she can from the both of you, is she? Eh? Christ, what a family. They broke the mould with you lot.'

Bud says nothing. His sidelong glance and his lightly

cocked eyebrow betray the keen interest. Snip can read him.

'Titheads. That's what I call them London policemen. Titheads.' Kevin is off roaring.

Bud says nothing. Snip lets it all lie.

Kevin is doing a masters thesis on the *tjuḵurrpa* dreaming stories in Walpiri paintings. And cleaning the Walpiri toilets by the oval for dolla. He lifts weights and captains the footy team with a freshly pierced eyebrow that was numbed for the darning needle with a wrapped Paddlepop. He lives intermittently in his Combi van and he's fathered two babies in the community who are both due to appear on the same day. His justification: that if he's not in a relationship his balls start shrinking and he's not having that. So the more fucks, the better, because the bigger his balls will grow.

Snip can't say why it is that she's here.

Kevin is debating whether to go through with initiation. He isn't sure. Maybe, maybe not. If one of his sons does, yes.

'You have to be asked, my sweet.' Shelly-Anne, dipping between them with her ladle of curry.

Being here for Snip is being in a place so far away Dave will never find her. And being here is because of Bud. As she studies him she thinks of the phrase she'd come across once, *bien dans sa peau*: good in one's skin.

He is now. She mentally draws him as he sits leaning back and observing, holding his energy in check. His slow, removed smile tells her he's comfortable now with the deep gouges on his face like river lines on a map, comfortable with the thin shirt that's branded across the belly with ochre, comfortable with the watch that stopped once and then never came off.

Shelly-Anne's told Snip that as far as she knows Bud hasn't been with a woman since he's been here. It's twenty-three years of abstinence. He's a man who's buried himself in religion and work and celibacy and God knows what else, and Snip doesn't know him now or the new ease that's in him. She's seen him fleetingly maybe ten times in the past ten years.

He was never comfortable before, that's how she remembers it. He was jittery and edgy and shy, as if he'd never quite worked out the person he was or where he belonged. And now there's a settling, and its origin is unknown. Nonetheless, Snip is reluctant to disrupt it with her grandmother's wish to pin him down and confront him over something she knows nothing of. And finish him off, in some strange way.

Shelly-Anne is filling Snip's plate and saying she can always tell if an old Yapa man has used the art centre toilet because there's urine everywhere, because his penis has been split during initiation – like a burnt banger, Shelly-Anne is telling her, and the men are laughing uncomfortably, the image vivid in their faces, and Shelly-Anne is telling them the urine sprays out like water from a watering can.

'Did you tell him where I was?' Snip says to Bud.

'Who?'

'The city-slicker.'

'Yeah, yeah I did.'

'Now, don't you go thinking about going off and doing something stupid, girl, like getting hitched,' says Shelly-Anne, stern.

Snip says, 'As if,' but Shelly-Anne powers over her words, not hearing them.

'You have to wait and see what he's like when he's pissed, you have to get him drunk, because you never really know a man until then. Do you, my sweet?'

Shelly-Anne holds Kevin's cheek, softly, in the cup of her palm as Snip tells her she's got no intention of seeking out someone who was such a bastard and Bud stands up from his seat and bows and they all laugh. We love the things we're not meant to, Bud says, but it's lost in Shelly-Anne's plea that no-one tonight is going to get cranky drunk, no cranky drunk please, it's her rising plea, and Snip sits quietly in it all and flicks and flicks at the lighter and Kevin slams down his beer and declares he wants to go on a float in Mardi Gras in Sydney. He's getting Marcelle the feral cat researcher to make him a pair of shorts from ginger-cat pelts, they're all hanging on her clothesline and he likes ginger streaked with black the best and in the evening distance the breeze through the louvres carries strange wails and snatches of chants, many voices.

'Sorry business, someone has died.' Shelly-Anne, sitting down, quiet. 'They'll be planted tomorrow, or the next day.'

There's the one protracted wail and then a chorus and then the wail again, rising sad.

'Old Maggie rang today, from Alice,' Shelly-Anne says. 'Her cousin's in there on a dialysis machine. He broke now she said, can't be fixed, all turn off. Like he was an old motor car.'

'What was that about a motor car?' Bud asks.

They all laugh and pick up their forks. Eat.

Long candles, unlit on the table, droop like flaccid penises in their tall candlesticks. The wax has been wilted by heat. There's a lull in the talk. The five of them listen to a long wail soaked in melancholy.

HOME, MATE

'I want Homer Hudson ice-cream,' Richard says as a checkered tea-towel is flicked away by Shelly-Anne to reveal a big tin can in her hand. Within it are little bitsy pieces of fruit, rigorously square in thick sugared syrup.

'I want sushi and Saturday papers and talkback radio and cappuccinos and concerts,' Richard says as the can, with its spoon, is placed on the table.

He's backhanded on the shoulder by Kevin. 'This *is* your home, mate.'

'I have to leave, I have to. I'm losing my own culture.'

Shelly-Anne tells them she can't stand her sister-in-law's flat down south because it's so stuffed full of objects and Snip thinks of the inner-city warehouse she lived in briefly and fled from, she thinks of the vaulting space and her search for spareness in the cram of the city.

Richard says he has to get out of the community because he's going deaf from the shouting, he's lost all patience with the loud talk, all the time, in his face, bashing at his ears. That's nothing, says Kevin, he used to work in an advertising firm, and Snip imagines him hyped by tall windows at the harbour's edge, slickly suited and pony-tailed and she asks him why he left.

'You know that Peggy Lee song, "Is That All There Is?" Well, after six years of flogging toilet rolls, that's how I felt. I'm thirty-five and I'm happy. I'm a slink-back – I left here once and I came back again, with my tail between my legs like a dog slinking back. I couldn't keep away. You know what it's like.'

The wailing comes again, rising sad.

Someone asks Bud how old he is and he shrugs, he's

lost count. Fifty-six, Snip says to his eyes and he opens them wide in dismay and together they grin.

Shelly-Anne says she completely missed her thirtieth birthday, until someone remembered and peeled her an orange.

'It was me.' Richard.

Bud says he remembers his birthdate but not his age and Snip tells him that's what homeless people do and Richard asks whether the Aboriginal people see them as homeless aimless drifters, do they think it's weird these whitefellas being out here, without ties to their own culture and community, away from their family and friends? Richard asks what the Aboriginal people think of them.

No-one answers.

'Come and sit on my knee,' Bud says to Snip.

They all laugh.

'No,' she says. 'I'm too old.'

MISTAKE

Over coffee with powdered milk the wailing builds and the talk slides to silence and they listen and then the talk begins again about what they'll be getting done tomorrow. Shelly-Anne says she'll be combing the dirt of her yard with a rake. Kevin says he'll be scrubbing away the new graffiti on the toilet walls – YOU BIG HOLE, JAPALJARRI LOVES NO-ONE, FUCK ME. Tomorrow, Snip's not sure.

'That city-slicker. He's driving out here, Snip—'

'WHAT?'

'Something about a mistake, he said, that he has to put right.'

Bud throws a hand in the air in a gesture of not knowing as there's a thumping at the door.

'A mistake? What – Bud?'

'Yehwah? Come in, open!' Shelly-Anne yells and old Queenie Nungala Mosquito walks in wailing and singing sad, clutching her handkerchiefed head in her hands, looking at the mess of bottles on the table and then looking at Bud and then sobbing to them all that they'll be looking for Bud, they'll be driving out to his place to talk to him tonight because of the cars, the cars.

'The cars, what do you mean Queenie?' Shelly-Anne says.

'All gone. Men's business. In cars, all gone. Old cars all gone. Big sorry.'

And Kevin, tight, is saying the cars, Jesus Christ, that's where the *tjukurrpa* is, the sacred items, in the gloveboxes of the old Holdens, that's the keeping place of the community's secret sacred items and Bud is saying oh, quietly, oh, quietly, oh, and Shelly-Anne is yelling what do you mean Bud what the fuck's happened and

Bud is saying oh quietly, oh, and Queenie wanders out of the house wailing and singing and then there's silence.

Bud has his arms propped stick-straight on his spread knees. His head is down and after a long while, very low, he tells them he got a scrap-metal dealership to come in from Alice to clear the cars away, that three blokes have been working solidly for the day and the old Holdens were the first to go, for scrap, and Bud's not looking at any of them and quieter and calmer still he's saying he thought he was doing everyone a favour, getting rid of some of the old rubbish, cleaning up the bush a bit, he's saying he had no idea about anything secret and sacred being in them and Shelly-Anne is saying why Bud, why did you do it, you IDIOT and Bud says again he thought it was a good thing, tidying the place up, and he says he got a bit of cash for it and Shelly-Anne groans and Bud says it wasn't much and for God's sake he'll write a cheque out to the council tomorrow if that's what they want. Shelly-Anne says oh shit oh shit, maybe he has to just get out for a while, oh shit, long way Bud, long fucking way. Maybe payback mate. Oh shit.

Snip stands, her mouth sapped of wet. Payback. Imagines. The spearing in the arm or the thigh, Bud crumpling to the dust, keeling over on his side, his agony, his exile from the community, his shame and possibly worse.

Bud surfaces. His face has crumpled into old age and Snip knows what's coming from his eyes.

'Pippy, will you come with me?'

'What?'

He's sinking. She can see it in his face. She can read the deep panic, the fear.

'I've got an old mate I could stop with for a while.'

'Where, Bud?'

'The border way, long way. No-one'll track me to there. Will you come?'

A fragment, twenty-three years ago. Another life on the run. Their caravan. And how he would put on the swimming goggles to chop the onions and Snip would be giggling and clapping her hands as she sat at the table slicing the carrots, and he would tell her he had to put the goggles on for onions because he couldn't risk it, because if he started crying he wouldn't stop.

She sits. His eyes at her. Their fear.

'But, but Dave?'

'You're only going to see him to give him an earful aren't you? You said yourself he was a bastard. I wouldn't give him the time of day. And my motto is keep 'em waiting, that's what gets to them.'

'But Bud there was a mistake, wasn't there?' She blushes. 'I, I fell for him a bit. I want to see him. To, to clear things up, get him out of my head.'

'Snip, I could really do with a hand with this one.'

Bud's never said that he needs her. And the city-boy did dump her.

'It'll only be a day or two. We'll leave a note for that Dave bloke. It'll be two days at the most, I promise. I'll get you back.'

Snip clamps her hand to her mouth in her furious thinking.

'The old man'll look after you, trust me. And to be honest, I don't reckon my clapped-out bomb of a truck'll make it. We'd have a much smoother ride in your fancy new ute.'

Snip puts her palms flat to her cheeks, masking her face from the eyes at the table. She's drowning, she's wanting to run: from Bud, from the mess of it, and from the pull of family. She doesn't want the weight of it, it's too much effort, it always has been. She prefers her own way, no obligations, no complications. Complacency.

Snip looks up at the dinner-party eyes, shiny and still around her. There's an expectant hush.

Shelly-Anne breaks it. She walks behind Snip and clamps her hands on her shoulders, locking her into the seat. She tells Bud not to force his daughter into something she mightn't want or that mightn't be the best thing for her. She says he can go out and get himself killed if he wants, but by God, he's not going to drag his daughter into it too.

'If I may be so bold,' says Richard suddenly, 'we may

be overreacting just a bit here. They might just want to know where the cars have been taken or something. I don't think we should be jumping to conclusions.'

'I don't want to risk it,' says Bud, his voice breaking under the strain. 'I want to stay away until things have died down.'

'Why don't you just wait and see what they say?' Richard says.

'I'm running with this one, mate.'

Snip surfaces. She examines Bud's deeply crevassed face. It's the face of a smoker, older than its years. There's something heartbreaking and vulnerable through it now, a need that he rarely lets out. She doesn't know if he's bullshitting or not about the ute and she doesn't know if they're all overreacting but Bud's never said before that he needs her. She feels as if he's hauling her into adulthood, daring her, in a way, to join. His hand is shaking as he runs it through his hair.

She smiles serenely at him. 'Yeah Bud. I'll come.'

'What about the dog?' Shelly-Anne says, tight.

Snip hesitates. 'I'll have to leave him behind. He'll never make it.'

'He should've been put down a week ago,' Kevin says.

Snip gives him a withering look. She skids her bowl across to him and tells him to wash up. 'It's good practice,' she says, 'for impending fatherhood.' Kevin pokes out his tongue. Snip says to Shelly-Anne they're going to need supplies. Richard says don't say I didn't warn you and then volunteers to look after the dog. Bud is still and ashen and silent and old among it all.

It's almost eleven. It's going to be a long, scrappy night.

CHAPTER FOUR

Silence Like Mould

Silence like mould has grown over Merv and Hazel's marriage. Shelly-Anne strides into it.

Snip doesn't. She stops just inside the doorway of their house.

She knows little about them. They've been here six months. They don't mix with the other white people in the community. They don't mix with Aboriginal people. They run the only store for 260 kilometres and order supplies a few days shy of their use-by dates. They buy in bulk, get a good deal and make a packet. Snip's watched their silence as they stand side by side behind the counter of the shop, as they walk home to their house when the sunlight loses its vividness and the day becomes gentle, and they don't seem to see it as they rake the dirt of their yard in the glare of the weekend. They rake Zen patterns, fifties-neat, then during the week some posse of kids will sneak open their gates and the human stools and plastic bags and chip packets will appear and they'll begin all over again.

No-one Snip knows in the community likes Merv and Hazel. Everyone in the community depends on them. There's a rumour, unverified, that they used to run a social club in Arnhem Land. That they cleared it after nights of big drinking with an electric cattle-prod.

Shelly-Anne's words gallop as she tells Merv that Snip has to get out of the community fast and she needs some groceries and she has a lot of dolla to spend. Shelly-Anne holds a bowl with the leftovers of the dinner-party curry. She offers the bowl to Merv. He asks what's in it and she tells him and he says, good-natured, oy none of that Chink food thanks. Like a judge at a country show Hazel, from her seat at the dining table, raises her chin and narrows her eyes. Merv heaves his body by his forearms from sagging vinyl in front of the TV. He flicks off the pushy noise, turns and props his hands in his shorts pockets. Jingles his keys. A peep of hairy white flesh rests over the elastic of his King Gees and he stares at Snip and doesn't invite her further in.

'The Paddlepop girl.'

'Yeah, but it's a bit more than Paddlepops I need at the moment.'

It's her cue and she jumps forward too quickly and pushes her hand into Merv's. It's a hand not used to shaking a woman's. His sliver of a touch barely connects and his hand slips swiftly away.

'Merv, can you help?' Shelly-Anne's voice cuts sharp through the niceties. 'C'mon, mate. The blackfellas are after her. It's about secret sacred stuff. Hear that wailing out there? It's big sorry and it's directed at Snip. Well, sort of. We don't have much time.'

Her tone's crossed the other side, it's redneck sweet-talk. Snip looks across at her. She didn't think Shelly-Anne had it in her.

Hazel coughs. A 'community cough', a scratch in the back of the throat some whitefellas get when they arrive in an Aboriginal community. They usually don't shake it until they leave the place for good. Richard's got it too. It's a niggling bugger of a thing and no amount of cough lollies will smooth it over. Hazel coughs again. 'It's past eleven. We've just done the stocktake. It's much too late, Merv.'

The voice is clipped and careful and warning him. The words are fenced, it's like she's surrounded herself with a boundary of No. Shelly-Anne throws across a grin at Merv. Snip catches it. His wife doesn't. It's a grin with secrets in it.

'Give me a minute,' says Merv, and ducks into a room.

Hazel goes pointedly back to her *Women's Weekly*. On the cover of the magazine is a European princess in a ridiculous hat holding to her cheek a newborn baby. Snip remembers that story. It's a couple of years old.

Shelly-Anne stands and waits, awkward, the bowl still in her hand.

Snip stands and waits, awkward.

Silence like mould.

BOX

Four long strips of light spit and flick in the darkness, row after row, and then hum into glary life. Snip clamps her eyes shut. The fluoro of the store is too blue-bright. Merv rummages for something under the weary counter and straightens and offers her a beer.

'I keep 'em in me own private fridge down here.'

There's the familiar sound of the ring-pull, the crackle of aluminium and the escape of the gas. Snip loves that sound. It's a Bud sound from her childhood, as tugging as the smell of a hose sprayed on hot wet cement or a new barbie camper or a freshly mown lawn. She takes the can from Merv. She'll only have a few sips for politeness. To humour him, and because she owes him.

'It's a good set-up in here. I've got me fridge and a town toilet. Some big-shot Abo committee from Darwin made us put in a loo, a public one. It was some sort of regulations. So what we do is lock the door and put an out-of-order sign permanently on it,' he says with a grog-stained smile, savouring his ingenuity. 'It keeps it good for us.'

Merv walks around the counter and stands in front of it and leans against it. Snip wishes Shelly-Anne had come to the shop with her, she wishes she hadn't gone straight back to her house to supervise the loading of the car. Merv takes another sip and crosses his ankles.

'We can turn the lights on in here and no-one'll know we're inside. You could run a brothel at night and no-one'd know.'

She snaps up a wire basket and walks the wide aisles, away from the talk. In the back of her neck Snip can feel Merv watching.

It's a store with no windows, a besser-brick box so there's nothing to smash. Inside the box, in a fridge by the far wall, are a few limp lettuces and shrivelled oranges. There are freezers of white bread. Roo tails in plastic that are four bucks each and as hairy and innocent-looking as tourist souvenirs. Freezers of purple, dubious looking meat and grey sausages and long tin buckets of flour and sugar. A plastic dispenser with heated cans of spaghetti bolognaise. Musk cigarette lollies. Hunting knives. Cowboy boots. Swags.

Snip stacks food items in the basket and dumps them on the counter and goes back to the aisles and does it again. She's panicky, trying to think things through, trying to remember the essentials. It has to be enough for a two-day trip. Better double it, just in case. Not that she'll be going any longer, she'll be holding Bud to his promise. She veers out of range of Merv's stare. Hopes Shelly-Anne's got enough water containers. Makes a mental note: check oil and water, check tyres, check spare. Make sure Bud's got his rifle. Oil. Water. Tyres. Spare.

Snip feels Merv's eyes still on her and she bristles her spine into a haughtiness as she thuds the last of the items on the counter. With a lazy grin he drops her purchases into thick brown paper bags. She hasn't seen those since childhood. Merv looks at her and flicks his eyes down to her chest.

Snip fucked a man like him once. The bloke had come all over her face and she'd thought at the time of a dog lifting his leg to a post and staking his claim. The cum had dried swiftly, had been thin and cracked like a face mask across her cheeks and she'd hated it, the humiliation.

She ducks away from Merv's gaze and reads the community noticeboard while he locks up the till. He's doing it slowly. There's a council notice: five dollars for full bags of rubbish brought in. He's pulled out a cigarette. There's a schedule for an upcoming sports weekend: football, softball, spear throwing, basketball, ceremonial dancing. He's taking his time. There's a schedule for a land-claim hearing. Another one.

'C'mon, Miss Paddlepop.' His big arms are around Snip from behind and she smells his sweat and then his soft forearm flesh is encasing her breasts and his quick-hot breath is close at the side of her neck and there's the wet smear of his tongue as his cock butts her back.

Snip jerks her arms instinctively. Her elbow goes sharp into his soft belly flesh and she doubles as if she's been socked in the gut, then moves from him quick.

'Oy! Miss Paddlepop. Steady on.'

'I *don't* do that sort of thing.' Tight.

'Okay. Okay. Jesus.'

They eye each other like boxers between rounds in their corners of a ring.

'You'll never carry all those bags by yourself. You'll need a lift home.'

'Fuck off. I don't want one. FUCK OFF.'

Breathing hard, both of them.

'It's close to midnight. I'm not keeping the shop open while I wait for you lot to get ready. It's gonna take you three trips, at least, to get this lot back to your car. And I thought there was a time factor in all of this.'

'Fuck *off*.' But he's right.

THE RELIEF OF AIR

There's clear plastic on the seats of Merv's four-wheel-drive ute. Snip sits as close as she can to the door and winds down the window and holds out her head like a dog, holds out her face to the relief of the air.

'Where you off to?'

He's attempting to smooth things over, to retrieve it all, to calm her down before they reach Shelly-Anne, Snip can tell. She doesn't pull her head back inside. He's not getting the satisfaction of an answer.

'I was only asking.'

A long pause. 'I don't know.' It's said to the night; it's said to herself, not to him.

'Oh?'

'The border. Lajamanu way.'

He'll never find it.

'You're Bud Freeman's girl aren't you?'

She's had enough. No more talk.

'The one that gave him so much trouble. I've heard all about you, the Alice roadhouse and all that.'

Merv shakes his head and snorts a laugh.

'Well, Miss Paddlepop, all I can say is good bloody luck. You'll need it.'

Snip squeezes further over to the edge of the seat and stares at Merv's house as they drive past it. The unpainted fibro. The government-issue, jerry-built construction. The rubbish bits flattened against the cyclone wire of the fence, as if they've been electrocuted trying to get in. There's a staircase out the back of the house that's never been completed, a scaffolding skeleton to nowhere. It promises the prestige of a stilt-house never built. Hazel's lean silhouette is in the front doorway, the glow of her cigarette tip like an obedient firefly. Snip pings a question at Merv, not looking at him.

'So, are you gonna retire in this place?'

'If there's one thing I'm sure of, it's that no white man knows their future in this town, you should know that.'

Hazel keeps watching as they drive on to Shelly-Anne's house. Her chin is high and Snip can just make out her eyes narrowed at them. She wants to paint the lean suburban hardness that's in her. The sharp, suspicious eyes. The skin across her cheeks that's tight and affronted and ungiving.

GUTTING THE UTE

Shelly-Anne, Bud and Snip work with economy and crispness around the gutted ute. Its doors are flung wide, its bonnet is up and the wings of its toolbox are spread. Water containers are swiftly filled and swags are rolled and cooler-boxes are packed. Oil's checked, the rifle's placed behind the passenger seat, toothbrushes are put in the glovebox and rope and sketchpads and paints and boxes are packed in the back.

Two tea-towels are slung to dry on the rail of the stairs. Richard and Kevin have done their domestic duties and gone home as the wailing builds higher in the air of the night.

No Food and his blanket will be going with Richard tomorrow and Snip worries over that. But she knows he'll be in safe hands. Richard's got the tightness of a perfectionist and he'll do everything he can.

Queenie Nungala Mosquito has returned. She crouches on the step and watches, holding her cheek in her hand and wailing and murmuring talk. A long time back, she used to visit each whitefella home in the community and sometimes piss on their couches. She was sent from house to house to get rid of her until one day Shelly-Anne peeled her an orange and asked her her story and suddenly, the pissing stopped. Now Shelly-Anne is her 'daughter', she's been invited to share women's business and ceremony, she's been told some of the secrets and painted up.

Queenie says to Shelly-Anne that maybe the men just want talking and Bud snaps that he's not going to risk it and Queenie takes up the wailing, softly, again. Snip asks Bud what place exactly they're going to. He says it's a mate's. She asks blackfella or whitefella and he chuckles softly and says no whitefella will have him. He doesn't say much else, he doesn't explain, he never has said much. There's a furrow cut jagged and deep between his eyebrows. It's new and Snip doesn't know if it's from squinting in the sun or worry or age.

The plan's to camp on the edge of the community in the ragged bit of night that's left and head quickly south in the fresh light tomorrow.

'Sharon,' says Queenie, snapping from the wailing. 'They got plenny fuel?'

Bud looks at Snip. She says almost a full tank and he tells her that's enough and she turns to Shelly-Anne and says she wants more than enough and how can she get a jerry-can of diesel at midnight.

Bud's furrow twists and deepens. He says nothing.

A GOANNA IN THE FRIDGE

The hand that leads Snip into the night is as dry as a leaf. Queenie walks her swiftly and surely through the black. They walk a long way to a besser-brick block of a room, her home.

'My family,' Queenie says proudly, flinging her hand towards the peopled mattresses in the flickering, doorless inside. There's late-night TV jangling, puppy puddles, stretched canvases stacked against a wall, dishes toppled in the sink, shy smiles, sleeping bodies turning away from the newness of the noise and air-conditioning pumping into the soft, still night. A canvas is lying on the floor. Its concentric lines have the beginning of some strange power and a hairless whimper of a dog is lying on it. Queenie says something sharp to a child of about eight who's sinking into sleep in a chair. His head is languid in his hand but he snaps awake and Queenie pushes him out the door.

'He my grandson. Kenny. Good one, coming up strong. Cheeky one.'

Queenie says something in Walpiri to Kenny. Kenny walks faster. He stumbles over a toy called a truck – a tin can on a string. He doesn't look back. He walks to a bush-battered jeep under a tree, hauls himself into the back of it and throws out a hose. Snip walks over with the jerry-can and Kenny takes it without looking. He opens the fuel cap and she goes to suck on the hose but can't do it and he softens and laughs and shows her how. He bleeds the car dry. In the jerry-can's hollowness Snip estimates it's a quarter-full. It'll have to do. Queenie takes her money softly and walks Snip back to the room, sweeping her arm at the sky and the land.

'Next time, Napaljarri, we go for more hunting. Swags, tea, pituri yehwah. Big bush trip. I show you how to catch goanna.'

They walk back into the room and Queenie opens the old fridge door and inside on the only rack there's a solitary goanna. It's cold and stiff and beautiful and as red as the dirt they stood on outside.

'Tail's the best bit, Napaljarri.'

They laugh and Kenny climbs on to Queenie's back like he's climbing a tree and together as one they wave Snip away as she walks into the black.

A WARNING

'My gypsy girl. You're always running running running, you're never stopping.' Shelly-Anne wraps Snip's fingers around a packet of chewing gum and jokes that it's a gift for the trip. Then she whispers close to her ear not to go, that's it's not too late to pull out. To stay here safe with the dogs. 'That Bud, he does things his own way. He hasn't looked out for anyone else for a very long time, he's all rusty. He's a dreamer, he just lets the world flow around him and does his own thing. I don't trust dreamers.'

'Shelly. He's my dad. It's one of those things I've just got to do.'

'Hey girl, you don't have to do anything you don't want to. Remember that.'

Snip smiles. Shelly-Anne told her years ago that life

is a series of difficult choices and Snip reminds her of that and they laugh. Look across at Bud.

'Snippy, for all your fearlessness and courage and adventuring, I sometimes think you're terribly naïve. You've got a lot to learn about men, my girl. You don't go on a car trip from Sydney to Alice with a stranger just because you like the sound of his voice. And you don't go running off into the desert at the drop of a hat with a madman called Bud Freeman. Even if he is your father. He won't tell me where he's taking you.'

Snip pokes out her tongue. Puts the chewing gum into the pocket of her shorts and kisses Shelly-Anne on the cheek and gets a slap on the bum in return.

'Get off with you, then. Scram.'

No Food licks at Snip's lips in her leaving. She laughs and pushes his nose away and whispers in his ear not to forget her.

She shuts the front door on his one quick bark.

HOW IT BEGINS

Bud tells Snip he'll do the driving. He knows the place they'll be camping the first night out and he takes the keys from her hands as she heads for the driver's door.

As they pull away from Shelly-Anne's house Snip says to Bud she wants to drop into his place by the abattoir, she has to, because Dave's heading to it and because she wants to leave a note on the door. Bud says no, NO, it's too risky and he accelerates the car.

'Bu-ud.'

'I said NO.'

In the loaded silence that follows, Snip knows that's that. She jerks down the window and holds out her head and dunks her skin into the night air's coolness.

It's not a good start.

WEARY

The place they drive to on the outskirts of the community has ground that's weary. Snip can hardly see it in the thick dark but she can feel the land's meanness, she can feel the barrenness thousands of cattle hooves have stamped into it. A twisted bit of muffler rears up at them like a petrified snake.

They lay out their swags and don't light a fire. There's no firewood and they're not in the mood and all they want is sleep. For Snip, a night out bush without a fire feels like a night without brushing her teeth before bed. But she's too exhausted to ask for one, or make it herself. Bud works in the dark with his old miner's caplamp strapped to the rim of his hat. She softens with a smile at that. The light's yellow, piss-weak.

Snip says nothing. The silence between them is taut. It's always the same, she's always wanting to say so much but can't, she never knows where to begin, she never knows how to talk to a father so changed. She always walks away from him feeling dissatisfied, feeling that no real talking has ever begun between them.

'How's your mother?' As if he's reading her thoughts.

'Since when were you interested?' Her snap-back. The moment's ruined. Now's not the time to begin. There's so much to say and it'll all come out wrong, Snip just knows.

She's ferociously tired.

Talk and movement peter away and they slip off their shoes and settle into their swags. Lonely, lame goodnights are thrown across the distance between them. The pillow and sheets are infused with Dave's smell and Snip rolls on to her belly and cups the pillow in her arms and breathes in deep and then pulls her nose away, cross at the craving, at her irrational, uncontrollable want. She's sure his family life has never been as fraught. It's not in his face. She lies on her back and stares at the great blanket of stars above her. There's a satellite moving in a stately path across the sky, then another. There's the blink of a plane. Snip's mind is jaggedly awake. Bud is wrapped in slumber nearby. A great mound of belly rises up from the ground. The sound of his snoring hasn't changed.

She has to go to the toilet, badly. It's Shelly-Anne's curry. She goes to the ute and scrabbles in the cabin, searching under the seats and behind the seats and in the glovebox and the toolbox.

There's no toilet paper.

Shit. Snip forgot to buy it. *Shit.* She's got to go to the toilet, it's coming on fast and she has no newspaper and no pieces of scrap paper and only one other T-shirt. She remembers what Bud told her once, years ago – Bread is your friend in the bush – and she grabs a loaf, an unfrozen one that Shelly-Anne's donated. The slices are stiff with staleness.

Snip walks far away behind a bush, kicks a hole in the dirt and drops her shorts to her ankles and squats. The slices crumble away in her hand as she uses them and with the toe of her boot she covers the messy lot of it and walks to the water container at the back of the ute, knowing that from now on, whenever she has to go to the toilet, she's ripping out the blank pages of her sketchpad until they're done with this God-forsaken journey and into a place where there's toilet paper and good food and relaxation and sleep.

She finally catches a ragged slumber and wakes, stiff, in a muddy first-light.

SNAP

Ants. Snip slaps at her skin and jumps from her swag. Bud's already up. He's making a flame on the grey depression of a campfire from some time before. Burning twigs crack strongly into the stillness. There's promise in the new day's cleanness. For Snip, things always appear better in the morning after the deep panic of a sleepless night. She's used to that now, falling late into sleep and waking up scrubbed.

Bud hands her a tin mug of tea. He hasn't asked her how she has it. It's blackfella tea – milky and thickly sweet. It's hot and strong and it slices through her sleepiness.

'So have you got a photo of this bloke?'

It's five-thirty in the morning and he's asking to see Dave. What a turnaround, Snip thinks. She does have a photo, it's in the glovebox. She got it developed in Alice after the roadtrip and she hasn't looked at it for a while. She gets it. The city boy. He straddles a single train track to nowhere across an endless South Australian flatness. Saltpans to the left and right of him. A straw cowboy's hat from Woolworths. Snip looks at his smile, at the openness that's in it. His thumbs are hooked in the rim of his jeans, his eyes stare straight at her and she's wet just looking at him again.

Dammit.

'He's got one of those faces that looks like it's never been anywhere.'

Knock the city in him, that'd be right. But Snip knows that buried in Bud's words are an apology and a relaxing and an opening to her and she laughs and doesn't bite back.

When the camp's packed Bud walks automatically to the driver's door and Snip thinks of Jackie O, who would hand across her car keys to the man she was with, who would never drive if a man was beside her.

'I want to have a go at the wheel.'

'Snip, it's a real mongrel of a road. I know it like the back of my hand.'

'Yeah, but I know the car.'

'Well, don't say I didn't warn you.'

He grins and tosses the keys over the cabin roof. They thud in the dirt.

'You bugger.'

Snip laughs and pushes the seat forward as far as it'll go and kicks the car over with the tips of her toes on the pedals. She powers along the narrow channel of cleared dirt that will take them west all the way to the border. She winds down the window to the lifting sky and feels a lightness bubbling up through her. Suddenly ahead, at a side-road junction, there's a skewed 44-gallon drum. ABATWAH is spraypainted on it, and an arrow. Snip drops the gears. Peers. Tries to read the road and the tyre tracks that are on it and a shudder begins deep in her bowels and travels up to her breasts, almost hurting, as she thinks of Dave.

'As soon as we get to my mate's, Snip, you can go back and sort out that city-slicker bloke. I'd like to ask him a few questions. I've got a list. You'll be back there in no time.'

Bud grins. So does she.

'I want to see if he has a sense of humour, if he's mean with his money, and if he ever wants to have squawkers. I'd like to live long enough to see some grandkids, Snippy.' He tips his hat to her. 'Just letting you know.'

She laughs and tells Bud that he's going to have a very long wait and then stretches at the wheel and accelerates, holding her hand high out the window, reading the strength of the breeze with the flat of her palm. Snip loves driving, the feeling of freedom and toughness and power it gives her, the sexiness of it. Dave's hand over hers on the gears and his fingers on her inner thigh and the touch of his cheek and his smell are with her as she pushes the ute west. She always recollects the good times more attentively than the bad, dammit. It's her faulty filtering system, geared for optimism. She wants the bastard.

They pass flying buttresses of hills, propping up the

push of the land. They pass rock serrations like ancient Roman battlements. Too much green stains Snip's recollection of the land. The soil is darker than what she remembers, it's still holding the memory of rains from four months back. A wide bush-car comes toward them, low on the ground and weighted with people, and as it passes a black hand pushes out from the driver's seat, flourishing a football trophy just won. Snip bips the horn in gleeful solidarity.

Bud starts singing along to her Nancy Sinatra tape, badly and joyously. She groans.

'Bu-uuud.'

He pulls out a roll of musk Lifesavers and offers her one. She smiles at him and says nothing, just rests it on her tongue, and they have a competition like they used to twenty-odd years ago, to see who can hold a complete circle in their mouth the longest. Snip always used to win.

'Bud, I've gotta have a pee.'

The stopped car twangs in the hot stillness and father and daughter sit side by side with the presence of a wife and a mother thickly between them. They compare their Lifesaver rings. Snip's has been shattered and swallowed a good while ago. Bud's is still a perfect circle, as thin as a sleeper from an ear as it lies on his poked-out pink tongue that trembles as vulnerably as a child's.

'I win,' he says with a triumphant crunch. 'You've lost your touch, Snippy.'

She can feel tears intruding into her smile, swift and silent and she's not sure why. Bud doesn't notice. Snip drags them away. They're dyed with dirt.

Snip gets out and pees then swiftly revs up the car and pushes on.

CLUNK

The hands on the steering wheel are a flurry of tough, dry grooves. They're the hands of an old woman. The set of Snip's face is turning into her mother's, she's caught it in the reflection in shop windows. Helen, if she saw her daughter in the desert, would be telling her to get on the moisturizer and the sunblock. Her grandmother would be insisting on gloves and a wide-brimmed straw hat. And would be instructing her to sleep on a silk pillowcase, to slow down the push of the wrinkles: 'Katie Hepburn would have done it.'

Bud hasn't asked how Snip got the money for a brand new ute. There's so much he never asks. For Snip people without curiosity are like houses without books: there's something unsettling about them. She's used to it with Bud now – having to tell him things because she knows he won't ask, being forced into talk, which she hates. He offers her another Lifesaver ring. They place them in their mouths at exactly the same time. Say nothing, mirror-grin.

The road deteriorates as they head further away from whitefella world and Snip thinks of how Europeans have overlaid the land, how they've threaded it with bitumen and concrete and how the touch of the Yapa is light on the land. She thinks of Dave and his love of foundations and brickwork and early settlements, his love of permanence and preservation and stone. She's not sure what he'd make of community life. Whether he'd ever be comfortable in it. Whether he'd ever understand her deep love of it.

She slows. On the track ahead there's a gathering of wedge-tailed eagles. Twelve or thirteen or fourteen of them are gathered Hitchcock-Hollywood style around some scattered red meat bits. Proud buggers, they're right in the middle of the road. There's the stand-off as the car roars upon them and Snip's forced to slow to a crawl as the last one pushes itself reluctantly into the air, flap . . . flap . . . flap . . . its strong haunches dangling . . . flap . . . flap as it abandons its precious dead roo for a temporary post in a desert oak. She drives on swiftly past the smell, and the wedgies watch and wait for the flurry of dust to move on so they can flap back down to their meat.

Snip drives into a different desert.

Sand dunes rise suddenly beside the road. They're like

high sea dunes with the promise of an ocean beyond. Snip drives on a colour-changing track. It's bleached white in parts and then sandy golden and then vivid ochre and then bleached white again. There are scattered cattle bones or car parts in the distance, she can't make them out but whatever they are they're wrong in the land.

She stops the car. They both get out and climb and stand side by side without speaking on the top of a dune. They feel high and heady with the silence, their ears ring with it. Bud puts his arm around Snip's shoulder and she curves, instinctively, into him. After several minutes they turn and walk back. Beside the car are the remains of an eagle, its two claws are detached and gnarled and curled and she picks them up and sticks them in the side mirrors. The claws look like furious little wings as the car's pushed fast along the disappearing road.

'Give it a couple of months and the track'll no longer be here, I reckon,' Snip muses.

'Don't bet on it. There's always someone who comes along.'

The land changes again and they drive into a valley of ghosts with a dust mist washing gently and strangely over the road ahead of them. There are vivid, almost fluoro-green bushes that hug the ground by the track. There are sudden mysterious spots of rain from a vastly empty blue sky. There are serrated hills, as if a giant's fingernails have been dragged across them.

And suddenly, there's bulldust.

Snip sees it ahead of her but she's driving too fast and too hard to stop. There are deep gouges in the track and she's powering, panicky, through the ridges and trenches and Bud is saying do you want me to take over and she's saying no, sharply, as she drops the gears down from fourth to first and repeats the mantra to herself, the cardinal rule, don't stop don't stop don't stop, as the car slips beneath her and dances and skitters like a thoroughbred on ice.

At the end of it Snip's shoulders are knotted with tension and tired and Bud says he'll take over and she says okay, but wait until they're out of the valley because she's too scared to stop because the car might get stuck, but she's not telling him that.

She drives on, hunched over the wheel, her teeth clamped together, her brow furrowed.

They round a curve in the track and Snip sees the rock in the middle of the road but it's too late to stop or to swerve and she knows she's got high clearance with the tyres but there's a God-almighty clunk as the car goes over it. Bud says Jesus Christ and when they're clear of the valley Snip pulls up, pale, her knuckles white around the wheel, and she lifts her foot that's jammed flat on the brake.

Bud leaps out and leans under the body of the car. 'Jesus Christ.'

'What is it?'

'A great big bloody hole in the fuel tank.'

Snip drops on to her belly in the dirt beside him. There's a slow, steady drip of diesel. And a dent. And a hole about half-a-centimetre wide.

The thud of a dead weight in her stomach.

Bud puts the pad of his thumb to the hole.

'I've got some chewing gum,' Snip says.

Bud tells her to start chewing fast, and she hands him half the packet and they chew, concentrated and panicky, until their mouths are hurting and then he rubs their wads into a grubby ball, slides under the car and sticks and smooths the gum to the tank. They fill it with the last of the diesel from the jerrycan. Snip hands Bud the keys and he grins at her and tells her about finding two blokes in the desert once whose car had broken down – they'd been lost a week and when he came across them they were stiff and dead and side by side in their old Falcon. 'Blackfellas turned into whitefellas, they were. Their skin, their hair, everything, it'd all been bleached white by the sun. That's not going to happen to me, Snippy, no fear.'

They head off in silence. Bud's hand reassures her, his fingers tug at her earlobe, tugging a smile from her. And then twenty minutes along the track the petrol gauge drops, quicker than expected.

They stop.

Get out.

The chewing gum is gone. They don't have any left. A knob of diesel is dripping on to the sand every five seconds or so. As they hurry back into the car Snip notices the back number-plate's gone too. Bud pushes the car fast. His big bull shoulders are hunched over the wheel like he's at a racecourse fence watching the last derby of the day and he's lost all his money and it's his very last bet.

'We'll make it okay.' His voice tight.

The afternoon slips into evening and as they push ahead in the falling light it's like a great hand has flung the soft, salmon-pink dust of the road into the sky. Hills in the distance glow red with the force of the sun, as if they've trapped the heat of the day within them.

The car slides to stillness, gently.

The petrol gauge is empty.

CHAPTER FIVE

What Children Do

Snip knows kids who've turned to drugs to shake their parents into noticing. Kids who've mutilated their bodies. Bodies that have become Chinese whispers of their father's and mother's, to rattle their parents into showing a love.

She spent a lot of her growing up bashing at Bud's indifference. She had a furious need to be touched: by attention, by love, by something. It came to a head eleven years ago, the year in her life she now wants to scrub. The year she decided to move from Wollongong to Alice Springs, searching for the pieces of her family and for a permanence and a new home. Snip arrived with a readiness to butt herself into it, and then gradually, gradually shut herself down.

The year as the town bike, in the room near the Alice Springs roadhouse. Small, she was told that a lot. 'Ooh honey, it's like velvet in there.'

'Bud's back in town,' she'd be told by Roslyn the

barmaid and he'd give it time before he'd let his daughter know. 'See you in the office,' he'd chuckle on the end of the payphone and she'd walk into the bar of The Alice hotel, tap him on the shoulder and say, 'Hey, Bud,' and he'd keep talking to his mates and finally turn. He'd put down his lemonade and say, 'Yeah,' gruff, like she was the new boy at the abattoir on her second day of work, coming to see him with a request. And the blokes around her would look at her, knowing, and laugh.

The two of them would go away, awkward, and sit in a corner of the lounge. Bud would order a glass of milk and the daily roast without asking if she was hungry or if she ate that sort of thing and he'd order nothing for himself. He'd say where you been even though he knew and he wouldn't say much more. Not wanting to face it, wanting out quick, Snip could tell. It was all in his fingers, deeply ingrained with dirty red, fingers that ran along the edge of a matchbox and turned it on its side and turned it and turned it again.

The meal would end limply. Bud would leave before she'd finished her mashed potato, saying he had business to see to. That night she'd go back to the room near the roadhouse with one of his beer-gut mates and she'd ask him to fuck her hard and he'd grin and open her legs and spit on two fingers and enter from the front and then flip her over and do it from behind and it never got to Bud, it never stung him into being the father she wanted. And she'd walk away from it all feeling quarried.

Some kids vanish from their parents' lives, to rattle them into a noticing.

So the relentlessness of the running began. First up, Alice to Sydney. There was the truck shunt from roadhouse to roadhouse, the sudden white glow deep into night four, a vast brightness ahead through the windscreen. The city seemed to Snip like something out of a movie, with its shine thrown up to the sky. She was let off in the fluoro-glare of a service station that was bright on Sydney's rim and within ten minutes she'd hitched a lift with a raucous family of four into the heart of it.

To bars on windows and boxed-in traffic.

Snip found a bedsit. Started to paint, building up a portfolio for entry to college. Picked up a cafe job. Began earning a bit of extra pocket money on top of it. The escort agency looked after her. She only did it once a week. Then sometimes it slipped into nightly. Her rule was never to do it with one man and then with another straight after, 'cause that'd make her a prostitute. One a night, just an hour, just now and then. Not saying much, never talking, never giving anything away. Learning the listening. Then it started sliding into overnighters. Tom the agency's driver dropping her off at the client's house and picking her up the next morning. Tom telling her not to fall asleep beside them, just in case something happened.

Wide-eyed as a possum, with her back to the snores.

She'd ring Shelly-Anne on a Sunday night, the loneliest night of each week. Her voice veering into a wobble, wanting to ping Bud with tears through Shelly-Anne, wanting him sleepless and haunted with the mess of her life, wanting rescue.

Snip knows kids who want to scar their parents, to make them notice; disappear for years to make them notice.

Indifference, Bud's trump card.

And now this.

AN UNPREDICTABLE BUSHIE

Within two minutes of the car sliding to a halt it's established that no-one's been told where they're going and no-one's expecting them at the other end.

'It doesn't work like that, Snip. You just appear.'

'Fuck it, Bud. What kind of bushie is that? *Fuck it.*' She turns away from him. 'Where are we going to anyway, Bud. Whose place?' Not looking at him.

'A mate's, Lajamanu way. They're not on the phone but they'll be there. And Snip, I wish you wouldn't use that kind of language.'

She stalks into the middle of the road ahead. She paces and squats and paces it again, like a dog in the back of a stationary ute.

CAMP

On day two and day three she's doing it again. Stalking, pacing, squatting. Snip's not very good at being still. You're never doing nothing, Helen had said to her once, recognizing in her daughter that which was deep in herself. The fear of stagnation, of complacency and routine, the fear of getting stuck.

'Fuck it.' Snip spits at the piss-weak road. It's a road that's exhausted itself, it's scuffed over and withered and she knows it'll soon fade into land. She sits crosslegged in the hurting glare. Narrows her eyes. Wills a puff of dust to dance in the distance, a puff to signal an approaching car. They need pursuers now, to rescue them. What a mess. Snip brushes the flies from the corners of her eyes and catches one in a tumble across her cheek. They're slower than the quick, flighty city ones. She sees a puff. Knows it's not there. Knows it's the heat, playing silly buggers in front of her eyes. She crushes the fly's body between her thumb and forefinger and wipes it on the side of her thigh.

Snip's head hurts and the heat bashes at her and there's a fury in her chest as tight and hard as a tin-foil ball. She had come to this desert three weeks ago with a specific wish to hunt down her father, a plan. She wasn't counting on a rock through a fuel tank.

He hasn't said anything about it being her fault.

The ute sits in the middle of the road. Its doors are wide and its backflap is down. Under a tree nearby is Snip's swag and on her pillow is a novel, *Perfume*, she can't concentrate on, and in the dirt beside it is a sketchpad she can't draw on. It's time soon for a new Sydney show and she needs to be doing some work for it. She can't. Her fingers won't sing. The sheets in her swag are spread messy and wide and sand is gritted through them. Snip pushes the sheet's cling from her at night and the material crackles, as vivid as a cat's growl. Sparks flit from the material's arc in air that's sapped of wet.

They have 60 litres of water between them in two plastic tanks. They have four days' worth of food. At a stretch, eight. The dregs of a campfire blot the sand between the ute and the swag. Beside the fire there's a squat camp oven and a billy, a toasting fork, tin cups and tongs.

They're having to walk further and further each day for firewood.

There's constant hunger and thirst.

They had taken this route specifically so they wouldn't be found.

Snip's mind gnaws at worry, at choices. To stay where they are or to walk out of the mess they're in or to split up. The bush rule is Stay With The Car if anything goes wrong; she's had it drummed into her since she was a kid. But there could be a rescue, an outstation or a bore, just beyond their sight.

Bud sits on a throne of a pillow and a spread-out sleeping bag under a tarp canopy. It's strung up, sagging, by the side of the ute. Sun through the cloth tinges him green. His eyes are closed, his head is back, his legs are loose and wide. His rifle's resting across his thighs, like a cat on his lap. The flop in his body registers utter dreamy unconcern.

He says nothing to her.

That's always been his problem.

Saying nothing to her. As if he's lost talk.

Snip spits at the road, she paces and squats and paces again, she spits at the road.

WHAT FATHERS DO

Bud treated Snip over the years like a lover scorned, except he's her father and fathers aren't meant to do that. And she reckoned early on that if she ever told him she loved him she'd feel stripped. So she never told him that kind of thing, she never gave him that gift. She'd wondered for years if she had the capacity for love in her. She'd turned long ago from loving too ferociously to not loving at all.

And then Dave comes along. Helen would tell her it's lust and infatuation and too soon. Whatever it is, Snip doesn't recognize it. The softness that plumed through her, the surrender in it.

The lesson Bud has taught her is never to give anyone total love because it's like a blanket thrown over them, smothering them. The lesson Bud has taught her is that absolute love makes you weak and does you in.

And now this.

WHEN THE SAND DUNES SING

Desert. Day four, late. Bud coughs and begins to talk, as if he's the host at a dinner party filling up silence. His voice is raw, it's pushed out through thirst and tiredness and wind and sun. He goes on about something he heard on Radio National, the different tones of the singing dunes in an Inner Mongolian desert that whisper and groan and make the sound of an aeroplane when a wind blows softly but he doesn't believe that dunes can sing because he's been in the desert for twenty-three years and he's never heard them, ever, and he says to Snip that if she ever happens to hear the dunes sing, then she's gone.

'Bud, have you heard that bald men's brains can cook in their heads when it's hot?' The sentence is snapped, like a rock from a slingshot.

Bud stops short. He puts his hand to the fine white hair haloed around his head and his face splits wide with a smile. It's hair that's sapped of all virility and in Bud's vague gesture Snip feels a sudden fierce flooding of something inside her, a swift contracting at the meanness of her words. She recognizes the playground nastiness that lies fallow within her and she knows she'd never direct it to anyone but him. And Helen. Because they're family she can hurt them more.

Snip looks away and says nothing, a flush shaming through her. She puts the mug under the plastic tap on the water container. They're five minutes shy of forty-five minutes and every forty-five minutes they share a mug of water. She hands the tepidness to him. 'Yeah, I heard about the dunes, Bud.' Sitting beside him under the tarp, not looking at him. Running her fingers like a rake through the sand. 'They had everyone baffled. It was something to do with the way the wind swept over them. No-one could make it out. It was something to do with hollow grains of sand rubbing against each other, or so they said.'

He savours a chuckle. He hands back the mug. 'There you go, Pippy, there you go. Those bloody dunes.'

Without looking at her his voice rises again and he talks about sand dunes and singing, wind and the sun, and then the words that he loves with two meanings.

'Spell, as in cricket, Snip, meaning to have a go at the wicket or be taken from the field. Then there's cracking up, which means laughing or going mad. And rival, that's a wily old one. It originally meant friend. Can you believe that? It came from river, but I can't remember the connection – river to separate, I suppose. And then there's cleave, I love cleave, it's such a strong biblical word. It means a splitting apart or a binding together.' And as Bud speaks he knots his fingers tight together and puts his fists to his mouth and grins from behind them. 'Don't you love that, Snip? A splitting or a binding. Isn't that something?'

'Yeah. I've got one too, Bud. *Heimlich*, I think it's a German word. It means something which is homely and comfortable and familiar, but also something which is concealed and inaccessible and unknown.'

'Good God, that's a beauty. Where'd you get it from?'

'Some book.'

Bud sees no irony in it. He moves on from favourite words to the Valiant Regal and a dog they'd found twenty-three years ago on the highway. It had been run over by a car. They called it Victim. It had a stale-smelling smile and a wheat-thresher tail and a dangle of a leg and Snip was never sure who out of the two of them loved it more fiercely. And then one day, it vanished.

'That was the male in it, Pippy, they're wanderers. You'll have to watch that new dog of yours. It's the girl dogs we should've been getting, they're the ones who stick close to home.'

'Oh, I don't know about that. I reckon you mucked me up a bit, Bud, turning me into a boy. Got my head thinking all the wrong way.'

They laugh.

'Do you regret me growing you up like that? Pip?'

Snip's tongue clicks the roof of her mouth. 'Bu-ud. Save the remorse for some other time, mate.'

His tone snaps. 'I told you, someone's coming. God's testing us. Telling us to be patient. I *know* this road. Okay?'

'Fuck it, Bud. Do you? Do you really? What makes you so fucking sure?' Snip shouts it to him, shocked at the new shrill in her voice.

Bud doesn't answer. She feels, again, a swift contracting. It's too easy to hurt him, she knows the formula now. Snip grabs the shovel and stalks away for a shit.

HOWL

Day five. A ferocious sunset falls away. There's the colour of blood in the sky and Snip stands and stares at it. She feels that Dave's looking at it too, she just knows. A scrawny dingo trots the track and then stops. It gives them one drop-dead look and ambles, casually, away.

'Ah, ya cheeky one,' Snip throws at it and slips into her swag.

The day's heat has soaked into the sheets, it's like lying on an electric blanket. Snip's so thirsty. She can't drink, it's not the right time. There's strict rationing now. They've set up some plastic over a dug hole to gather moisture, but it's never enough.

Darkness seeps into the sky. From somewhere near the softening campfire there's a bawl and it's deep and throaty and unearthy. Snip jumps up, all skin and senses and whamming heart. Her eyes flit, she can't make anything out. A stick cracks on the fire and she sinks down and lies alert, awake to the night.

Crisply and suddenly there's a chorus of howls that seems three hundred and sixty degrees around the camp and it's chilling and thrilling and beautiful, like some ancient choir of young and old voices and it goes on and on, as if the souls of the dingos are talking to the moon and the very marrow of her bones.

'G'orn,' growls Bud from his swag.

The wailing snaps shut.

'Git.'

There's a hum of breeze in the desert oaks. There's a whisper of song in it, it rises and falls and drops to silence and then rises again.

Wind comes deep in the night. It skips over Snip's body like a lover's sweet murmur in sleep. She can't drop her mind into slumber, she can't stop the thinking. The gnaw of worry, of choices, of staying with the car or splitting up. She's gorged herself on resting and it's like her body, now, is spitting out sleep. Dave said to her once, deep in their drive, 'You worry too much,' and she'd laughed. She's not good with worry, she knows.

The smell of his hair oil is still soaked into the

pillowcase. Snip wants to gather his body to hers, she wants to flood his dreams like ink into water. The soft wind skips. Her hand slips between her legs and comes back dry and she flits her fingers under her nose. She should be menstruating and she's not. She curses the heat, sucking her insides.

Bud is snoring unevenly on his swag under the tarp. They've both been sleeping too much, there's little else to do. There'll be another day like all the other days tomorrow. They have half-rations at six a.m. and eleven and five and they have cups of tea to fill out their stomachs and the long days are dulled by a routine grimly unvaried. Snip can't draw, it's all stopped up inside her. Her hand is listless around the charcoal, she's not able to hold its lightness down right. Her days dribble away with reading fitfully and dozing and taking the shovel off and shitting. Her piss is coming out hot and concentrated and too deeply gold and her shit is small and dry and meanly hard. She flops early into bed with the coming of each night. There's nothing else to do.

No-one'll come, she just knows.

They'll have to haul themselves out of it, but God knows how. Her head screams with the strain of the thinking.

TO RUN AS FAR AWAY AS LOST FOREVER

A muddy first light. Snip wakes to ants like Lilliputians over the hills and valleys of her body. She snaps the strings of slumber and sits up. Bud's walking away over a dune, the rifle clenched in his fist and his gait fresh and focused. It's day six, five a.m., 'the stillness hour', Queenie calls it, the hour when voices carry furthest.

'Why was it that you ran away from Wollongong, Bud?'

Bud snaps to a stop as if he's heard a shot. He turns. He looks at the lifting sky then looks at Snip and he laughs as he says something about wanting to run as far away as to be lost forever, further than complicated air can get, and then he turns and walks away, shrugging his shoulders and leaving it at that.

'What do you mean, complicated air?' He's not getting out of it that easily.

She lies on her back with her arms behind her head, the mirror of her mother in the shape of her mouth and her eyebrows, she knows. She's been told it before, that her mother is in her hair and her laugh and her morning clearing of her throat, that her mother is in her cough and some of her clothes. Bud takes off his hat and walks back to her. Squats.

'Snippy.' His tone is playful and reprimanding and warning her. He's filtering furiously what's to be said, she can tell.

'Well?'

'When . . . when your mother and I got married, the night after we returned from our honeymoon, she said that my family were the type that washed up in lukewarm water.'

Snip's composure wobbles into a grin which she tries to put out. Bud grins too. He pokes her briskly on the shoulder, punctuating his words.

'Now that to you, Miss Marple, mightn't sound like much, but by God my heart dipped. I knew then that it was going to be the start of something. I just didn't know what.'

She sits and her toes dig hard at the dirt, colouring her toenails ochre with dust.

Remembering a fragment, the photo in the darkened sliver of her grandparents' hallway, the portrait a foot high in the gilt frame chipped to chalky white in the corners. The glass smeared with years of Mr Sheen wiped away with dirtied cloths. The photo was taken the hour before Helen's debut. There were fusty fifties not-quite-real colours and happy little Vegemite cheeks, too rosy, too silly-pink. There was Bud with the glow of adoration and possession and there was Helen with her face saying hello to the camera. Helen was Miss Illawarra 1956 when

Bud met her on the coalfields, he a good-looking man and she a knockout of a woman, Snip knew that much. Helen had the self-sufficiency of a beautiful woman and she was an outsider because of it, aloof in their small community and often alone.

Bud lays down his rifle by the side of her swag. 'I had won her with my little MG and my trick of lighting matches on the sole of my shoes. Crikey, Snip, I was flash.' He runs his fingers through his disappearing hair, Elvis style. 'She worked the cigarette trick out a day into the honeymoon. I used to cut up the sides of matchboxes and glue them on my instep, you know, tuck them in next to my heel. It worked a treat.' A pause. 'For a while.'

Laughter spills loudly into the new day's stillness.

'After we got back from the honeymoon, that's when I started calling her Helly. Then one day it slipped into Hel.'

The lights screaming on, digging into Snip's toddler eyes, and the growls and the shouts and the stabs of words from two people she'd never heard before. The thumps and the whimpers, Bud Bud no. Years of it. The whimpering, the quiet and the thumps again and again. And one day the police. The wailing growing and growing and then stopping blunt at their house. And screen doors slapping from across the street and up the street and pyjama huddles hushed on verandahs as Bud was led away.

The memory of that incident was seared into Snip, from her vantage point between the bannisters of the stairs and the railings of the front verandah. And he was home the next afternoon, lifting her high on his shoulder, and nothing was ever explained to her about the night of his taking. 'Ssshh baby, sshh,' as hands were placed over her ears at her questions, 'it's not for little girls to know.' As she grew older she dropped the asking. It never seemed right anymore, it became too long ago.

'Cuppa tea, Snip? By jingo I'm hungry. Where are those croo-sonts?'

'Right over there, mate, just by the champagne and the caviar. And don't you go getting sand in the jam, or you'll have me to answer to.'

THE ENEMY

A spider of sweat slips down Snip's torso. Liquid pools in her belly-button and in creases across her stomach. She collects the sweat with two fingers and runs it across her lips. It's not enough, it's never enough. She stares at the dot painting by her feet that ants have made with beads of dirt around their nest. She slashes a stick sharply through it. Bodies scatter, frantically, and Snip envies the energy that's in them. When their panic stills she slashes the stick again.

Mealtimes twice a day now, instead of thrice.

'How goes the enemy? The Chinese say that, Snip, when they want to know the time. How goes the enemy. Isn't that something?' Bud's voice is cracking and splintering, losing its strength.

'Eleven. Just past.'

Eight years ago his watch had stopped at twenty-to-three and he's worn it, stopped, ever since. Helen gave it to Bud. Its silver band is almost buried by a flurry of whitened hairs that have trapped the red dust. The watchband is tight, it looks as if the skin will close over it soon. Snip had asked Bud once about the silliness of wearing a watch that had stopped. He'd said to her too swiftly that he lived in a place where he didn't need a watch because he didn't have to fit in with other people and that was the best thing about living in the place that he did. He'd said to her that things like the time and the date he just didn't care about anymore.

Under his tarp Bud tells Snip about the cops in Wollongong who told him the one sure way to get rid of the smell of a dead body in a flat is to go to the stove and boil up a fresh pot of coffee, that kills it every time. He tells Snip about the eighteenth-century Neapolitan death tradition where lead would be run through the arteries and veins, and as the body decomposed all that would be left was an extraordinarily beautiful knot and twist of lines. 'Now what I want to know is, surely the person would have had to be alive to get the lead through their body in the first place? Imagine that.'

'Bud, I wish you'd stop going on about all those things.' Snapped.

So they sit without speaking in the sullen stillness of the midday heat. The land is thick with it.

'How goes the enemy, Snip?'

'One-thirty.' Snapped. 'Just.'

Bud stands and stares down the road. Then he says very quietly for the first time since they've stopped that he doesn't reckon a car's going to come. Not looking at her.

'So what should we do?'

'I'm thinking, Snip, I'm thinking. Give me time.' The voice is hard and short with her.

She drops her head between her knees and tries to remember how many days it's been, her mind a muddle of headache and weariness and hot. She can't work it out. The heat's demanding, like a toddler fresh from sleep, always at her, not letting up.

A butcher bird sharpens its beak on a nearby branch, oblivious to the two humans rank and still right by it. Its industry thaws their dirty silence.

'You know why they're called butcher birds, Snip?'

'No.'

'Because they spear their insect victims on the thorns of barbed wire. I've seen it, the prey slowly rotting and the bird tearing the flesh from them. Clever little buggers. Survivors. Not like me.'

'You're a survivor, Bud, you always have been.'

He doesn't answer. Says yeah, after a while, then talk drains away into silence.

The rations are going off. They're down from half a serving to a third. All that's left is dry Weetabix and biscuits and a bit of rice. The curries and the stews have long gone.

Snip tries to go back to *Perfume*. She's read it through once. She's starting again.

The words dance and won't hold on the page. Sweat from her forehead drops on to the paper and a slow diagonal streak bisects the text. The droplet at its head magnifies a letter, blowing the type up and illuminating the page's grain and then the droplet rolls slowly over another letter and another until it's stopped and spread by the paper's rim.

The folded-up instructions that came with her grandmother's cheque are Snip's bookmark. The words nag still and yet she has so little energy for anything and she's not sure what the instructions mean anyway and her head is too thick with the hurt of the heat and all she wants to do now is lie very still and do nothing. And drink, and eat.

Above her, clouds congregate.

Flies are at her eyes.

A panic is softly whispering in her chest that maybe, just maybe, there's no way out of all this.

CHAPTER SIX

Blood Rain

Hushed light. Dirty red clouds gather behind the distant ranges. They rise and then stretch the length of the sky. The world cows and stills under the spread of them. Twenty minutes later the whole sky is stained an eerie, apocalyptic pink and the desert holds its breath before the dust storm smacks into it.

A sudden wind whips. Lightning snaps. Rain hits, the first fat splats – it splashes like crushed cherries on the white of the car, and Bud and Snip's bodies are buffeted, they're pinged by the furious pink. Lightning sparks around them and the rain splashes on in great ragged drops and then the thunder comes and comes, great bellowing growls of it across the breadth of the sky.

'Am I the only one scared?' Snip yells as she drags her sodden swag under the car.

'No bloody fear! Stick close to me.'

Father and daughter grind cups and bowls and billys

in the sand, twisting them in deep to catch any water they can and then when no container is left they scramble for the cabin of the ute, sweaty and panting and soaking wet and they slam the doors shut. They catch their breath and stare out at the lightning all around them, spitting and flicking like a faulty fluorescent light as the ute shudders and rocks in the bash of the wet.

'Jesus Christ, the tarp!' Bud slaps his forehead with the flat of his hand.

Snip opens the ute door and the wind snatches the handle from her and smacks the weight of the door back into the side of the bonnet with a wrenching crack. She jumps out into the mess of wind and wet and scurries to secure the canvas that's jumping and flipping like a wild horse just roped and Snip's blinking and half-blinded as she wrestles with it and eventually overpowers it and ties it down snug. She falls in the push of the wind and pulls herself back to the side of the car, hauls herself inside and then can't shut the door. Bud leans over and puts his hands over hers and together they haul the door closed with another wrenching crack and they slam the storm out and sit back, the talk whipped from Snip.

Bud grins and hands her a musk Lifesaver. She laughs.

'There's only one left, Snippy. I found it under the seat. It had your name on it.'

The rain slows and stops.

Bud and Snip wait in the car in matey, exhausted silence.

The sky hangs, sullen.

SMELLING TEARS

Sly sun warms the car and Snip's too tired to move and she shuts her eyes and dozes with a warm lemon glow collecting in her lids. She wakes later, body skewed, neck kinked, arm asleep. Bud is looking at her. The smell of their rank wetness is thick. The rain has stopped and the desert is sodden and meek. Snip grizzles and stretches and looks at her father who's now looking away, as if he's caught her in a state of undress.

Her memory: Bud walking into her little pink bedroom on a night long ago and Snip smelling tears like the coming of rain. Bud tucking her blankets too tight across her neck, smoothing her hair, and finally coming out with it – that he isn't going to be here anymore, that he'll be in a little flat just like poor people, in a little room with a little bed just like hers. And Snip remembers screaming and sobbing and choking and making herself sick with the crying as she clamps on to the hotness in his neck and won't let go. 'I'm coming too, I'm coming, I'm looking after you!'

Bud never made it into his little flat. He didn't leave the house until they both did.

His fingers dig and scrape at sleep in his eyes.

'Why did you leave Wollongong, Bud?'

Sleep is flicked. The pause that follows the question isn't swiftly filled.

'How come you've never gone home?'

He sighs. Starts to talk and stops, feeling his way, as if it's all clogged up rusty inside him. He winds down his window to dampened air and puts his face out into it then sits back in the seat and stares straight out of the front windscreen.

'All I could see stretching ahead of me, Snip, was the life of a divorcee before every second bloke was a divorcee. In my little town the word then was something that only happened in the movies.' Bud's hand thumps down viciously at a stray ant on the dash. 'All that was in my head was the thought of coming home from the pit each day to some cold, cooped-up box of a flat. To a room bashing my ears with silence, with no woman's smell in it and no life in it. Dishes stewing in the sink and my mates and their wives asking me around for tea all the time and ahead of me a whole lifetime of bloody sympathy.' Bud gets swiftly out of the cabin and gathers up the last of the twigs in the store under the car to wake up a fire on the sodden sand. 'I knew the only way to get under Helen's skin was to take the one thing she loved more than anything in the world. Clever, eh?' He looks back at Snip, pointing a stick and grinning.

She says why on earth did you have to take me with you, you bugger, that really messed things up. He laughs and laughs.

'Darling, darling, I wanted Helen haunted. I wanted to find a way to wriggle right into the marrow of her bones for the rest of her life, to never, ever let her go. And it was all because I loved her that much.'

'Did you?'

The fire won't start. Snip gets out of the car.

'Is that really love, Bud?'

He doesn't answer. The two of them hover over the twigs and Snip coaxes a smoky flame from them and Bud talks about all the stops they made at the pubs during the running and all the ladies fussing over them and he says those bloody women and laughs, he says every single one of them had said to him he was too young to be a father and he'd replied to every single one of them that yeah, he probably was.

Bud hands across the lukewarm tea. It's thickly sugared, there's no milk. The ice that kept it went hot and was drunk days ago. The milk was flung out. The powdered milk has all been used up and the tea is tinged pink from mud in the rain. Snip drains the cup.

'I used to tell 'em all that we didn't have a mother,

that she ran off with this city-slicker and didn't want anymore to do with either of us.'

'So why did we end up here, Bud? Of all places. You could have picked Cairns!'

'Snippy, that's simple. Helen knew I loved the water, she knew that the surf lifesaving club and the beach and the mountains and the pit were in my blood. I'd had coaldust jammed into my nails since I was knee-high to a grasshopper. I'd never been much further than Sydney, I was never very adventurous that way. I knew she wouldn't think I had it in me to get beyond the border of the state or away from the ocean. The plan was to go to a place she wouldn't dream of looking for me. But you, Snippy, you were the worry. I didn't know what she'd do, plaster the country with posters or what, I just didn't know. So the idea was just to keep on putting a little more dust between us and her and the police and the world. Until I finally stopped in this goddammed place,' he grins, 'where the silence was just about yelling at me.'

The only sound is the gulp in his throat as he drinks his tea.

'The plan, Jesus I thought it was good. The cops'd never guess. And I knew you were smart enough to carry it. When you really started showing as a girl, I was just gonna move us on to another town and you'd be my little daughter again. Just like that. I was counting on people forgetting. You know, we'd be modern-day swaggies, moving from place to place.'

Bud finishes off his mug of tea like it's a schooner of beer and wipes his lips with the grubby side of a fist. Ochre stains his chin like a lipstick smear.

'I didn't think it through. That's my problem. I never think things through.'

He grins. Snip does too. It runs in the family, the not stopping to think things through, the running.

UNDER A MOON

Day seven, evening. A full golden moon, warm and plump as it hangs in the night. Snip remembers the moon of their first roadtrip together, the sliver of cold white that was racing the car, always a little ahead of them as it shunted swiftly through the sky.

There's an anonymous rustle of something in the black. She lifts up on to her elbows and her ears and eyes strain.

She can't make anything out.

Under the wide yellow moon Snip gets up from her swag and picks her way to Bud and lies softly beside him on her stomach, thigh to thigh. He says nothing, just nudges his body a little aside and strokes at the skin at the back of her earlobe and says softly, 'My little man,' and strokes it again. Then he slows, and stops, and rests his head in the shallow of her back.

A soft snore.

Snip shifts.

Bud wakes with a start and moves off her and settles again, jamming his leg by hers.

He's now sleeping neat on his back and Snip feels a deep tenderness for him. She moves her thigh from his and wills herself to drop into sleep because it's the only thing now that stops the roar in her stomach. But she can't catch on to slumber, the relief of oblivion. She tries to seduce sleep with thoughts of cool wetness: surf rushing at her toes that are burrowing into the weight of wet sand; Bud as a young man diving into a wave and then flipping and ruffling the water; surfers off North Wollongong waiting like blackbirds for the heave in a flat sea; her slicing through the coldness of the ocean baths, waking her muscles to the memory of the stroke and kicking away at a lap swimmer behind her, whose fingers feel like seaweed as they softly brush at her toes.

Dave's fingers on her neck in the dark, like a trickle of cool water.

BEING THE MAN

A large cross stretches the width of the road in front of the car. It's made of clothes and pillowslips pinned down by silver fists of sand wrapped in tin foil. Maintenance is Snip's job. The cross is her idea. Bud has not come up with a single scheme for attracting attention. Every morning Snip pointedly brushes the dust from the clothes, keeping them stark for the sky. She wills herself daily to tend to the cross, to get up and clean it when all she wants to do now is lie in her swag. She needs blood through her legs, she needs distraction from thinking.

Too much thinking. About Bud and Helen and Before. It's driving her crazy, the not knowing. Her grandmother knew and she wants her granddaughter to find out. Snip needs Bud to comply and she's not sure if he will and she has to hunt him down subtly or he'll clam up completely and be lost. She knows him.

Fragments. The threat in her seven-year-old head. That if she doesn't go along with Bud's scheme and turn into a boy, Daddy will get into great big trouble and be taken away and she'll never see him again and never see Mummy again and she'll be locked up in a big stone building, like in England, an awful-nage. So Phillipa, the name her mother had insisted on and loved, was turned into Snip.

Rehearsing and rehearsing the story she has to say.

'I want to have gone to cubs, Daddy!'

'Oooh, that's a difficult one, darling, I'll have to teach you lots of badges.'

'I want to have a GI Joe!'

'You little bugger.'

Grabbing the big nozzle of the petrol pump from Bud's hands and sticking it into the fuel tank of the car, practising being the boy. Reaching across and honking the horn at passing cars because that's what boys do. Tossing chip bags out the window and snapping bubbles, doing wheelies on a bicycle, hating girls, spitting, farting, swearing.

'Now don't go too far, my little man.'

Hands coming at her on the first day at the new school at the desert place where they've stopped – Alice Springs. Playground fingers sweaty and grubby and rubbing and stroking and oohing and aahing at the bristles on her head. Snip fed up quickly. Deciding before playlunch is over to make a buck from it. Charging five cents a go for each hand that comes at her and making eighty-five cents by the end of the day. At the corner shop after school striding up to the counter and buying five banana Paddlepops for the ones she decides are going to be mates.

Snip is the littlest boy in the class, the worst catcher but the best speller, and she has a city haircut and has been to the beach and a roller-skating rink and has seen Mario Milano at the wrestling and has a cool name and a cool dad with cool eyes who's been a lifesaver and a spy and who lights his cigarettes by striking his shoes, just like in the movies. She's the boy who gets her mates on to cigarettes, she steals them from Bud and smears them with Vegemite because she's heard somewhere that it gives you a kick – like a rocket up your bum, she tells them. And the smoke sears down her throat and she vomits up a banana Paddlepop with the hurt of it all and never learns to like cigarettes. But the others do. And she's still cool. And Bud's scheme works. The two of them dissect her days in their caravan at night, while Bud makes baked beans on toast and bacon and eggs and baked beans on toast again and continues the lessons on being a boy. Teaches her cricket names and football, camping and cars. Teaches her overhand snatch-catching and wolf-whistling, collecting bubblegum cards and doing an alphabet of burps.

As the weeks go by the games at school get into chasings: girl-boy-pull-down-your-pants. Snip is always disappearing at the start, he's always running off to the toilet, the cubicle bit and not coming out for a very long time. The mates begin asking and taunting, wanting to know why. And one day after school all of them are walking across the oval and the mates suddenly grab him and pull him down to the ditch by the drain and she's screaming and tugging and twisting like a rodeo pony and the mates are holding her down, one at her chest, two on her legs, two on her arms and they're pulling down her shorts, underpants don't look right for a start, bloody strawberries on them someone is saying knowingly, and Todd the biggest and her best mate is pulling and tugging off her pants and then there's the mates' sudden hush, their voices chopped still.

They spread her legs wide.

There's prodding and poking and twisting down her arms and she's sobbing and screaming and choking out something about being born strange and she's finally pulling from their hold and running and tripping and stumbling and the humiliation is swallowing her up and her face is flaming with the running and a stitch is screaming into her side and when she barrels into the caravan there are great walloping gulping sobs to Bud, to his chest, that she's never going back to the school, evcr, but she won't tell him why. And gradually the choking and hiccoughing and crying is stopped and all that's left in the caravan is a muddy silence. Because she can't talk with the knot of it all. Because she can't look Bud in the eye.

There's the letter from school.

The polite enquiry about her absence.

The visit by the teacher to their caravan on the abandoned chicken farm on the edge of the town.

The knock on the tin door unanswered.

And Bud and Snip, head touching head, peering from behind closed curtains at the fresh dust ball from the teacher's car that's disappearing into the distance.

The mess of it hangs about, it stews like a sewage-pond smell. When Snip tries to speak the words come out twisted and jagged and wrong so then she doesn't let them come out at all. She doesn't want to play anymore. No more boy, no more swearing and spitting and burping and laughing. For two weeks she refuses to leave the chicken farm, kicking and squealing and scratching like a caught tom-cat when Bud bundles her, determined, under his arm and tries to shove her in the car to take her to town, to see the doctor, to get her talking. She draws blood on his face and his neck and his chest and one day he stops trying to bundle her into the car, he lets her run wild.

One morning early he leaves her without saying where he's going. By lunchtime Snip's snivel of a sob is a howl. Then Bud comes back late that night and holds her so tight she thinks he could crush her with his love. He shows her a slip of paper that says he has a new job at an abattoir, eight hours out of Alice. He tells her they'll be driving to a very special place, a place few people on the planet have ever been to. And she's so very, very lucky to be going there.

They drive west, deeper into the desert than they've

ever been before, and they end up in Queenie's Aboriginal community where the old Valiant Regal splutters and coughs and lurches to a stop. It's a town that doesn't have a school in those days or a pool, bitumen or lawns or a church. Snip is quickly taken under the wings of the old women of the place. She's given a skin name, taught how to catch goanna and read stars and smell winds, and as she learns the new way she stops wanting to keep up with her running writing and her reading and her sums. She tells Bud that's okay and that she wants, very much, to stay.

The day after they arrive Snip draws Bud a picture of a goanna but can't write its name on the bottom of the paper because she doesn't know how, and she says she doesn't want to learn because the name bit isn't important, really. He tells her very softly and without looking at her that it hasn't worked out. That she has to go back to school. And he's staying put. Snip drives the ball of her head hard into his belly and hits and punches at him and he clamps tight her wriggle in his big bear arms and he says ssshh, very low, ssshh, because his heart is splitting like a tree trunk just axed.

Six months after the vanishing Helen gets a phone call. Snip is squashed into the phone booth beside Bud. His voice is flattened and hardened by gut-weariness and distance and the land he is in, and defeat, deep, right through him, Snip can tell. He asks Helen to be at

Central Station in Sydney on the first Thursday of the next month and her daughter will be there, but if there are police or welfare or anything else her daughter will disappear and Helen will never see her again.

Helen told Snip later how she got to the station at six a.m. with her two uncles and the husband of her best mate. They spread out. Searched and waited and walked the length and breadth of the station and then did it all again, and again. The day hauled itself into late afternoon and they wondered if Bud meant the car park or the country platforms or the lost property office or if it was all a cruel joke, the bastard, and suddenly it dawned on them – that the little boy sitting alone on the big flat bench, who'd been sitting there all day, still and silent and screened behind the plastic palms, was Phillipa.

Snip remembers seeing them early but being stuck to the seat, not able to get up and run to them and shout here I am because she didn't want to be where she was. She wanted the desert. She knew she couldn't go back to it. And although Bud was watching her from somewhere in the shadows, he deliberately hadn't told her where he was so she couldn't run back into his arms. And she couldn't run away. So she stayed stuck to her seat for the length of the day, unable to move, until she was found.

Helen told her later that the first thing she heard in a very grown-up voice that was bleached of all its elocuted vowels was that Phillipa was called Snip now. And that she'd been a boy. And that she would never tell them where Bud had ended up.

She was whisked away to the house on the cliff, the house of solid walls and mean windows that never let in the sky.

She didn't see Bud for a very long time.

And the absent parent became the idolized parent.

She didn't see Bud until the year she came back to the centre, the year in her life she now wants to scrub. Alice Roadhouse and all that. Bashing at his indifference. Never breaking through the barrier of Bud's giving up.

And now this.

WHY PEOPLE END UP IN THIS PLACE

In the desert sky, a distant drone. Bud and Snip sit up and stiffen like dogs, reading the breeze. She looks at the cross of clothes and the scum of sand settled over it and the drone is faint and is carried away on the wind and is gone.

Snip looks at Bud. He says nothing. He savagely flicks away the dregs of his tea and in a ferocious, despairing panic she builds up a campfire, hot and high right by him.

'It's no use, Snip. The plane's gone.'

'It might come back. We've got to do something.'

Bud says nothing.

The sun sucks up the morning softness. Snip flops into her swag. Her fingers toy with the letter marking the page in her book.

'Why did you never come back to Wollongong, Bud?'

He mock-groans and mimes throttling her neck. 'Snip, I *wish* you'd give all that a break.'

'There's nothing else to do.'

'Okay, okay. Someone told me once that if you stay too long in this place you get the disease. Well, I got the disease. I'd go mad if I couldn't dig my toes into the dirt. You know that.'

It's the place for runners, she knows. The Territory's full of them, runners from parents and the law and cities and lovers and children and wives.

Bud chuckles, coaxing a softening from her. 'I'm a modern-day swaggie, darling. You can't pin me down.'

She laughs, despite herself. 'We're both hopeless, Bud.'

'No-one would have me if I went back to Wollongong. It's like with chicks, Snippy, I've seen it. If one of their siblings is bleeding from the bum the others will peck it to death where the blood's coming from. They'd do that to me, you know. That was probably someone from Wollongong in that plane, having a go at me, saying ha bloody ha, you old bastard.'

She tells him he's got nothing to worry about now, that it was all so long ago. He says people have long memories and he picks up the shovel and stalks off, shutting off the rest of her questions. 'Forget it, Snip. You've got to with those sort of things, just get on.'

Snip looks up at high clouds sliding across the sky, marching from them. There's a prickling in the back of her eyes as she stares at them. It's as if everything's bailing out.

THE SANDEATER

Day eight. A howling hole in Snip's stomach. A smell stewing in the cooler-box. All that's left is some bread gone green, a bit of rice and two flaking crackers. With four mouthfuls each, every four hours, the food will last two more days. Snip drains the last of the day's water ration from her mug. It's ten-past-two. Her body grabs greedily at the last dribble of liquid.

She's still thirsty. She can't close her mouth anymore.

Bud sighs into the silence. He rises, with great effort. He snatches up the rifle and his fingers pick at it. He says nothing.

Snip runs her hands through the sand, she scoops it up and lets it cascade through her fingers. She used to eat it as a kid. From sandpits and at the beach and when

Bud first took her into the desert. The sandeater, he dubbed her. Like a pregnant woman with a singular obsession she'd suck up grains from the cup of her palm and drive Bud crazy with the crunch of it against her teeth.

Her gut feels as empty as an abandoned stadium.

She picks up a handful of sand and holds it to her lips and it's soft and smooth and feathery against them and she opens her mouth and her tongue tests the dryness. She can't swallow.

'What are you doing?'

'Trying to . . . to eat sand. What do you think I'm doing?'

'Good God, Snip.'

Bud runs his hand through his hair. She crunches. He smartly snaps the barrel of the gun and she gags and spits a string of gritted saliva. Flings the rest of the sand from her hand. Goes back to leaning on the side of the car.

Bud turns and walks, determined, away, spraying dirt across an arm of the cross. Snip clicks her tongue, annoyed. Bud's rifle is horizontal across the back of his shoulders. His hands are loose and their flop is incongruous with the purpose in his walk. Snip watches his back. She doesn't ask where he's going or why, she doesn't have the energy for talk. She just wants to lie.

The day drags itself into lateness. Bud's not back. It's been three hours. She hasn't heard shots. She wills herself into stretching her legs and walks to a rocky outcrop and sinks on to the heat of a rock and it's warm and good against her skin and after an hour or so of lying and staring and dozing Snip wakes to a wallaby feeding, oblivious, right by her.

Her eyes are the only movement.

The animal moves closer, its nose intent on a rock.

The smell of the bush has soaked into Snip. The animal's trust is humbling. Her gut twists in agony. She feels in her pocket for her Swiss army knife, opens it, barely moving, and tenses, barely moving.

She lunges.

Snip's on the wallaby but in a mess of limbs and tail and twisting neck and frail, thumping body, all ribs, it slips through her clumsy arms. She manages to grab it by the thinness of a leg and she pulls out the knife and drags the small animal trembling and fighting to her, and in that moment when her hand with the blunted knife is against the softness of the fur and the galloping pulse she can't do it, she can't kill it. The wallaby's mate has appeared, quivering and still and fearfully watching at the bottom of the outcrop and Snip stares at it and then loosens her grip on the struggle of limbs in her arms and, swiftly, the two animals are gone.

She's too weak to snap shut the knife. She sinks back to the rock and curls, clutching her stomach. Her whole body screams hunger.

The camp is empty on her return, it has the look of something that has no faith in ever being found. There are gutted swags. Both doors wide open on the car, like the aftermath of a crime scene. A cross of clothes disappearing into the dirt. Half-buried tin cans. A tampon stiff on the ground like a petrified mouse. Snip had menstruated a trickle and she'd tried to force the tampon in but the barrier of dryness inside wouldn't let her and she was too tired and too heat-addled to then bury it.

She sinks into Bud's depression in the pillow under the sagging tarp and idly corrals some bull ants. Viciously grabs one and crushes it and rubs it between her palms. It explodes with bitterness in her mouth. She spits it out.

She curls and whimpers for Queenie. She'd know what to do, she'd know what to eat and what not to. Snip knows the wiliness of this desert – there are deadly plants that mirror the appearance of the edible ones, and she has no idea which is which. She wishes she was curved around Dave's sleeping back with her hand slipped under his arm and across his chest to his heart, fed and full, in a place with just-washed sheets dried in the wind and the sun, in a place very cool and very safe.

Above her, around her, is the vaulting, hurting sky.

She wonders where the hell Bud is. Hunger claws at

her insides like fingernails scraping down the insides of her stomach. She's hot, so hot, with her hair clinging to the back of her neck and in her face and her eyes and she's sick of pushing it away. She feels the years-old seething at Bud coming into her again, the familiar smudge of anger collecting in her chest. It's all his fault. Snip grabs up the knife and hacks at her hair, chopping at its length. She goes shorter and shorter until there are only tufts left and she lets the air come into her head, she's digging and bashing and wrenching at her scalp, cutting her fingers and then there's blood and tears and the knife is flung from her and there are great howling sobs at the sky, at the stately, oblivious migration of clouds.

Snip goes to the cooler-box and like a bulimic on a binge crams the last of the bread and the crackers into her mouth and scoops up crumbs gone green and rams them in too until there's not a speck of a thing left, anywhere, to eat. And with a feeling of sweet, exhilarating recklessness she drops back into her swag.

Tosses and turns. The sheet is twisted into a sweaty rope around her. She finally catches on to an angry sleep and wakes and thinks fragments and falls into fretful sleep once again and dreams of a young Bud's swimming goggles and Dave's cowboy hat beside her and a plane dropping water from the sky and a coming storm and then iceblocks from high clouds, a beautiful hail like snow carpeting the sand.

SKY GIFT

The drone of a plane is in Snip's sleep and she's flying over ice and a whole sea of cloud and then Bud's shout from the top of a distant dune is dragging her fighting from it. She wakes to the full-throttle glare of late morning. Bud's running up the road, gesticulating to the sky and waving the rifle and jumping like a ten-year-old and she's swiftly up too, shedding sleep like a silk sheet and running and screaming and dancing to the thrumming blue.

They're saved! The cross of clothes has worked!

The plane passes to the right of them, arcing, its tail a vivid green. It dips beautifully, turns, flies almost over them, veers to the right, keeps veering to the right, veers far away from them.

And is gone.

There's an enormously empty sky.

'It'll be back,' Bud says, no conviction in his voice.

'It didn't see us.'

'I know.'

'It won't come back this way because it'll think it's done this area.'

'Jesus Christ, Snip, I fucking well know. Just shuddup, shuddup, get out of my head.'

It's a voice Snip hasn't heard since she was a toddler

in a room next to her parents, in a time of Bud being led away from her world by two policemen, a time of slapping screen doors and sirens and thuds. There's a violence in his voice that makes Snip want to curl up in a ball, far removed from it.

The thrum tails away. A silence settles, thick. Bud stands very still in the centre of the road and holds the rifle with the nozzle under his chin. There's a tension Snip doesn't like to his stillness.

'Silly old Richard has this note, Bud, pinned to his wall.' Her laugh skids too high into panic. 'It was when he got stuck out bush, after his battery died. He'd just got the teaching job, he'd only been in the community a week.' Her mind is thick with heat, it scrabbles to grasp at the story she's now too far into to abandon. 'A plane dropped a water bottle and a note, Bud, saying that if he had any injuries to stand in front of the car and if he needed water to stand at the side of the car and if he could wait six hours for the cops to arrive to stand behind the car. Or something. He's got it pinned on his wall like a boy scout certificate. When I saw it, all I could think of was what a fool to get himself into that, what a stupid bloody fool.'

They both laugh.

Bud lowers the rifle. 'In Australia, Snip, bad luck is almost seen as a virtue. They love you for it.'

She stands beside him. 'Where've you been, Bud?'

He stops laughing and lets out a sigh and she burrows her face into the familiar smell and the darkness and warmth of his chest. He puts down the rifle and his arms wrap tightly around her and his fingers run over her head.

'What have you done to your hair, my little man?'

'I, I don't know. I missed you, Daddy, it was horrible.'

'Well, there was no need to cut off your hair! And you've done a bloody awful job of it. Your mother'll kill you. And me.'

Snip giggles, soft. 'Where've you been?'

'I've been out hunting, Snippy, a long way away. I kept on shooting at this rabbit. I'd shoot and hit it, and it'd explode, and then when I went to get it it wasn't there. Four times I went to get it, and it wasn't bloody well there.'

His voice is cracked and broken, it's almost sucked away from the sand and wind and silence of the land that he's in. And defeat, Snip can tell. His hand keeps running and running over her head.

'So after a while, I stopped shooting at the bloody rabbit and tipped my hat to it and just let it go.'

They whisper a chuckle.

'There's hardly any food left, Dad.'

'I know, I know, little man.'

'There's not—'

'—enough for both of us, I know.'

A long silence.

Snip doesn't want him voicing possibilities, not just yet. They're all too grim and her head hurts as it is with trying to dam them, because they're pushing her over the brink into something that frightens her very much.

'I reckon we should walk it, Snippy. You know, light spot-fires along the way. I did it once before, when the car chucked a spaz on a hunting trip.'

She flops to the road and lies belly down in the dust.

'Bud, that was close to home! This isn't. We haven't got any food to keep us going and we haven't got any energy. It's forty degrees out there. We can't even shoot a rabbit and the water's down to three inches. A storm comes once every blue moon. It's fucked.' Her fingers dig deep into the warmth of the sand. 'It's all fucked.'

'I told you, Snip, bad luck's a virtue. I bet that was bloody *Sixty Minutes* out there.' He chuckles.

Snip does too.

It hurts in the thinness of the skin across her stomach.

In the dryness clogging her throat.

In her eyes.

CHAPTER SEVEN

A Letter

Bud hauls out an old cardboard suitcase from the back of the ute. He kneels on the ground and opens the case. Something in him has changed.

Snip can sense it, in his lean over the case that's shutting her out. She can sense that sun and heat and stillness have drained the hope out of him, that it's sunk like water into sand. The plane is gone and will not come back. They both know it and don't say it.

Snip knows that without the gift of optimism Bud will slip through her fingers. She tries to think fast, to haul him back. She can't. It's as if her brain has wound down with the heat.

Bud puts on his wire-rimmed glasses, placing them carefully over his ears. A knob of stickytape, like a squat caterpillar, clamps the frames together at the bridge. A crack slits a lens clean down the middle. The glasses transform him, they cast him as vulnerable and fragile and old.

Bud holds out an envelope to her. The paper's worn thin from being carried long distances, by being held by different hands and being shuffled from pocket to pocket to port. On the front of the envelope it says, barely, Snip's name. The writing's fraught. Her thumb strokes the words, learning the hand. Bud keenly watches. The letter's been sent care of his address and the community's spelt wrong. An outsider. Snip doesn't want Bud reading her face as she opens the envelope. She turns it and turns it.

Her mouth feels dry, as if spiders' webs have grown in it.

With a great calmness over him, as if everything from now on is mapped out, Bud takes off his glasses and he puts them in his pocket and snaps shut the case, like a doctor who can do no more. He looks up at his daughter and tells her to throw the letter in the fire. It's as if he's rehearsed what to say. He tells her the letter will just put worms in her head and she suspects he's opened it and looked at it and closed it again but she's not sure enough to say something to him. She can't read him, he's shutting her out again. He tells her, once more, to throw the letter in the fire.

I'll make up my own mind, Snip says but the sound is clagged in her throat and it comes out ragged and tight and sapped of voice. She turns from Bud, angry at herself and at him, not liking the new resolution that's in him and not liking the not knowing. She walks away swiftly with the letter in her hands. It's folded across her chest like a book or a Bible and when she's far from Bud's ears and his eyes she slides her thumb, trembling, under the loosely stuck flap.

Her fingers feel oddly light and weightless and disconnected, like when they're very, very cold.

She keeps walking, fast.

I don't understand, Snip. You were going to stay. You told *me. Alice was the stop and you know, I was going to tell you the next day that I felt like we'd been kinda married out there, by the land and the sky and the storm and the air. And then I learned from Kate, your (very fierce) mate, the story of the city bastard who fucked you on the road and left you, and him saying in parting don't crowd me, I'll see you in a week, I've got lots of people to catch up with and lots to see. And it hit me horribly, it made me sick in my stomach. Because it was my stupidly shy, stumbly way of saying you were at the top of the list and everyone else was down below and I would take you out for a big restaurant dinner and all that. And because it meant that much to me, and because I was all rusty with that sort of thing, it came out all silly and wrong. And then you moved on to the next town or the next and no-one would say. I rang your father, Christ, out of my mind! And he told me not to bother, that you were busy and tied up with somebody else for a while.*

Oh Snip, missed lives.

At the end of the third reading Snip's walking stops. Her fingers hover over the text and cover it up, trying to shut out the slug of the words. A curtain of tears comes and goes and comes and she rubs dirt into her eyes as she rubs away wetness with the rim of her fist. She licks tears from the side of her hand and holds her face up to the sky and blinks in sharp flicks to stop more precious liquid leaking from her.

Oh, missed lives.

Snip wonders where he is and what he's doing and whose life he's entangled with at the moment. She's got to see him again. She's got to get out. She looks around her.

Grass, like a dry ocean of wheat. Grass a metre high and sapped dry and stretching as far as Snip can see. The desert surprises her, it changes so often.

She's utterly, utterly lost.

A fury at the unfairness of it all tightens the skin across Snip's cheekbones and her throat and constricts the breath in her chest. She feels a despair and a hopelessness washing over her and dumping her hard like a wave at the beach and she weeps great gulping sobs to the sky over the promise, now confirmed, that was in the relationship: so he felt it too, so it wasn't just her.

The connection between them, the knowing.

Scrunched tight in her hand is the slip of paper, flimsy and tear-streaked and wrenching and wrong.

The weeping subsides with the shock of Bud's betrayal, the breadth of it. Snip's mind shunts back to the beginning of the envelope's journey. She can hardly believe it, that her father could do what he did. To say that to Dave and to lie to her. If she'd been given the letter when she first saw Bud, that night at Shelly-Anne's, she'd never have come on the bush trip. She'd never have chosen Bud. She'd be with Dave now.

And Snip knows absolutely as she stands lost in the grass that she'd be prepared to stop running to be with Dave, she'd be prepared to try a new way. Her armour against hurt is not to commit herself too deeply, not to love too fully, to hold herself back. But with Dave she'd be prepared to surrender all that. She trusts him.

Married out there, by the land and the sky and the storm and the air.

Snip strides and then runs, rage pummelling through her. She pushes at the cloth of her T-shirt, it's clammy and clinging like a whiny child. She flings off the shirt. Throws it away. Strides briskly on in just shorts and a bra, jagged like a walker in an Olympic race. A stitch jabs at her side. She stops, her breath rattling and rusty through her. The skull of a brumby is by her feet, its teeth are bared as it sinks into the dust and it leers up at her. Snip hooks her fingers into the eye sockets and wrestles the skull from the hold of the ground and flings the dirt-clogged heaviness far from her and the skull spins, skewed, and thuds a short distance away. She spits in the direction of it. No saliva comes out. She slaps the dirt from her hands like a cleaner. Looks around her and can't read the land. Tries to think behind the thumping in the front of her head: the sun's to the west, so the camp, the camp is, where? *Think* – her knuckles grinding at her temples – the sun is to the west – her knuckles grinding, grinding – so the camp is behind her.

She turns around to drag her feet back.

Her tongue is like a dead grub jammed between her teeth.

Snip spirals down into the grass and keels over on her side and curls in the sand. She weeps roaring choking sobs, as abandoned as a toddler lost in a crowd. There's no way out. Her body's failing, it's slipping from her, she's bogged by the sun and the sand and the grass and the heat and she can't get up and she can't get out.

And there's Bud. Snip scrunches sand in her palm until her nails find blood. She wants him savagely haunted, she wants to run far away from him, she wants him to come upon her body, face down on the ground, with the letter screwed tight in the stiffness of her hand.

After a very long time Snip forces herself to stand, wracked. She heads back to the camp.

She's ferocious about surviving all this. She's not giving up.

ROT

A hum of nothing.

A carcass of a cow sitting upright, propped too neatly on the grass. The hide is stiffened and frilled around the edges of the bones like a sheet of rusted tin. The nostril bone is poking through frayed skin and ants are delirious with it, still.

The sun beats down. Snip's head pounds with the mind-nag of Dave, with the possibility of a relationship. The chance she had fleetingly at the kind of love she'd always aspired to, a quietness and connection she witnessed once long ago. Had given up on. So much so that when she turned thirty she'd thought that was that: she'd probably never love anybody now.

Snip carries with her a scrap of a memory, like a blurred photo treasured in a locket:

Her mother in a hospital bed.

Her big toe poking from the end of the sheet and her father holding on to it.

No words, just the clean humble holding of a toe.

And a room thick with love.

Snip aspired to a love as clean as that.

The rot had set in between her parents and she'd never been told why. It was something so terrible, 'You won't be able to bear it,' her mother had whispered to her once, dropping to her knees before her. Snip remembers the grave, quiet words said to her close, 'It's something you mustn't go on about, to your father or to me, promise me that, promise,' and the words were soaked in perfume and silence. Her mother had shut her beautifully manicured hands over her little daughter's ears, she'd shut off her questions and Snip had sensed even then that it was her mother who couldn't bear the telling of it and had locked it all away.

She'd asked them all repeatedly – her mother, father and grandmother – and realized very young that none of them were going to budge. And as the years went on time softened Snip's memory and she stopped insisting on knowing, so that by adulthood she never thought much about it anymore. It was all in the past and it could lie there. Lots of families split up.

And then her grandmother's letter arrived, freshening it all up.

Snip walks heat-bashed and panicky and lost through the desert, feeling as if some resonance of that terrible energy of long ago is with her now, dragging her down. She feels pulled into some strange, fateful family cycle that she doesn't understand and doesn't want to be a part of. It's a family of silences and secrets and hands over ears, a family fractured to far places.

She heads back to Bud, maddened by questions. Why did he get her out here, just the two of them, why did he keep the letter from her, why did he keep Dave from her, why did he leave her mother in the first place and why did he never come back?

It's taking too long to get back to the camp. Snip's feet feel like they've been mummified in Gladwrap. She kicks off her sneakers and pulls away her sodden socks and puts her shoes back on. Her feet begin to drag. Dryness like razors catches in her throat. Her feet feel like dead fish, colourless and bloated and floating in shallow water. She throws away her shoes. On her soles are pricks and scratches and searing hot but she keeps on walking and then it's too late to go back for her sneakers and she can't remember where they are anyway or why she took them off in the first place. A headache shudders in her crown at each step. Her feet scream. Her legs push on.

There's too much thinking time and too many questions, they're like insistent prickles caught deep and hurting in her socks.

At last there's the road. The winged ute. The bleak remnants of the cross.

SKINNED

Bud is on blankets and a towel in the tray of the ute. His back is against the rear windscreen, his hat is over his eyes, his chin is resting on his chest. The tarp is rigged up crudely above him and the canvas is wilting, propped on two sticks. He looks like Queen Cleopatra on a stationary barge.

Snip stops before him, exhausted, her thighs twitching like a pony's, her hands shaking.

Bud's stomach is serenely heaving. The scrunched-up letter pings off it. He jumps awake, as if he's been poked with a cattle-prod.

'Pippy. You're back.' The fuzz of sleep is deep in his eyes and his voice. His hand reaches up and haloes his hair.

'You bastard, Bud. Get up, get off your backside. We need to talk. I need some answers.' Fury and fierce tiredness clog up her voice.

Bud wakes up fully and looks at the letter and

calmness shuts over him like an armour-plating as he tells her, slowly, evenly, that all he was doing was trying to protect her.

'Yeah. By bringing me into this fucking hellhole.'

'Watch your language, Snip. And it was you who put the rock through the fuel tank.'

She gasps. She feels as if a netball has come at her, hard at her chest.

'Don't forget, my girl, we have you to thank for all this.'

It's the first time he's thrown any blame. Tears prick her eyes. Fathers aren't meant to hit like that, they're not meant to aim below the belt. Mothers, yes, but not fathers. Snip tilts back her head and shuts her eyes to catch a hot sliver of a tear. There's a flood jammed behind them and it won't take much.

Bud picks up the letter. He smooths it and folds it and puts it in his pocket, like a policeman retrieving evidence. 'The Freemans have this fatal flaw, Snip.'

Snip says nothing. She's suddenly, enormously, tired. She doesn't want a lecture, she wants to curl up on the ground and put her fingers in her ears and shut out his smugness, she wants sleep and the forgetting that's in it.

'We love too much. I can recognize it in you because I know it in me. And it frightens the hell out of me.' In a voice soaked in stillness Bud works at lulling her back. He looks straight at her and tells her the idea that someone's out there for you, the one, the only one, and you just have to find them, is bunkum. He says he can read it all over her face, she's a Freeman through and through and she's fallen. He says it's not love it's infatuation, and like foundations sunk in mud, there's nothing solid to it. And it will eat and eat into her until one day it might kill her.

'What?'

'Give me the old Aboriginal way any day. Where it's all decided for you. It's much bloody easier.'

'You, you read my letter.'

'I didn't. I just know these things. Up here for thinking, mate.' Bud taps his head.

Snip can't respond, her mind is too heat-bloated, her sharpness has been drained from her, it's all happening too fast and her head's hurting too much. 'Well, well *you* fell for it. With Mum.'

'Exactly. And look what happened to us.'

'What *did* happen, Bud?'

He looks at her in disbelief. He says she must have told you and he repeats it, slower, testing the waters.

'She didn't.'

'I don't believe you.'

'Bud, she, *didn't*. I, I don't understand.'

'Snip.'

He looks away, as if the hills to the right of him are whispering what to say next.

'I read something once . . .'

His voice skids into quietness. It starts and stops and starts, picking through a minefield of words.

'It's . . . it's the only way I can explain it from my point of view. It's all I'm going to tell you, and that's that. You can make of it what you want, but you mustn't keep on at me about it.' The voice gathers volume. 'In Russia, Ivan the Terrible, he had the eyes of the architects of St Basil's Cathedral put out, so that they would never build anything so lovely again. And that's why things happened the way they did. Don't drag me through this, Snip.'

He smiles slowly and sadly and in his face is a warning that it's finished and Snip's got the explanation and he won't be talking about it anymore. Clamming up is what she dreads most. His words don't make sense. She wonders if the heat and hunger are addling his head. Like they are hers.

'I don't get it, Bud.'

'You little bugger, get out of here. I know you do.'

He rolls over. He drags his body to the rear end of the ute and pisses with his back to her over the side of the car, like a man incontinent in a hospital bed. Snip walks away in disgust. Flings a last question at him. 'Why've you been lying in the back of the ute anyway? What's wrong with the ground? Are you too good for that?'

Bud rolls slowly back to the centre of the tray and tells her that an Englishman went mad in the Tanami Desert, from ants. That he ended up putting honey on his calves but it didn't work. Bud tells her he's sitting on the car because he has no honey and he doesn't want the ants to eat his body and Snip feels in her gut, again, the fermenting dread of something coming to an end.

He's shutting her out. He's got something worked out. He's not letting her in.

Snip walks back to Bud and asks him very slowly and very quietly what made him finally give her the letter. She tells him there are some things she has to know or they'll rattle in her head and give her no peace until she dies, they'll sap any shred of serenity left in her. She asks him was it something to do with his fucking God rules, with living in sin. She asks him was that why he wanted Dave out of the picture, was it because he knew that a lover would always be chosen over a father, because that is the way.

Bud looks at her with an expression she can't read. It gives nothing away, it's blank. He says he gave her the letter because he didn't want to have any loose ends between them and before she can jump in with why, what does he mean, he's not making sense, he asks what she's doing in just a bra and shorts.

Snip looks down.

She can't answer.

She's not able to explain it to herself.

The bra is ragged and stained and the lace is torn and one of her nipples pokes through and her hands flutter to her chest in a half-hearted gesture of modesty and then they drop, giving up. Her head's thick and thumping. There's a memory as filmy as a cobweb, a memory of reading something long ago about the last stages of dehydration, about dragging away all your clothes being the beginning of the end, but she doesn't tell Bud that.

She's holding in her hand some bleached bones from a roo skeleton. They've been picked up from somewhere, she doesn't know where or why.

They're slender and snappable and beautiful.

Edible.

Snip turns and walks away from her father. The bones are hers. He can get his own food.

NIGHT WATCH

Roo bones rattle furiously in the billy in the last of the day's water. The liquid rolls joyously, shaking the bones clean. Snip stands over the shafts. Fierce heat bashes at the skin on her face which is tight and furiously flushed from the heat pushing through her and from anger inside her still.

Bud lies asleep, neat in the back of the ute. On his head is his hat and its material has morphed into something solid-looking, like oil-stained tin. As always in slumber, he's on his back. He'd read soon after he was married that sleeping belly up caused snoring so on his honeymoon he'd slept with Helen's bra on back to front, with tennis balls propped in it to stop him from turning on to his back. When he first told Snip that they'd laughed till their bellies hurt.

She looks across at him now. He's like an old drunk very still on a city step whom people walk carefully past, and pause. And their moment of quick doubt – is he dead? – is swallowed by the energy of the street.

Snip doesn't check him.

She lifts the billy from the coals with the tongs and then grabs in their jaws a roo bone. It's brittle and light and gleaming white and she holds it for a long time in front of her and lets the night's coolness seep into it. Her stomach whinges. She stares at the bone. It's slender and ghostly and as beautiful as a Brancusi and she's not sure what to do with it next.

She looks again at Bud. He's so still, so wrapped up in his own world, so deeply removed from her. He swallows all her questions inside him and lets so little out, keeping his secrets too well. Not telling is a family trait and the Freemans are masters at it.

Snip looks at the bone. There's nothing in it but the

dryness of the desert. She shanghais it sharply into the black and kicks the billy over the settling fire and liquid spits and fizzes and snakes away and is swiftly gone.

'I was waiting for that, Snip.'

'What?'

'Them bones are riddled with disease. There's nothing else in 'em but rot. You know that, don't you? Never meddle with something that's already dead; it's an old bush rule.'

'Thanks for telling me now, Bud.'

'Mate, it was me Saturday-night movie.'

He whispers a chuckle and rolls slowly over and his broad naked back leers at her. Snip throws the billy at him. It clatters loudly into the side of the car and she yelps with the pain of searing her palm on the handle.

'Fuck you, Bud. Why can't you answer a simple question. Why? *Talk to me.*'

'Oh, for Christ's sake, let go of it. It's for your mother to tell you.'

There's a contempt loud in his voice and its ugliness rings in the dunes. Snip shuts her hands over her ears and curls in the dirt by the fire, one hand pressing at her stomach, pressing at the pain, and the side of her other hand is deep in her mouth, searching for wet and cold. Her teeth bite into the source of the pain and compete with it.

Silence, and then out of the darkness Bud's voice

comes at her soft. 'The best cure for a burn is a spider's web. Oh hang on, no, that's for cuts. You heard that one, Snip?'

It's as close to an apology as he'll give.

'Eh, Snip? You heard that?'

She can't bring herself to answer him. She turns, pointedly, on to her back.

There's a sickle moon, frail in the sky. It's the mirror of the crescent that's high on Dave's shoulder, the tatt on his back that her fingers had kissed as he'd murmured to her that he always liked checking on the moon and she'd laughed softly and said yeah, me too, as she moulded her body into the curve of his back.

She's losing the clarity of Dave's face. She holds in her mind just scraps of him now, it's all that's left. The knot of hair at his belly, the vivid veins in his forearms, his vigorous tallness, talking eyes, tender hands. She'd been taught in anatomy classes long ago that each palm is a square with a halo of fingers around it. But Dave's palm is an oblong. She loves that strangeness, his sifter's hands, his enquiring fingers. And she has his handwriting now too. His seduction by text, the one fresh thing of him.

Married out there, by the land and the storm and the sky and the air.

Snip's legs flop wide apart and she smells her hot gamy stink. She tries to remember how many days they've been stranded and can't now – eleven, fourteen, sixteen – she's not really sure. Her head's thick with thinking, it feels like her brain is shutting bits of her down. She falls into a jagged sleep.

Snip wakes with a start, blurred, stiff, disoriented. Her mouth is smeared with sand and her bones ache. It's like after a night on a too-soft mattress, as if her body in sleep has been struggling with the softness of the sand, has been tensing against it and getting no rest. Snip crawls to her swag and on the way murmurs across to Bud you old bastard, hoping to unlock him in sleep. There's a suck of a snore in response.

The sheet in the swag twists between her legs. She holds the material tight at her chest and keens softly, like a fretful toddler. She rocks and can't sleep.

There's a low kick of a stone.

Snip stops moving.

Her breath and body are caught still.

She senses, in the prickle of her skin, she's being watched. Blood thuds loudly in the sides of her neck. She shoots up her head and searches the black.

Nothing.

A cool breeze whispers and Snip feels as if God is carried in its voice. The thumping in her neck subsides. A wave of tiredness washes over her, dragging her under, and she sinks back into her swag. She rocks and keens, the sheet bunched thick at her chest.

THE KICK OF THE BUTT

Late morning. Snip wakes stiff. She opens her lids a sliver. Dozes. Snaps awake. Licks her pillowcase as slowly and softly as she has licked a lover's back. But she licks her pillowcase to drop saliva on to it, because her mouth won't let her swallow, because her tongue is swollen.

The wind kicks up, playful, across her body. The sand dunes sing, soft and ghostly and low. The back of her watch has stamped her wrist with a coin of sweat. With eyes still shut she takes off the strap and licks the liquid trapped on her wrist and swiftly it's gone and she dozes again.

A rifle clicks, cold by her ear.

Her heart gallops.

She opens her sticky eyelids.

It's Bud. He's crosslegged beside her, with the rifle demure in his hands. He tells her she has to know how to use the thing.

'Oh bloody hell, Bud, you scared the shit out of me. *Why* do I have to know?'

''Cause every bushie does. You need it to get by.'

Snip clamps her head under the pillow and tells Bud that her head hurts and she just doesn't have the will to learn. He flops on his belly hard against her, plumped up with energy and purpose. Snip moves an inch or two away from him. With a swift grace Bud cocks the rifle and aims at a rock fifty metres from them. He doesn't shoot. He puts his hand over hers and places it on the gun, his fingers are twice the size of hers and he guides her hand gently and quickly over the safety catch and the butt and the eyepiece and the trigger and then he does it all over again. 'She's a good worker this little one. She's looked after me well. She's never complained and she's never got sick.'

Snip watches Bud. It's like a stranger has stepped into his body as he swiftly and surely handles the gun. She examines him objectively, like a person who's only just met him and has heard a few scraps about his loner life. He's someone who's given himself over so completely to his singular existence that he's got within him an odd kind of purity amid the strangeness of it. As he scrunches an eye and aims at a rock Snip sees for the first time the grace that's in him. It's a grace that comes from no compromise and is as frustrating as hell but there's a kind of nobility in it. He's given up so much and she knows that the word sacrifice, in a wider sense, means to surrender to God.

He hands the weapon to her.

The rifle's all wrong, it's made for a righthander – she's a southpaw. Her left eye is awkward and craning in the eyepiece and her left hand arches oddly over and fumbles with the safety catch on the right side of the butt.

'I reckon I'd be the first to be shot in a war.'

'You're not wrong,' Bud chuckles. 'Have a go anyway. Just try it.'

'Bu-ud.'

'Snippy, you've got to learn. I'm not leaving you until you do.'

Snip aims at the rock. The rifle wavers. She fumbles, all fingers, learning the weight of it. Fires. The butt kicks back into her shoulder and the adrenalin shock of it is like a shot of whisky through her. She hands the rifle back, buoyant, with a feeling of power pluming through her. She suddenly, inexplicably, wants to give Bud a hug. He's sharing something with her, he's letting her in. And it could be a way out. Snip feels a shattering of all her fierceness and tightness, as swift as a rock through a pane of glass.

'You know, I reckon I could grow to love someone like you, you old bugger.'

A smile floods Bud's face. 'You have the gun, Snippy. You'll need it to get by.'

She strokes the weapon. Her fingers start to own it. The clean wood of the butt, the cool barrel, the intricacy of it, the odd beauty in it.

Snip looks up and asks Bud if he feels like a cup of tea. He says there's none. She says oh. He says there hasn't been for three days and she's forgotten, she's forgetting a lot now and she falls floppy and giggling on to her back with the rifle across her stomach and Bud's stroking her earlobe and saying the words softly you'll need it, you'll need it to get by, and it's like a sweet red wine murmuring through her and her mind is hurting too much to ask why she'll need the gun and not him. She reaches out and traces a scar on Bud's hip that stretches across to his belly. He shivers like a horse at her touch. The gouge in his flesh is ovoid, it has a slit down the middle and is fifteen centimetres long and puckered angry and deep. Snip has never seen it. She sits up to look closer at it.

'That's from when my tractor rolled.' His talk answers her eyes. 'I was chasing this bloody bull, and the tractor rolled in a creek bed. My mate ran four miles to get help and when it got to me I was five minutes off dying from blood loss. Old Jakamarra it was. I've never seen anyone run so fast.'

'Oh Bud.'

'I loved working for blackfellas. They make good bosses, they're not mean. Christ, I'd never seen so much blood. We're bleeders, the Freemans. You almost died as a kid when we had to get a tooth pulled. You soaked the towel with blood. It was as if your throat was cut.'

Snip remembers the sound through her head of the tooth being dragged out, the grind of it, like mice in a skirting-board. And Bud's hand clamped over hers on the chair arm and his body lifting her high to the ceiling at the end of it and blood at his shoulder, deeply spotting his shirt. Bud telling her as he carried her to the car park that he was going to make a souvenir of that shirt, he was never, ever going to get it washed.

'Five minutes off dying I was, with that bloody tractor. I never told you that one, did I?'

Snip picks up the rifle and aims at the rock she'd missed widely before. 'Those sort of things wouldn't be happening if you'd come back, Bud.'

'Yeah,' he chuckles. 'Back. You know the only thing I miss, Snippy? The one thing?'

'Nup, what?'

'Crayfish. Catching them. Feeding them up with milk and honey and then boiling them in milk. That was something. They tasted like heaven. You know, I haven't had a crayfish for twenty-five years.'

'There's still plenty of them out there, mate.'

'Yeah.' And he pauses. Snip's fingers stay with the rifle, learning the trigger and the butt as Bud tells her how he heard on the wireless once that some prisoners in a war, rather than be taken back to their place that was soaked in blood and ghosts, smashed their heads through the train windows and turned their necks from side to side and cut their throats on the glass.

Snip puts the rifle down, talk sucked out of her. She

stares at the sky, at the clouds shunting from them. Bud drags the cardboard port to him and Snip feels once again the fermenting dread of something coming to an end. Her breathing shallows, her body stills.

'CHRIST, I could do with a Scotch,' she says and laughs nervously, looking at Bud.

'I don't do that sort of thing anymore, Snip.'

'Why not? I've heard you used to be able to drink a bar under the table back in the good old days. Weren't you a twenty-six-can-a-day man?'

'They weren't the good old days.'

Snip clicks her tongue in annoyance. They're on the backfoot once again when everything had been loosened and lubricated between them but Bud reads her exasperation and laughs. Says okay, you win. And he begins it, halting, just like that. Snip knows from the tone of his voice it's something drawn up from deep inside him and now is absolutely the right time. That all it's taken is kindness and collaboration and sharing and trust. And that it's so much easier this way. *Hunt him down* – with love, of course.

She doesn't move, careful not to distract him, careful not to snap him out of the talking. The subject's as fragile as thin glass in hot water. Bud speaks without looking at her, working his way in. He begins by telling her something that Archie, his undermanager at the pit, said to him long ago: that when he began going out with

Helen there was a spark in his eyes that had never been there before, he became, in a sense, three-dimensional. Bud was nineteen, Helen sixteen. She the mine manager's daughter, the district beauty queen, he the pit boy who lit the matches for his cigarettes on the soles of his shoes. And who promised her the world. People all around them said it was too soon to fall in love, to give it time, to grow up.

'But we just knew.'

Snip smiles and curls around her father's back, her arm a scarf across his neck.

'I felt, Christ, as tall as the sky. Me, with *her*. The most beautiful woman I'd ever seen, and the daughter of the boss to boot. I was obsessed with Helen, Snip. She was the love of my life. I felt like we were made for each other. You know, destiny and all that. The memory of love is so bloody permanent. It's never going to let up on me. When I slipped that wedding ring on Helen's finger, I thought, Ha, I've got her, she's mine now for life. And then we had a child. She was the most beautiful little angel, my little princess.'

Snip giggles, her hand slips under his singlet and absently strokes his chest.

'And then I started calling her Hel.'

Snip's hand stills.

'It hit me at some point, Snip, that you can never have any idea what's in another person's mind. All the deep-down secret stuff, no-one else can ever dig that out. And it hit me that happiness never, ever lasts. After the mayor visits, there's always the dunny cart. Always.'

Bud stands. Moves away from Snip, shakes her off, paces and runs his hand through his hair and then stops and squats and looks at the hills with the rifle across his knees. His fingers oil the gun with his sweat as he talks to his daughter about the place he didn't understand, that her mother shifted herself into, in the years after their wedding. How she'd be beside him at night and the bed would feel as wide as the Sahara. How he used to dread getting into it. Love is attention, he says, he was giving it but he wasn't getting any back. Bud aims the rifle at a rock as he talks. Fires and misses. The echo ricochets in the dunes. Bud tells Snip about the Tuesday nights when Helen would go off to the View Club. Or so she'd say.

'And she'd come back late, flushed and sparkling. Loose and light. It was how I'd seen her years ago when I'd first met her. She started reading the modern magazines, she got into takeaway dinners, she talked about a job. She began turning her back on me at night in bed. She'd snap off the light and clothe her body away.'

The rifle fires at a different rock.

'One morning there was a cave-in at the pit. No-one was injured but they shut everything down early, so I came home unexpectedly. I heard her yakking on with the neighbour over the back fence, and something made me stand there and listen, not come forward, and as I listened it was like a fist squeezing at my heart. It was like every last drop was wrung from it.'

Snip is very still, her hand hovers at her mouth, her fingers are suddenly dry.

'I remember it exactly. Moira her neighbour going on about syringing carbolic soap up inside her and combining it with a huge dose of laxatives and gin, and then jumping off a table. Saying that was the way. And Helen saying no, no, she couldn't, she really wanted another child, she just couldn't do it. And then I heard the name Arch, and that was that. I'd lost her. *Archie*, for Christ's sake, my bloody *undermanager*. I turned away from her. I felt oddly still, it was like I was floating. I went to your grandmother's, we'd always had a soft spot for each other, and I made her tell me. You know what she said? She said the only thing she knew, the only bloody thing that Helen had told her, was that he smoked in bed during sex. Like that was the most dashing thing in the world. I could see where *she* was coming from. Her and her bloody movies.'

Bud swings the rifle and aims it at Snip absently, lost in his talk. She laughs nervously and wavers away from the barrel and Bud swings the rifle to another rock.

'Another man, someone else touching her.' His voice drops into an ominous quietness. 'And she wouldn't sleep with her husband anymore, no bloody fear. She was going to have another beautiful little princess, but it'd have nothing to do with me. I began thinking. Something so beautiful wasn't ever going to come from her again if it wasn't going to have something to do with me too. She was my wife. She belonged to me.'

Bud goes to say something and stops, his rhythm bogging. Then he forces himself into ending it.

'I, I snapped, I just snapped. It was a Tuesday night. I was drinking. I'd started doing that a lot on Tuesday nights. It was like . . . like I'd turned into someone else. This anger was right through me. It wasn't going to let me go.'

Bud's face is a terrible, still blank.

'This rage, it was – Christ, how can I say it? It was like a wind, you know, that carries a fire through the tree tops. I, I held her down. I'd been working on a bakelite radio, trying to fix it. I had the screwdriver right there. One of those long, slender ones. I held her down and opened her legs and I made sure she'd never have that other child.'

'Wh—what?'

'I made sure she'd never have the child. I fixed it.'

There's just Snip's ragged intake of breath.

The low hum of wind.

Bud looking at his trembling hands held low before

him as if there's blood still on them and he's caught by the sight of them and he doesn't know what to do next.

'I collected my little princess and drove as far away as I could, as far away as to be lost forever. I drove from an absolute fucking mess.'

Her scraping, hurting breath.

'And I drove into an absolute fucking mess.'

Everything changed. Snip shivering in spasms as if a fever has been injected into her. Trying to clamp the tremors down but they're shuddering right through her. A screwdriver. Her mother. A screwdriver.

'So that's why I left, Snip,' said softly, crashing into her thinking, 'and that's why I'm never going home. You can reach a point where you say you've ruined your life and there's no going back on that. I reached that point twenty-three years ago. I stayed in the desert because I had to. Helen was the love of my life. It's my punishment. I put myself on trial. I deserve this.'

Snip's saying shit, softly, over and over again, the sound is trapped in her palm by her hand over her mouth, it's trying to stem the panic gushing out. She wants to cry but she can't, she wants to weep for her mother and herself and her father but her body won't allow her the luxury of tears. It's as if the will to survive is leeching the last of the liquid from her innards, it's as if her body is now feeding on itself. Bud comes up to her and touches her enquiringly on the shoulders and she shies away like a spooked horse, revolted by him, and strides from him and then runs, wanting to get away from him and not able to look at him or talk to him and not knowing, yet, what to do.

Hunt him down. Now it all makes sense. She walks away, dazed, reassessing family conversations through her life, reassessing clamped hands and cryptic messages, bitternesses, silences, bleakness, and then she turns and walks back to the camp.

Bud's not there. Probably off for a piss, Snip thinks. She curls up in her swag. She can't speak. She's tired, so tired. She clings to the sheet at her chest and between her legs and at her mouth, and there's a rising acid of nausea, a bile in her throat, but nothing comes out.

Slugged. Her eyes are wide as a possum's, for a very long time. Bud doesn't return.

And then she's asleep.

It's a dirty, scrappy, dishwater sleep.

A SACRIFICE

Snip wakes with the rifle butt hard and hurting against her cheek. Her mind in the heat and exhaustion and hunger and thirst feels jagged and unable to cope with the slam of the knowing.

It changes everything between them.

There's no sign of Bud. His watch has been placed beside her hand. Snip picks it up and feels its familiarity – the scoured glass and the worn leather band and the face with the crack clean through it. Ochre dust has worked its way inside, joyriding on the hands and clustering at the numbers. Snip automatically winds the dial and stops herself and stares at the dead hands and turns the watch over quickly, feeling as if she's opening a secret drawer in her parents' bedroom. The back has been engraved. It's the copperplate of a suburban shopping-centre booth.

To Bud, with love. Forever. Helen.

And Snip knows, now, why Bud finally had the courage to tell her.

He's gone. Given up. Run.

He's sacrificed himself but there's nothing holy about it. The fucking, fucking coward. All he's left her with is an empty esky and a frozen watch and a rifle she's not sure she'd be able to use. She's not going to let him get out of it that easily. The hunt has only just begun. She stands.

Then notices a page of her sketchpad under a stone behind her pillow.

I didn't pass on that bloke's letter at Shelly-Anne's
because I really wanted you to come with me on

the roadtrip. And right after we broke down I thought it was too cruel to give it to you then. Knowing you, you'd start bloody well walking back to my place by yourself, right there and then.

Snip scrunches it up, furious, and throws it away. Screams his name and her voice rings shrill in the dunes. She grabs her sandals from the ute and pushes her body into a run. She stumbles, sick in the stomach, her head thudding and the breath through her mouth grating with tiredness and thirst. She spots footprints. Then Bud's shorts. They're discarded, twigged by a bush. Then a sock, jolly on a branch, then another, desultory in the dirt. And his hat. He's heading due west. She spots one shoe, then another. And then she sees him, ahead of her.

Screams his name. He keeps on walking. Screams his name again and she knows he can hear. He keeps on walking. She fires the rifle in the air. He keeps on walking. She aims at him, to scare him. Fires just to the right of him. He keeps on walking, the bastard. Fires again.

He vanishes into the ground.

Snip stops.

She drops the rifle.

Walks to him slowly and then, panicky, disbelieving, she runs.

She cannot find him. No blood. Nothing there.

Dune after dune, nothing. All around her, nothing.

Her hands clamp at the pain in her head.

Snip can't push her body into any more walking and her body is screaming to stop and to rest and to sleep. The camp is far gone. Bud is far gone, God knows where. She lies on the ground. She's tired, so tired and her stomach howls and she can't remember now what direction she came from. She spins. It all looks the same. Her eyes are losing clarity.

Snip tries to fight the sleep dropping over her but her body is demanding it. It's shutting itself down.

Snip knows she can't do anything to stop it now.

A BODY BURNT BLACK

There's no moon, Snip can't find the moon. Thick black is all around her and she has no torch and her eyes aren't working properly. She crawls a little in the dark. The kiss of the wind has smoothed any footprints away.

She's even less sure now of the way to the camp but there's nothing for her there anyway and she feels she's turning her back on it for good.

Snip sinks belly down into the still-warm ground and ruffles her hands and her toes through the sand.

Something jabs into her hipbone. In her shorts pocket is Bud's old Zippo lighter for the campfire. The sand is so soft she could lie there forever, her bones are so tired, the ground is so good. But something within pushes her awake, away from the lull of it all. It's like a hand between her shoulder blades pushing her up a hill. She wants to find Bud, she wants to finish things off. And she wants to survive, to be rescued. It's a furious need, and Snip recognizes it as something that's fiercely in her mother as well. It's a tenacity that's pushed Helen through her life – the refusal, to the last, to be eroded by failure, the continual fight against giving up. Snip doesn't want to die face down with the sun on her back. She doesn't want to be found by the police with a mouthful of sand, her body burnt black and her hair bleached white. She's not like Bud, she's stronger than that.

Snip drags herself to a nearby bush on her elbows, too weak to stand. She flicks the lighter under the leaves.

They're tough little buggers, they won't light.

She scrambles on to her hands and knees, roused by the stubbornness of the leaves. She scrabbles for kindling and heaps the scraps beside the stem of the bush and hardly has the strength to roll her thumb over the flint but the flame catches and crackles and licks at the bark and is off. Snip rolls away from the bash of the heat and it melts the tiredness in her and she stands and pushes herself to another bush and another as the heat wakes up the last of her energy.

She torches the desert around her, leaving a trail of

crackling, burning bushes in her wake. Heat sears the skin on her face, stretching it tight and forcing out tears that are laden with smoke. She moves greedily from bush to bush, leaving none in her sight untouched, grating away at the skin of her thumb as she lights her world to find Bud and to find Dave, as she lights her world to find rescue.

On the top of a high dune Snip sinks slowly to her knees and folds her body into the warmth of the sand. She can't go on. As she lowers her cheek to the ground she surveys what she's done. Before her, vivid on the black, is a vast pocking of orange. It's a magnificent carpet of brightness across the world, like a Turner painting aglow.

Snip slowly shuts her eyes and a smile spreads deeply through her. She can do no more.

The glow dances in her lids. The flames rip and crack in her ears. She smells smoke nestled in her hair and on her skin and her clothes and it smells sweet and sensual and familiar and good.

Snip tries to yell Bud but she can't push a voice out.

Hunt him down. Everything changed now.

TONGUE

Snip smells lightning sharp on the wind and there's a coming cold, breaking the back of the heat. She burrows deep into sand that's collected the day's warmth and then rain comes, the first fat splats and there's hail as big as hen's eggs, there's ice festooning the desert a Christmas white. And she's crying out Dave's name and then he's holding her and rocking her and soothing her and rubbing her, he's kneading her back and her legs and her arms as if he's drawing the hunger from deep within her bones, and then his tongue is at her throat and at her breasts and at her stomach and then his tongue is nudging apart her legs.

She wakes with a jolt.

Her fingers are hard on her clitoris.

The sand she lies on is bone dry.

She wants to pee but she can't.

Breathing hurts.

She's bone dry.

LIPS SOFT AT HER MOUTH

Snip wakes to a hand gentle and firm at her chest and her back, a hand sitting her up, rubbing between her shoulder blades and pushing the curtain of hair from her face, her eyes are glued shut and her mouth can't close and her head flops back and the hand catches it gently and tilts it forward. She opens her eyes as much as she can and in a palm before her is a slice of bread, thickly white. Her head moves away and the hand keeps rubbing and rubbing her, rubbing her body into life. Dave, she thinks, and all she can do is smile, just, and the bread comes at her but she knows it won't scrape past the thick dryness in her throat and like a toddler she tightens her lips and pushes her head away and she's crying and fingers are wiping the tears and the dirt from her face. She leans her head on to the strength in the arm and can feel herself floating deep into sleep. Bud, she asks, where? But there's no voice in it. Dave, she smiles and the hands leave her and her body totters, her spine wilts and then the fingers return and they're firm on the back of her neck, and near her mouth is the flattened palm with chewed-up sodden bits of bread and she closes her eyes. Dave, she smiles. And then lips are soft at her mouth. They're kissing her, they're passing the masticated bread to her and she swallows without tasting and then slowly eats like a horse from the palm laid flat and as she does so she realizes the ochre-dusted hand before her that's been rubbing her back and propping her up and wiping her face and feeding her isn't white, it's black.

CHAPTER EIGHT

A River of Voices

Consciousness comes and goes and comes. Snip's body is slung over a shoulder and the bones of her hips are sharp through her skin. All she sees is a Levi's red tag and a rim of jeans grimed with dirt. The down of hair on the carrier's spine is pocked like pollen with ochre. Her saliva is a snail's trail down his skin. Snip feels in their long walking as if her flesh is melting into his and her consciousness seeps away and she's dropping back into sleep and then she's set down on the ground and a trickle of water is wending its way down the tightness in her throat and her body is grabbing at the liquid's cool path and then shc's under, deeply, again.

Jolted awake. A car rattles, cranky over corrugations. It speeds through the black, slipping across the dust. The corrugations grow smoother and the slipping stops and Snip reads the road with her cheek against the seat. There are shouts and horns and directions in a language she doesn't recognize and lights arcing in and away.

An abrupt halt. The whinge of the handbrake. She lies along the length of the back seat. She moans. She can't sit, she can't move. Hands are at her, hauling her out. There's the bustle of community. Someone kicks away at a snappy dog. There's a yelp, a flashy-heeled boot. There's the curiosity of children, their small hands are like whispers in her hair and on her legs and at her fingers and then her body is slung over the shoulder again and there's the rim of the jeans and the blonded hairs and the hills of the spine and then she's set down, gently, on the ground.

The hand is steady at her neck and at her back. The hand doesn't leave as directions are barked in the language Snip doesn't understand.

She has no idea where she is. She doesn't recognize the community and doesn't know any of the faces. She feels no fear, just a deep, restful trust that makes her want to lie on her back and float in the river of voices.

A bush runway is four times as long as the huddle of houses and shacks beside it. A long row of car headlights illuminates the tarmac of dust. The car beams are strong through the black, floodlighting the runway in broad ghostly bands that are threaded with dust. Aboriginal people are in the bush-bashed utes and Valiants and four-wheel drives, Aboriginal people are around the cars and on the roofs of them and in the back of them. Children crowd around Snip. There are old women's eyes and a still squat of old men. The man who's been carrying her is strong by her side. His hands are still firm at her back and her neck and he holds taut the sag of her spine. Around them all is a clutter of dogs, skinny and runted and three-legged and barking and wheeling and snapping.

A white man comes at her, walking briskly, the energy of city soaked through him. The man at her spine stands. His tallness fills the space and Snip falls back and is caught swiftly by him and is lifted strongly and placed on a stretcher.

Hard white sheets.

The scratch of washing powder in them.

The smell of bureaucracies.

She tugs at the jeans and mouths Bud to the man and he says yehwah, and nods, and points back to where they came from and flashes a smile. She catches the spark of his face but before she can ask more, about who he is and where she is, the white man takes over.

His hands are blunt and stained and his nails are rimmed with black like a coalminer's. The fluster that's in him spreads through her.

His plane has a flat. It's the front tyre, it's shredded and the replacement's in Alice. The last thing you want to hear, isn't it, he throws to Snip absently and then he flings a yell to someone and his distracted hands come back at her before his face does. Then his fingers are at her forehead and mouth and throat and the shock of cold metal is at her chest. A child of about twelve trundles up triumphantly with a squeaky wheelbarrow. The doctor whips around and there's squealing and shouting and laughing and then it's hushed, expectant, as the doctor stands and surveys, sceptically.

He kicks, once, at the wheelbarrow tyre. 'Yeah, what the heck. Give it a go.'

There are whoops and shouts and laughter and instructions as the wheelbarrow is pushed off, triumphantly, for dissection.

Snip's voiceless laughing stops as her eye catches the delicate plume of pale liquid from the syringe, she holds her breath and her arm is lifted and the needle slips in, hurting and deep.

The man who found her is close beside her, his hand still in hers because she wants it to be. The man is saying that doctor, and chuckling, he's saying that whitefella, he's always fixing fixing fixing fixing the plane, always trying to get the grease off his hands before the babies come out, and as the cloud floats through Snip, shutting her down, the rescuer's eyes laugh with hers. She taps him on the chest and asks the question, who is he, and her fingers on his chest slip to his belly and he says I'm your Helicopter, just call me Helicopter and she shakes her head grinning and not believing but she can't get her voice out because the cloud is shutting her down.

'Bud?' She mouths. It's all she has left in her to ask as she's carried across the dirt to the plane by the two young men from the community who don't look at her once.

'Bud, yehwah. Looking looking.'

Helicopter is beside her, his hand is still in hers. She can't let go. Children and old women and dogs are around them, voices are like cool water over her. She wants to say thank you, she wants to be with it all longer, she wants to stay but the cloud is coming in thickly over her and then she's deeply, vastly asleep.

WHITE BRIGHT

Snip tries to get her eyelids to part but she can't push them wide, it's as if her eyes have been drowned in milk. She opens her lids a sliver.

'Welcome back to the real world, Miss Freeman.'

To a place seared by white. A nurse is before her, that much she can tell. Her eyes snap shut.

Blackness, oblivion, again.

AS TALL AS THE SKY

Snip wakes to hands tying a cloth around her eyes, propping her up, smoothing her down, and then other, stronger hands are taking over. She's lifted from the bed. Placed in a wheelchair. The cold of its metal is under her fingers. Her feet are wrapped in the firmness of bandages. Her throat still won't let her talk. 'Where?' she mouths.

No answer.

She's wheeled down the smoothness of the hospital corridor. No talking, not a sound, the thick of night and settling down, of sleep and calm all around her. She's taken into a lift, she feels the closeness of the space and its smell, hears the pressing of a button. 'Where are we going?' Her voiceless whisper is again unanswered.

The lift doors open. A small push to another door, a heavy one, and she is wheeled outside into the caress of a warm night. The wheelchair is stopped.

'I think people fall in love with you, Snip Freeman, for your unattainability. You're very hard to hold on to, you know.'

The familiar voice, the ease and the humour and the gentleness in it. The blindfold is removed.

He hasn't changed.

A smile floats through her and a tear takes its time

as it meanders down her cheek to the corner of her lip. Her hand is taken. Nothing is said. A cheek comes to hers. Wet to wet. With that gesture she crumbles like a building imploding and she weeps with the vast sweetness of it. They hold and hold and say nothing.

And then she surfaces. Looks around, incredulous. They're on the roof of the Alice Springs Hospital, alone. Surrounding them on the ground are small candles, glowing softly inside their brown paper-bag cages. The night is still, as if the breeze is holding its breath. The lights of the town are below them and the hills to the right of them glow faintly red with the heat of the day still trapped in them. In the sky, in a far corner of it, there's a small sliver of red like a rip in a black curtain.

A brand new swag, with pillows and cushions tumbled on it, is in the middle of the roof. Snip is lifted and carried to it, laughing and hitting at Dave.

'I bribed a nurse to get you up here. She said you needed some pampering, it'd do you good. I figured you'd need some fattening up, so I had a think about what you might've been craving out bush.'

Mangoes from Darwin. Brie from Tasmania. Belgian chocolates. Olive dip, hummus and taramasalata. Black grapes and white grapes. Mineral water, a velvet wine, the softest bread.

'The nurse told me only gentle things. For your throat.'

They lie on the swag into the night as the sky deepens and the stars gather, and Dave lights a kerosene lamp by the pillow and reads to her from his favourite book, Michael Ondaatje's *Running in the Family*. He reads about the grandmother in it, 'Because grandmothers are important, I think.'

At the end of the night, back in her hospital bed, Dave is quoting the line of a poem, 'I will not let thee go,' and the words are like a finger moving slowly over Snip's stomach and then they're gone and Snip's deeply burrowing into sleep once again and a smile is seeping through her, warm like a glow.

Rescued. The sweetness of it. She wants to hold the memory of it forever, she wants to bottle it.

SCOOP

Snip lurches awake to lightning, to the galloping thud in her chest. A photographer's flash. She holds in her eyelids the negative of the figure at the foot of her bed as a doctor and nurses scurry and shoo and hush.

'No press, no press.'

There's wet in her sheets. A nurse's sure hands. The tart sharpness of smell. Shame. Memory: Bud peeing down the side of the ute. And then the nurse is gone and there's no-one in the beds around Snip or across the corridor from her and she feels a vast sense of being alone and everything hurts. A fly zooms past her ear. It turns wide from her bed and comes back and is gone. She dozes. Wakes to the sour taste of mid-afternoon in her mouth and the spit and flick of an insect caught somewhere in a fluorescent light. She rubs and rubs at the milk in her eyes and thinks of her craving for Dave and then Bud and asks for him, her voice cracking. She cries out his name, asks where is he, wanting to know is he injured, is he lucid, is he dead, and nurses are at her arms and she's holding their wrists and not getting answers, later later they're all saying, later, and then the needle's in deep once again.

Snip wakes to Helicopter at the foot of her bed. To his grin. He says he's in town, on business, passing through. Just checking he says. Where's Bud? she asks. Don't you worry about him he answers and then he's up and gone and Snip watches his tallness amble loose down the corridor and the cowboy boots and the hat never off. She grins at his back.

She used to say to her mother, as a teenager, that she was going to run away and have a black baby someday. To get under her skin.

Helicopter doesn't look back as the corner is turned.

THE VANISHING

In the flat air of mid-afternoon Snip sits with mended eyes and voice, her body pillow-propped.

Dave is grave and tender near her hand when all she wants to do is hit at him to see that he's real, all she wants to do is play like a puppy, silly and soft with joy at seeing him.

'How did you get here, white boy?'

'I was just passing through to see my girlfriend, the nurse down the corridor, the blonde one. And then I saw this skinny little thing all by herself who looked as if she'd weigh six stone in a wetsuit. And with her hair all sticking out as if a whirlwind has had a disco in it.'

Her hands rush up to the tufts. She'd forgotten.

'What happened to it, Snip?'

'I got cranky with it.'

Dave's face firms into seriousness. He says we need to talk and his hands are at her shoulders, bracing them, and Snip nods, a dryness sapping her mouth. Dave tells her he was back in Sydney after he lost her in Alice but then as soon as he heard she'd come in from the desert he flew straight back to her. He's in town for ten days. He asks her if she's still cross with him about the mix-up after the roadtrip. God no, she says. Good, he says, just checking, we're all so bloody cautious. I almost lost you, he says, when you booted me out of the ute, I almost had you slipping through my fingers because I didn't talk things through with you, because I was too bloody cautious.

They smile.

Then Dave tells Snip that Bud is still missing and his hands drop firm over hers, holding them down. He tells her Bud has disappeared and they've been searching for three days and they're still searching, the police and station choppers, planes and dogs. Her fingers curl tight and her nails find her flesh and his hands clamp hers down.

Dave asks her, very gently, how he can contact her mother. Snip shakes her head and says she doesn't know, she's out of the country and it's all too hard and she'll tell him why some other time, not now. Dave says wouldn't Helen want to know about Bud. Snip says no, no, don't ask, shaking her head violently and shutting her eyes, no, no, and she tells herself that Bud deserves absolutely his prison of sand.

Some people aren't qualified to be parents. Or spouses.

But in her gut is Bud's howling screaming absence, a ferocious wanting of him alive, a love overriding all the revulsion she has. She shuts her eyes and catches the tears and feels a deep confusion like a blanket falling over her, muffling and throttling. She wants the sweet oblivion of the needle. There's a silence and then Dave's lips are softly at hers, his cool hand is on her forehead and his lips are at her temples and his cheek is resting on hers and she can smell his closeness and she breathes it in deep. Ssshh, ssshh we'll get to him, he says to her close, ssshh, and he whispers like a soft moth in her ear. He whispers that he's so glad he found her again, because it wasn't until then that he realized how much he cared for her, how deeply she's seeped into his consciousness and won't let him go.

Then he's gone. Snip falls into sleep cupped in a giant palm of security and containment and knowing at last the rescue of love. And wondering why she shut out the possibility of it, so resolutely, for so long.

BUD ON A BED

Night. Snip jerks upright feeling she's falling, owl-awake. The hospital is drained of life. She looks across to a soft glow in the ward on the other side of the corridor.

Bud.

The blood thumps in Snip's neck.

He's sitting up, bug-eyed, fully clothed on top of the bedspread. He's wearing brand new moleskins and a shirt of crisp checks. He's staring as if a TV is before him, but there's nothing. His eyes are slightly askew. His wild professor hair is upright, as if it's in shock.

Snip yells to him. Nurses are swiftly at her and their hands are pulling her back by her shoulders and their soft soothing words are all over her like thick cream. And through it all Bud is not looking at her and not acknowledging her, just staring straight ahead.

The needle's in deep.

Snip wakes late the next morning. The blanket is stretched tight on the bed across the corridor.

SOAK

Dave holds Snip close to his chest like a child and kisses the top of her head as he tells her the police search is being called off soon because nothing has been found and she should be glad but she's not. She wants Bud alive, facing her, she wants to have it out. As Dave licks and kisses the tears from her cheeks Snip smells his hair oil, it's deeply familiar and it wakes something up in her and she pulls him down with her on the hospital bed. She wants him inside her, ferociously, wiping away the hurt of Bud, she wants Dave's fingers in her vagina and massaging her clit, signalling the start of it all. His fingers come to her lips, stilling them as he pulls away from her. Without a word Dave turns her over. He lifts up the back of her pyjama top. He kisses the small of her back once, softly, and then without another word he walks out.

Snip feels in that soft gesture that he has her and he holds her. She's never felt so soaked in want. And as far as she knows it's reciprocated. She clasps her fingers behind her neck and squeezes the points of her elbows tight, wriggly with delight.

SEARCH

Crisply at midday a policeman comes at her with forms. He's younger than she is. There's a beaded moustache of sweat above his lip, like a youth's first down.

He's insistent with the statement. He's tight with the rules. Snip's head is hurting with the thinking of it. Bits are all she can recall.

A cross of clothes.

A plane.

Bud in the back of the ute.

Grass like a dry ocean of wheat.

'Grass? There's no grass out there, Miss Freeman.'

'Yes there is, I was in it.'

'It's impossible. It's all dirt, and rock and scrub.'

'I was there.'

'Whatever you say.'

The billy thrown at Bud.

A watch.

A rifle.

'A rifle was never found.'

The constable's voice is both a question and an accusation. Snip doesn't understand it and can't answer its tone. She's tired.

The constable snaps shut his folder and looks at his watch. He leans on the bed. He softens his rigid constable-speak and tells her that he's very sorry but the police search has been called off. They can spend no more time or money or resources on the looking, they've done all they can. Then he says a non-official search has just been initiated and a few station owners are helping out. It's being privately funded.

Snip sits up straight. 'Who, who's paying?'

The constable checks his notes. 'Someone called, um, let me find it . . . Helen O'Connor. Not a local by a long shot. A London address. That's all I know.'

Snip feels as if a hand has grabbed at her heart.

Helen.

Anyone but her.

The policeman departs and Snip flops on to her back. Her *mother*.

Snip's palms press into her cheeks and her fingers

cover her eyes. It's all too hard, she hates the not understanding, it's too soon for this news, it makes no sense and she feels utterly, utterly alone with it.

After many minutes Snip uncovers her eyes.

It could be a good thing, Helen's involvement.

She doesn't know what's been going on between her parents. She has to find out.

WHIPCRACK

Dave's hand is over Snip's on the gearstick. 'You feel beautiful,' he murmurs.

And then they hit bulldust. The car skitters and slides.

Shelly-Anne pops her head through the gap between the front seats and says she should take over. Dave and Snip look at each other and laugh.

'Whatever you say, master,' Dave says.

On firmer ground he stops the car and moves into the back and Shelly-Anne pushes the front seat forward and roars expertly off into another bulldust patch. The car slips like an eel and Shelly-Anne guides it back with the flick of her wrist. They shudder along corrugations and Shelly-Anne yells hold on to your hats!

Champagne, Snip demands, this minute! She is shot through with exhilaration and it's as sharp and as clean as a whipcrack. Exhilaration for survival and the hospital release and the new Bud search and Helen's involvement, whatever it is, and Dave, glorious Dave, by her side. And news that a white dog is up and limping and waiting for her. Snip feels as if layers have been scrubbed from her, she feels as if she's all skin and senses and surfaces and she wants to hold on to it, the high, the cleanness that's newly in her.

The three of them are on their way to Bud's place. It's twenty k out of the community, along a bad track. Snip wants to examine his house for clues as to where he might be, for an address or a phone number of the mate near Lajamanu. She wants to know Bud's life beyond Wollongong. She's sure he's not dead.

Dave pops the cork out with a soft *plumph* and collects it neatly in his palm. He passes the bottle to the two women in the front seat with a smack of a kiss that misses Snip's cheek. There's the spill of sweet sticky froth and the rattle of teeth finding glass.

Shit, says Shelly-Anne, suddenly tight, craning at the rear-view mirror and bunching her hands at the top of the wheel. 'Cops! You'd think it was the bloody Hume Highway.'

They're five hours' drive from Alice. They're passing through community land where grog's not allowed. They're driving very fast, on bulldust.

Dave whips off his shirt and stuffs it in the neck of

the champagne bottle and hides it all under the seat. The cops pull past and Shelly-Anne nonchalantly lifts a finger at the wheel. 'They must be on the prowl for grog runners, they're not interested in us.'

The police truck roars off and is quick over a rise in a flurry of dust. The wind fans its dust-wake elegantly sidewards, like a flare left smoking on the ground. Their car jiggles and there's shuddering laughter and they flop back into seats with the sweetness of relief. Dave picks up the bottle from the vibrating floor and lifts the champagne high and with a whoosh the T-shirt shoots out with the pressure. There are startled hoots and the shock of champagne flecking their faces and smearing their arms and dripping like a chandelier from the rear-view mirror. Dave flings the bottle out the window before Snip can stop him and it cartwheels like a Catherine Wheel into the bush and their whoops and screams and laughter are flung out wide to the land. She should be reprimanding him, but she doesn't have the heart to.

Snip feels flooded with happiness. She feels like a sea anemone uncurled, soft and silky in the water. She loves these people and this place.

Bud is alive, she just knows it.

STOPPING

Shelly-Anne stops the car when the trunks of the river gums glow golden with the remnants of the day and the world for a moment catches its breath. Talk is sucked out of the three of them by the settling quiet of the land.

Dave and Snip wander before nightfall in the bleached dry bed of the oldest river of the world, the Finke. They say little. Words are suddenly awkward and wrong between them. They pick up stones, their bodies and fingers nudging and bumping and pulling away, shy. The stones they want are worn smooth from millions of years of water and wind and grit, they're nestled like beautiful coins among pedestrian rocks that are grey and white and dusty brown. The prized ones are of a concentrated ancient ochre colour, as if the rock has trapped the impermanence of sand deeply within it. As Snip walks the soft breeze caresses her and the light glows golden still and it feels like a wedding night to her, it feels as if the land is sanctioning what is to pass, whatever is to pass that evening between them.

Dave and Snip keep walking along the riverbed, weighting their pockets with stones. As darkness takes over the day she puts her hand on his sleeve and they turn without a word and walk back.

Back at the car Dave makes a campfire, brusque with manliness. Snip laughs as he does it. 'You whitefellas, you make 'em so bloody big. Wasting all that fuel. The blackfella way is a little-bitty one, economical way. They're minimalists.'

Dave – eventually – laughs too.

Over dinner little is said. It's as if the beauty of the night and the land is seeping into them and forcing a silence through them. They're all early to bed. Shelly-Anne rolls out her swag far away from Dave and Snip.

There's the shock of familiarity in Dave's lovemaking: his fingers tickling the hair between Snip's thighs and stroking her wide and massaging her into wetness, his fingers hard in Snip's vagina and the rhythm of their fucking, building and falling and building again until she comes and then he quickly withdraws, splashing her stomach and her breasts. There's the softness of his cheek as they nuzzle like ponies, the smell of his hair oil, her kissing of his tatt and curling around his back. And then half an hour later it begins again and this time Dave bites Snip's flesh and bruises her in lovemaking, as if he's trying to brand her.

'I want you to be my woman forever,' he whispers into her ear, trembling and still deep inside her. 'I never want to lose you again.'

Snip's legs wrap around his back in reply.

She feels scrubbed. She wants to begin a new way. She looks up to the stars. Their witnesses, their wedding guests.

COMMUNION

They're simultaneously awake in the still-dark of the early morning and they whisper and giggle face to face. Snip's foot rubs at the softness of Dave's calf and the back of her hand listens to the quick thump in his chest. She feels a line of communication with him, as uncomplicated and honest and clean as the sky. But more, a communion. She loves that word, a word of grace, spiritually softened.

Snip whispers gravely to Dave that being found has given her new eyes, has swept all the cobwebs from her. She flips to him and props her temple on the heel of her palm and tells him that she feels how people must feel after surviving plane crashes and near-drownings. Scrubbed. New. Humbled. Changed. Not wanting to throw away life, but to nurture and grab it, to be still with it. She tells him she wants to settle, that she's ready to paint strongly again – she's spoken to her Sydney dealer and there are tentative dates for a show, she's got a new palette and a new energy and new ideas. She tells him she wants to stop the running for a while, to try being still in some way. With him.

Dave affirms and stills her chatter with a kiss.

FROZEN ROSES

The smell of roses is thick in the car. Dave's got them for Shelly-Anne. It's her bush rule: anyone who comes and stays with her in the community has to bring her fresh flowers. It's the only demand she makes as a hostess.

'I can tell a lot about people from what they get me, it's my test. Like whether they bring me Woolworths carnations and throw them in the back of the ute, or forget completely, or go to a bit of effort.'

Dave has found flowers flown into Alice Springs from Melbourne. They're white, and tinged the faintest lemony-blue.

'They're called iceberg roses, Shelly-Anne. I thought they'd keep you nice and cool.'

'You'll do, mate. You'll do.' She winks at Snip.

Dave is sitting behind Snip. He leans forward and dances an iceberg rose in front of her, then whispers it across her throat.

A SAGGING BED

Bud's empty house screams his absence. Snip feels a contracting inside her as Shelly-Anne's car approaches. She's never been to this place. It's Bud's private domain and she's respected the sense of privacy that's fiercely part of him so they've always met in Alice, or the community.

'Anything nice out here, nature rips it down.' Shelly-Anne gives a soft commentary as she slows the car. Dave leans his head keen out the window.

For Snip the house's emptiness is like the open mouth of the newly dead. She moves swiftly toward it as soon as the car has stopped, shaking the two of them from her. She strides protectively towards the sagging building. Faded, painted aluminium is buckling under years of heat bash and oven-baked wind. And neglect.

She tries the door. There's no lock. Of course. No-one else for twenty kilometres in any direction and he'd never get visitors dropping in by chance. Dave and Shelly-Anne catch up with her. The three of them step inside and they move through the small rooms like real estate agents, they run their hands over surfaces, open cupboards, pry.

The temporary nature of the tin construction is made solid with a cram of books. Bud never let on. Snip stops with the shock of it in the doorway of the living room. Like a forensic scientist gathering evidence she moves into the room and reads her father through his deeply bowed bookshelves. It's more affirmation of how little she knows him, of how little he lets out. She smiles remembering what he'd said to her once, quoting Merlin: Learning is the one thing that never fails. It had gone into her journal and she'd thought at the time, Where on earth did he get that from? 'Some book,' he'd said.

There are books from charity shops and pubs and libraries and mates, books that have been passed from hand to hand in the bush, from glovebox to port to saddle to swag. There are books that are coverless and dog-eared and grubby and worn. Most of them look voraciously read. Their pages have absorbed the dryness of the desert and the thick texture of it grates on Snip's hands.

She feels like she's stepping into Bud's thinking. There are books on the history of plagues, wildflowers of the desert, wind, the surrealists in Paris, commonsense cookery, crime scenes, Churchill, cricket, the aesthetics of fascism, schoolgirl French, romanticism, cattle-breeding, the stars. So little of all this leaks out of him. The vigour of self-learning is crammed into his space and it's a home not much larger than a caravan. The books have overrun every spare bench and chair and resting place, like a cluster of cats taking over a house and infusing it, absolutely, with their presence and smell. Snip's hands run over the volumes, she picks them up and feels them and smells them. Their dryness, the covers curling and ripped, the pages fanning out like accordions. There are wisps of paper floating from them, covers coming off, stacks teetering at her disturbing hand. The smell of reading is thick in the room.

Dave calls her to him. His movements are careful and his voice is battened down, like a tourist who's snuck into an empty church.

On an old kerosene fridge is a snap. The photo's edges are curled. It's stuck by a piece of deeply yellowed stickytape that's almost completely lost its potency. Snip lifts the snap away. Sun over the years has leeched the colours of any brightness.

A little boy by an old Valiant Regal.

A cub scarf around her neck.

Hands held to her head.

Hair shorn like a sheep.

A face full of grin and light.

Snip can't stick the photo back, her hands tremble with the trying, with the swiftness and the recklessness of her disturbing. She props it by a jar on top of the fridge and her fingers hover around the snap, holding it and putting it back and placing it again.

Dave touches her on the shoulder and points.

Above the door is a studio portrait of Helen, glued

to a piece of foxed cardboard. It's pre-marriage. Red softly and fakely colours her cheeks and her lips and the fingernails resting on the side of her face. There's the strong stare into the camera, even then. And the arch look – don't touch me.

A single bed hugs the corner of another room. A stern black Bible is the only book by it. An old patchwork quilt has slipped on to the floor. Ochre is nestled deep in the bed's sheet, staining the white a soft pink where Bud's heavy body has rested on it. Snip kneels beside the mattress. She wants to cry at its narrowness and the dip that's left behind.

She feels like an intruder. The house tells her everything and nothing, it's as inscrutable as Bud is. It locks away his secrets just as he locks away the learning in his books. And it's all of no use to anyone but him because it's never been shared, and that, Snip realizes as she stands in his house, is what sums up his life. His chosen way is selfishness. And there's something fundamentally wrong with that.

Snip stays very still by the bed for a very long time, beyond her knees hurting on the hard lino, beyond Dave and Shelly-Anne retreating softly outside.

CHAPTER NINE

Home

The sour smell of desert flowers pushes into the car. Dave leans out the window and takes a photo of the community. Snip swiftly takes the camera from his hand. Puts it on her lap, annoyed at him for seeing it all as spectacle. Dave stares at her. She turns her head from him. Says nothing.

It's the annual sports weekend. Twenty desert communities have gathered to compete. 'Good timing, girl,' Shelly-Anne says to Snip as the car joins the slow procession on the one road in.

Snip barely registers, thinking of Bud. She's not sure what lies ahead of him. She doesn't know whether he'll ever be welcome in the community again and this place is the closest to a home that Bud's got. He loves the community just as she does. She can't imagine how he'd cope with another banishment. He's an old man now, it's not so easy to be slippery, to run.

An electricity Snip can almost rub between her

fingers pushes through the windows. The frisson of a big occasion is in the air. She holds out her head and breathes in the breeze. Shelly-Anne is telling Dave that in the community Alice Springs is now referred to as Kumanjayi Springs, it's been given the generic name for someone who's died because a woman called Alice in the community has just passed away and the name of the dead can't be mentioned. Dave is laughing, saying wow. He gets out his pen and rushes them both with questions. Snip ignores him.

They pass the jangly stalls of sideshow alley squatting on the dust like newly sprung grass after rain. They pass congregations of men and cars and boys and barking, wheeling dogs. They pass young boys sitting backwards on the roofs of high utes, dangling their legs down to the trays and lightly holding on, swaying on the slow cars like they would on a horse.

By Shelly-Anne's house there's a gathering of black-fellas and whitefellas with No Food in their midst and at the sight of the group Snip moves away from Dave's questioning stare. She's yelling out joyously to the gathering before the car has rolled to a stop. She's out fast and ruffling No Food's neck and hugging Kevin and brushing Richard on the cheek. He's blushing and then she is too and they're both laughing and hitting at each other in mock shyness. Two fierce desert girls by the fence watch keenly and say nothing. Snip doesn't know them. They're from another area.

Snip buries her face in No Food's neck and the dog is licking her cheek and her lips as she tugs him by the ears in welcome. Kevin turns to Dave, who's lugging in the swag behind them. 'You're going to have to watch this one, mate. Cheeky one.' He squeezes Snip's shoulder. Dave says nothing. Snip puts her arm around Kevin. It's good to be back among her community mates.

The whitefellas gather inside and call for drinks. There's a thumping on the door that has the heartiness of lumberjacks in it and Kevin lets in a rush and screech of kids over Shelly-Anne's rising wail that she's just de-kidded the house. She holds high in her fingers, by the tail, a just-discovered dead mouse. Kids cluster about her and reach for it and scatter, they bang open cupboards and the fridge and they run their hands along walls and find a juicer and pore over it and pull it apart.

They see Dave. They stop. They stare at his city-black jeans and his big-buckled belt and his very new hat. They see Snip. She kneels down to Caleb.

'Hey, remember me?'

He steps back, unsure. He stares at her hair.

'Napaljarri. Truck lady.'

A grin like a lightbulb snaps on his face.

'You belong to Bud!'

'Yehwah. I belong to Bud.'

Snip smiles. It feels wrong now, saying it. She pulls Dave to her and the kids are off squealing and racing and thumping again. Caleb is instructing little Daniel Bly that he has to sleep with Snip and Daniel Bly is obediently laying his head on the pillow of the swag in the spare room, waiting for her to join him.

'No,' Dave says. '*I* have to sleep with her.'

Daniel's head cocks.

Snip's arm slips around Dave and she pulls him in close. 'Bugger it, you can all sleep with me!'

There's Shelly-Anne's high wail.

UNDER HER SKIN

At seven the light softens into night and a stillness falls over the community. Queenie's household has gathered in her front yard with Shelly-Anne's. Two small fires flick and crack neatly on either side of the group, pushing away mosquitoes and flies.

Queenie sits. She reaches up a hand and pulls Snip down to the dirt beside her. She swiftly strips kangaroo tails from shop plastic and throws the tails on the flame, singeing the fur away and scraping the stubborn bits off, talking to Snip all the while, 'That way skin crispy, Napaljarri, good one,' sharing her way. She wraps the tails in alfoil and buries them in the ashes and leaves them in the heat. Says, 'Smell when they're ready, Napaljarri,' and taps Snip on the nose.

Snip watches the flame and eventually moves from it. The push of its heat is bringing the trauma of being lost too freshly back, reawakening the nag of Bud's disappearance. Dave steps back to her. He sits with his thigh pressing against hers. Says nothing. Queenie carries to her the first tail. Glutinous flesh fibres cling to Snip's skin and without a word Dave takes her hand in the shadows and he licks her fingers, he sucks softly at the roo flesh stuck to them, he sucks and licks as if he were sculpting her nipple into stiffness. She draws away, shy with it. Queenie brings her more meat. 'Fatten you up, Napaljarri,' she laughs, telling her that she must stay. 'I take you hunting. Teach you things.'

As they walk from Queenie's at the end of the night Dave's hand slips into Snip's, as if he's trying to lay claim to her thoughts. 'You know, I have this fear sometimes I'll lose you to all of this. You're so hard to hold on to, Snip.'

His voice is tired and there's something new and ungiving in the back of it. Snip doesn't like it. She kisses Dave full on the lips, kissing it away, and then she turns him softly around and stands with her belly pressed into his back. Her hands are light on the vulnerability of his stomach.

'We don't belong here, Snip.'

'I know.'

She doesn't like his lecturing tone. She drops her voice low and speaks close to his back. 'I, I can't stay away from it, Dave. I can't really explain why. But I love these people, and I love this land and this place. This is as close to a home and a family as I get.'

Snip rubs the dried fibres of roo tail from her fingers as Dave breaks from her and tells her in a city voice that she's so fucking naïve, she's blinded and bewitched and not seeing. The stink of the place, the sores on the kids, the dripping noses, the scraps of houses and dogs, the wife bashing, the grog. He speaks to her in a voice she hasn't heard before, a voice that's cold and accusing and short with her.

'Dave, it's a lot more than all of that.' Her voice has a new tone with him in return, tight and defensive and wounded. Snip recognizes her mother in it. 'It's, it's under my skin and it isn't going to let me go.'

She tells him – stumbling and trying to get the words out right – that she only knows what she sees. That for her it's something unique and good. It's got to do with family. And spirituality. And sharing. And land. And she respects it and envies it.

As she speaks she rubs and rubs at the roo fibres, rubbing away skin with the fret of the talk.

'You don't see straight, Snip. You don't really know them and you never will.'

Snip walks ahead of Dave, shaking him off with her stride. His voice comes hard at her back, telling her loudly she doesn't belong in this community and has no right to assume there's a place for her here, telling her loudly it's time to go home.

Snip doesn't really have one. She's not telling him again. He's not listening.

'I think this is going to be a problem between us.'

It's as if he's flung something at her back. Snip halts, momentarily, and then walks away, swift, into the black. She doesn't look back.

She's not sure where she should go next. They haven't discussed it. She'd assumed since the night of camping out that wherever it was, it would be with Dave. And now the gypsy sings softly again in her blood.

FLUSH

Morning. Dark. Dave and Snip in the swag on the floor at Shelly-Anne's, fuming still. No Food awake, ear cocked to the new tones in their voices.

Dave says to Snip in a hard stab of a whisper that if

she loves it all so much why doesn't she stay here permanently. She says fiercely back that she doesn't know what she would do. She couldn't paint side by side with the Walpiri, it wouldn't be right in their place. She says they do it differently: that she works alone, isolated from humanity, but they're the interpreters of everyone's humanity in the community and they're not set apart from it. She says she'd have to have a function, a purpose, as a white person living in this place.

'Anthropology,' Dave says. 'Go back to uni, try something new.' He rolls to the wall. 'Your chum Richard says there's a good course in Melbourne. Why don't you go down there?'

'Painting is my profession, Dave. You know that. I'm following my heart, I always have. Anyway, what . . . what about you in this place?'

Snip is close to tears.

'Oh come on, I could never live here, Snip. There's absolutely nothing for me here in terms of my work. The people touch the land too softly. I need foundations and bricks, I need certainty, something more solid to work with.'

Dave draws the sheet around him and curls up. Snip hovers angrily over his sleepiness, trying to drag him from it, talking in fierce, jagged whispers about how she reckons the measure of a civilized society is how badly off its poorest people are, not how many tall buildings it's got. But Dave keeps his face firmly to the wall.

Snip flops on to her back and looks at the back of his head, knowing he won't understand if she tells him the land she grew up in feels like corrupted land to her, because it's been swept clear of the people who told stories about it over thousands of years, it's been swept of the people who sang for it. She wants to rattle him into talk by telling him the land she's in now feels rich, it's singing with spirit and community and family. And she doesn't have any of that.

She doesn't tell him. She jerks a bit of the sheet over her and stares at the moth-spotted ceiling in the coming light. She can't drop back into sleep.

Shelly-Anne gets up to go to the toilet. The house vibrates with her footfall. There's the slow shudder of the frame in the dark and Snip knows she has to leave, very soon, this living, responding, flimsy house that she's grown to love too much. It's not hers and it's not Shelly-Anne's: it belongs to the community's council. Snip twists her fingers in the skin of No Food's neck and listens to the generator's hum. She shuts her eyes and for a moment feels like she's on a ship, swiftly moving through the black and not able to escape the soft engine hum.

Snip knows she has no right to a permanent place in this community. Shelly-Anne only has a temporary place in it. And Snip doesn't know what either of them will be leaving it for.

A CIVILIZED SOCIETY

A slush of faeces and urine on the concrete floor. Smears on the wall. Lumps on the floor. Snip hovers above the toilet seat rim. The chain doesn't work. There's no paper. There's a child's wail and a nappy stink and women coming and going past the doorless cubicle and beneath it all there's the stench of shit and it's almost sickly sweet, throttling her nose.

Snip picks her way across the floor's wetness and in the dirt by the toilet block door is an abandoned stroller skeleton, kicked up jolly on its hind wheels, frozen like the statue of a horse in mid-rear. She smiles at it. There's a sculpture for a suburban shopping centre in there somewhere.

Spindly goalposts define the length of a football field. The surface is defiant ochre dust and the players are barefoot. Underpants, bras, T-shirts and skirts hang like dead chickens on the barbed-wire fence that's sagging around the field. Dave is sitting on the dirt of the sidelines. His hand is in his pocket on his camera. Snip watches him from a distance. He's wanting to use the camera but he's not daring, she can tell, he's not wanting to cross the divide into tourist. She's heard about the whitefellas who come to bush communities and freak out because they're in Australia, their own country, but they've entered a place where the culture and religion are alien and they can't read the paintings or speak the language and they don't have access to the intricacies of the law.

She doesn't want to sit near Dave. He's too much the archaeologist, dissecting and appraising and cataloguing. She can read his hungry visitor eyes.

Snip strides from the football match through the community, wanting to feel the place. Time is running out. She's made up her mind. She has to find her own country, she has to stick with her painting for a while. She's not sure whether it'll be with Dave or not, whether she'd be completely comfortable with that now. It's such a big U-turn in her life. So this is domesticity: compromise. Bud hasn't chosen it. And she's not sure, now, whether she could.

The referee of a netball game blows a whistle with a baby loose and comfortable on his hip. Old men gather for a ceremonial dancing display. They're painted up in white ochre and on their heads are headdresses made from green cardboard beer boxes. Snip walks by it all, fiercely loving it.

'Hey, Napaljarri!'

Snip turns and screams too loud with delight.

Helicopter's tallness and teasing and ease strides towards her. Sexy one, yehwah.

'We got to feed you up, Napaljarri. Skinny one. Get some bush tucker into you, take you hunting.'

They laugh. She softly hits his shoulder in greeting. He says he's visiting the community for the sports weekend. And keeping an eye on her. He tells her he's got a present for her and points. Up the road, under a tree, is Snip's ute. It's cloaked in a deep dusty red. It looks sorry and bush-bashed and alone, like a kid who's been found after running away from home. Snip feels a tightness in her throat as she looks at it – there are so many memories soaked into it. She's not sure she wants it again right now. Helicopter tells her the car jumped like a roo when he put the diesel in it. That he managed to patch up the tank.

'How?'

'Ah, I'm not telling you. You're a whitefella, you'll patent it!'

'C'mon, Helicopter. I need to know.'

'Bush way, Napaljarri. My secret. Bit of plants, bit of gum. It worked real good.'

She thanks him again. Thinks of Bud. Lifesaver rings. His hat. Being on the run. Whitefellas turned into blackfellas by the heat of the sun.

Helicopter tells her he almost didn't give the ute back because he's been busy making use of it, getting into town for business. 'Whitefella mining, Napaljarri, lots of talking talking talking.' Helicopter tells her all the old fellas are worried the mining mob might get sick from a sacred site they want to dig up. That the old fellas say when they see the mining mob ripping up their ground, it's like their arms and legs are being ripped off.

Helicopter tells her she should stay for a while, she should get Queenie to fatten her up. They laugh and Snip plunges in with asking about Bud and the *tjukurrpa* situation, about what he'll face when he comes back. It's the first time she's had the courage to ask an Aboriginal person, and it had to be an outsider to this community – she couldn't raise the subject with anyone from Bud's area, she's too fearful of the response.

Helicopter chuckles. He tells her not to worry, that the blackfellas have no intention of any punishing because they knew it was an accident.

'You white mob, you're always getting it wrong.'

He tells her the blackfelllas went to the scrap-metal dealer in Alice the very next day and got the secret sacred items back and put them somewhere very safe, where there'll never again be any chance of whitefella tinkering.

Snip feels a collapsing through her as she listens. She crosses her arms over her shoulders and draws her face to her chest as she reels with the news.

There was no need to go on the run.

Bud wasn't being targeted.

They were all being too careful.

She looks up.

'Is . . . is there any news of Bud, Helicopter? Have you heard where he is?'

His face shuts down. He tells Snip not to call Bud back after he's gone. He says some people choose to go, she's got to let them, and a young boy comes up to him and tugs him away and Snip's not quite sure what Helicopter means and she wants to ask him but he's striding away and is gone.

He's swallowed up by the crowd. The moment's lost.

Reeling still.

No need for running.

Too careful, too cautious.

Getting it wrong.

A HAND LOOSE IN HERS

Night. The big top, open to the stars.

There's a roof of frenzied moths delirious with happiness as they batter the spotlights. There's a country-and-western concert in the rodeo ring. On one side of the ring are Aboriginal elders, stately in cowboy hats and boots and shirts. The men are lean and sexy and still.

And on the other side of the ring, crammed on low benches, are wriggly, squirmy, squealy kids.

Dave and Snip are with the young ones. The two of them are distanced and tight within the aftershock of their first fight. Dave is resolute, wanting her out now. His ten days are almost over. He's got a new, short-term contract coming up. He has to prepare for it. He wants to go home.

Shelly-Anne is back at the house, grabbing the peace.

In a racy song one child bobs up and then another and another in little spot fires of dancing. The children are around five and six and seven. They swivel sensuous hips, they thrust their pelvises forward and throw their arms behind their heads and close their eyes and open their mouths wide. They surrender to the ecstasy while the teenage kids beside them are silent and watching and not daring because inhibition and a sense of responsibility and impending adulthood are shutting them down.

Snip pulls Dave up to dance, knowing they can never compete with the young ones. The kids laugh and squeal and one grabs at her hands and jigs with her and runs giggling back to the safety of her mates and then another comes up to them, and another, and Dave's awkward with it all. Then the whole tent roars with laughter as Helicopter gets up and with one hand behind his head and one hand on his waist swivels his hips and shows them all.

Snip laughs so much it hurts. She glances at Dave. She can't read him, his closed smile.

The silence between them is as taut as stretched wire on the walk home. Snip doesn't know what to say. Dave doesn't get it, the pull of the community. His closed-off walk is telling her he's seen enough and he wants out. The place tugs at Snip and her heart tells her she's not yet ready to move from it. Dave represents attachment, a shedding of the old way, a dropping of the defences that feel as much a part of her as her painting does.

His hand is loose and noncommittal in hers. Snip looks back at the big top, at the frenzy of moths. They're like a soft cloud, circling close above the tent, wanting in.

HER MIND MADE UP

On the track back to Alice the smell of Bud's sweat stains the ute. Snip can hardly drive it. She slows over corrugations and bulldust, she almost stops at rocks on the road. Shc's addled with thinking about Bud. It feels like betrayal, driving so soon from the land that he's in.

Queenie had said she'll try and visit but Snip knows she won't. She gets physically sick whenever she leaves her land. Snip will have to come back to see her again. She doesn't know when.

The car is so coated with dust inside and out that

she can't read the dials on the panels. Snip cleans them with the side of a fist like she's wiping a misted mirror. She slams on the brake for a startled calf in the middle of the road. It has the affronted look of someone caught looting. She curses the animal and jams her clenched fist on the horn. It heaves sideways in shock and ambles off.

Bud's slipped through her hands once again. Just as she had him. Always one step ahead of her, impossible to pin down.

Dave and Snip hardly talk. The silence between them feels grubby. Dave's head is turned resolutely to the window as they drive through the land that is bitten into by hard cattle hooves. Snip stops without asking at a tourist tearoom. They climb out sapped of words. Examine the desultory blackboard menu. They don't consult. What's the soup? asks Dave of the man behind the counter. Shredded Aborigine is the matey reply. What? Snip says, her cheeks blooming with flush. Something dawns in the face of the shop assistant. She turns and walks briskly out, slapping the screen door, before he can reply. Waits in the car. Fuming, cursing this country, her fists clenched on the wheel. After what seems like a very long time Dave saunters out with a milkshake. I had to eat, he says and shrugs. He offers the carton. Snip shakes her head and says nothing and roars the car to a start. Food can wait.

The wind has blown the desert into the town they

pass through, coating its signs and windows and benches and poles. It's a town that clings to its Woolworths following the local mine shutdown, a town fighting the seep of the sand. It's not winning. They slow as they drive down the bare main street and stare out the windows, assessing the emptiness. Snip looks across at the head turned from her. Ghosts are the price of love – she remembers that line from a movie. Something between them has turned. They're not talking, proper way, anymore.

Dave checks his watch and tells her they've got three hours to get to the airport. He asks if they'll make it. She says yep. Relationships are hard work, her mother had told her once. Snip's always running at the first sign of waning, that's her way, and she's not good with telling men why. Snip can feel Dave's jitter for home in the thump of his palm on the roof outside. His head's in another world and she doesn't try hauling him from it. The hills around Alice glow golden with the last of the day's heat. Neither of them comments as they drive towards them. They would have once. The silence between them feels weighted, like a shelf bowed with books.

At the airport, at the boarding call, Dave asks Snip when he'll see her again and she says soon, she doesn't know, she's got some business to do. He says he doesn't want to lose her, he wants to take care of her, he wants to introduce her to his family. He says he's not into long-distance relationships and if she doesn't want to make a commitment to him, well, that's that. And she's so bloody slippery to hold on to.

'You won't lose me,' Snip says, 'I'll call,' and she walks away without looking back.

She can feel Dave's eyes following her. She's never felt this way about someone, but she's fighting the pull of a habit that sings through her. And she never grew up with the expectation that someone would look after her. It's not her way. Dave's offering to wrap her in the one thing that's always eluded her – a strong sense of family.

She doesn't turn.

PAST TENSE

The bar of the Alice Hotel. The three men around Snip have all asked her to marry them during the stretched evening and she feels her sentences slipping. She tries to tighten them, tries to scrub her mind clean as one man buys her another gin and tonic, and then, swiftly, another. She runs the palms of her hands flat over her head, trying to pull her body into straightness.

Snip's waiting for the bar to empty, for a moment alone with Roslyn the barmaid. The gin no longer slices but soaks through her. The three men drift away. It's late. There's the drag of communal tiredness around her. Roslyn clears her glass and there's no-one else left in the room. Snip's ready.

She leans forward and asks Roslyn does she miss him, warming her up.

'Bud?'

'Yeah.'

'God yes.' Roslyn smiles. 'He was the bugger who always sat down in front of me and asked me for the beer that made him cry. And then he'd say hang on, no, you're too beautiful to be inflicted with the sight of that, just make it a lemonade, that's all I'm allowed now. God he was an old smoothie.'

Past tense. Snip pushes the sting of it away.

Roslyn moves down the counter, grabbing up glasses and rattling and clinking them on to trays. Snip gets up from her stool and stands in front of her and asks if she knows anything about where Bud is. If she's heard any little scraps, because the second search has come up with nothing. Snip tries to sound casual. She's been waiting all night for this moment. If anyone would know, it'd be Roslyn.

'Heard something? Lord no. He's dead, isn't he, love? Isn't he?' She smiles sadly at Snip, pity in her eyes.

Snip feels like she's cracking under the strain. She rings her mother from the pub's public phone. Gets the answering machine. Isn't sure what number she should leave because she doesn't have one. Tells Helen, via the machine, she'll ring back when she can.

That night, on Kate's closed-in verandah, Bud pushes into Snip's dreaming like ink into water. Bud wandering, mouth open, Bud stumbling and falling and not getting up. The sun on his back and a mouthful of dirt. A shallow grave slowly swallowing him, his stiffened hand thrusting through the sand, a wrist with an engraved watch still on it.

Snip jolts awake. Just a dream. Sweet relief. Her thudding heart stills.

THE LONELINESS OF A LONG-DISTANCE RELATIONSHIP

The next morning Dave's out. Snip's question careers into urgency, she can't contain it: When will he be home? She has to know. The flatmate doesn't have any idea. It makes Snip know, absolutely, that she wants him. That he's all she's got.

Snip rings again in an hour and then another and he's back. She takes a deep breath. Tells him she's flying into Sydney tomorrow and she wants to stay with him and she asks him, stumbling, if that's okay. He goes quiet. Then out of the long pause he tells her that sometimes he's in pain, missing her so much. He says she soaks through the skin of his days and it's torturous and wonderful all at once. He says she's the one thing in his life he can't seem to have. And it's been driving him absolutely crazy.

'I'm, I'm sorry Dave, I'm sorry, I'm not very good with relationships. I've got to learn so many things. And God, what do you see in someone like me anyway? Why on earth do you love *me*, of all people?'

'I love you because you're unlike any other woman I've met. I love you because you're not one of those neurotic Sydney girls. I love you because you're courageous. You say exactly what you mean. You're honest. And I'm comfortable talking with you. I love you because your ears blush when I kiss them. And you're a pretty damn good fuck. I love you because of the way you draw and paint, as if it's coming from way inside your soul. I love you because you've got the strength to do what your heart tells you to. And because you're beautiful and you don't plaster it over with make-up. You don't go on about your weight. You don't mind tucking into chocolate mud cake and milkshakes with me. You've got one hell of a ute. And I love the way you smell. And I love you, Snip Freeman, because you're a huge challenge in my life. Um, is that enough for you?'

'Okay.'

Dave laughs softly. He asks her what she's doing

with the ute. Snip doesn't know. She tells him her brain feels cobwebbed, breaking up with the strain. That there are too many things not tied down, too many questions. She feels as if she's only tackling everything halfway and then moving too quickly on to something else. And nothing's getting properly done. Something within Snip baulks at taking the ute. Bud's presence is seared into it. She can't bear to drive it on another long trip and she can't bear the stress of driving in a big city. She could leave it with Helicopter, but she's afraid of community kids taking it over and trashing and bush-bashing it. She'll leave it with Kate for a while, until she works out what she's doing with her life.

Snip hangs up from Dave, drenched with him, wet, wanting. She has to give this a go, she has to try compromise. The neophiliac.

And she has to speak to her mother. She rings. Gets the answering machine, again.

LEAVING THE LAND

Initiation time. Night gathers in the sky. There are old Aboriginal men being driven into town in the trays of utes, men with vivid red bands across their foreheads, men still and silent and unsmiling. And there are white-fellas in high four-wheel drives heading out of town, roaring and speeding and honking, gathering at the speedway gouged in the desert. It's a big night tonight, for both black and white.

Snip walks for a long time, feeling the insistence of the land through the clot of buildings and car parks in the ugly tourist town. It's a town threaded with sacred outcrops and trees and rocks. She walks to let the smell of eucalypts and the hills and the air and the sky soak through her. She steps into the riverbed to say farewell to Zacharia, a senior man from the community who's living now in town. His art hangs in public galleries all over the world. His mattress is the Todd riverbed and his plate for meat is a ripped-up piece of cardboard box. She tells him that tomorrow she'll be up in a plane, leaving this place, and he says seven sisters, Napaljarri, don't forget the seven sisters and she looks up to the knot of stars, following his finger, and says yehwah and smiles and holds her hand out in farewell and walks on. Every time she comes back to Alice she walks down to the riverbed to him, with a gift of a fresh piece of canvas and paint. She doesn't know when the next time will be.

Snip hasn't painted for a long time. She's feeling the need for it now. The hunger for a studio, her own space, for blank canvases and the sensuality of them, for silence and spareness and the glittering alone.

She's not sure how Dave will fit in with all of that.

Snip tries Helen again. This time there's the familiar

brisk hello. The connection to London speedily gobbles Snip's coins and it's a conversation made jagged by the crackle in the line and the drop of the money and the half-second delay, but in it Snip establishes that she knows what happened twenty-three years ago and she knows Helen funded the search. She asks why. There's a long pause. Helen tells her, speaking carefully, that she'll go through it with her when she next comes out, that she can only do it face to face. Then she asks if Snip is okay and before she can answer, the line drops out.

No, I'm not okay, Snip tells the dead line, I'm rattled by what I'm leaving behind me and I'm rattled by what's ahead. She hangs up the phone.

Over the MacDonnell Ranges lightning flicks and sparks in a cloud like some super-fast mosquito trapped in a net. It's a fluffy-white, sunny-day cloud but it's night and the rest of the sky is star-stained and clear. The lightning flicks and flicks, trying to get out. The air in the night is odd, stamping Snip's memory with its vividness.

She walks back to Kate's, to where Dave had come six weeks ago and demanded to see her. But she'd already gone, leaving instructions to tell the city bastard that when he calls, if he calls, she'd moved on, to the next town or the next, no-one could say. Snip smiles at that, at the circle they've come.

The axe head is shunted under the studio door,

propping it wide. Snip stares at the half-finished paintings, ferociously splattered and streaked on the night she came back from the roadtrip. She can't go back to those paintings now, the energy in them is all wrong and she turns their fury to the wall. She doesn't want to linger in the studio with its daddy-long-legs and dust, she wants to move away from it all and scrub herself clean.

Snip rests her belly against Kate's shower wall for a very long time, washing away the lipstick Kate had earlier put through her hair to deepen its red at the roots. It was an experiment. Kate's always mucking around with her own appearance, and anyone else's she can get her hands on to. Snip smiles. She'll miss her. The shock of her hair. Her spikiness. Her chocolate-covered honey ants. Her latest girl crushes. Her fierce loyalty. Her tolerance of Snip's ways.

She smiles at the sweetness of the water sweeping over her. Snip's studios in strange towns often don't come with showers, so her nomadic painting life has often included a ritual of swimming every day in public pools for the sole purpose of showering afterwards in their changerooms. Sixty cents usually buys three minutes of hot water and it never seems enough. Snip's sick of wet concrete floors and besser-brick blocks and of water dribbling to a stop, she's sick of carrying soap and shampoo and scrounging for change and never feeling quite clean enough, she's sick of the jagged, fraught life that she's led.

She scrubs at her skin, sloughing off the grime of a couple of months in the desert. She scrubs with her nails until it hurts under hard, hot water and at the end of it her skin is tingling and red. A ring of ochre marks the bathtub she stands in and a clot of hair matts the plughole as scummed water seeps through it.

Snip doesn't know when she'll come back to this place. She feels as if this way, her way for so many years, is coming to an end. She's come to accept that Bud's dead. It's allowing her, finally, to leave this place.

She's jittery and anxious about going. Kate senses it. Asks her to sleep inside in the spare bedroom of the house for her final night.

'Practice,' Kate says and softly laughs, 'you're going to have to get used to it, girl.'

Snip gives her a long hug in reply, she ruffles Kate's hair that's now cropped silkily short, running her fingers over her head, learning her scalp.

Kate puts her hands over Snip's. 'This is all because of you, Snip Freeman. I knew you hated that bleaching job, I could see it in your eyes. Your face always tells people exactly what they don't want to know.'

The two of them stay up late, split a bottle and smoke a joint, talk about girlfriends and kids and marriage and men. Snip says her periods are becoming heavier, more insistent, as if they're telling her body that it's time. Kate says me too, and grins.

'But I don't have to worry about all that.'

She asks Snip flippantly if she'd ever get hitched and Snip laughs and says God no, explaining it to her by explaining what she knows of falconry, the practice of running a fine thread of silk through a bird's eyelids and sealing its eyes to make it tractable. She tells Kate that being made tractable is the thing she fears most. She lies down along Kate's couch, her feet on its arm and a glass of wine in her hand, and talks of her fear of losing the sharp flint that sparks her paintings, her fear of losing the exhilaration of the savage, creative alone. She says she loves the masculine energy, the selfishness of it.

'You got to do what you really want to, Snip. You've got the choice.'

'Yeah, we'll see.'

Snip falls into sleep sideways across the mattress of the spare double bed, her body nudging the line of pillows and her feet poking out, caressed by the coolness of the night. She always sleeps like that when she's alone in big beds. Dave doesn't know of the habit, it's born of too many bedtimes alone. And she's grown to love it too much.

Snip wakes deep in the night and feels a welling of sadness coming up through her. She has to leave Bud behind, to move on. She has to move on. She has to give Dave a chance, she has to test the pull of being ferociously independent and alone. Because Snip knows that it's something she's grown to love too much, that it's settled over her like a shell.

KISSED LAND

The day Snip leaves Alice Springs, with No Food perplexed in his new plastic travel crate, there's a mist of rain like a whisper. Clouds drop low over the MacDonnell Ranges, obscuring from Snip the outline of the caterpillar dreaming that crawls so starkly in stone along their ridge. The smell of the desert is concentrated in the wetness of the air. The dry rivers are flowing. Chains are across the causeways of the Todd and there are cars and people with cameras at them and a festival atmosphere and parents yarning and dogs barking and kids splashing. The drama of occasion is soaked through air made soft by rain.

As the plane taxis down the runway Snip puts her hand to her mouth and sniffs her palm. A strange smell has nestled there over the past few weeks, it's a smell of sweat and ochre and desert and sadness and she can't scrub it away. It's as if the smell of grief is cupped permanently now in her hands.

Bud is gone, he is dead. And she is leaving Central Australia.

As the plane climbs high Snip glances down at the rain-kissed land. It looks like a sheet of mottled, rusted tin. As they climb higher they pass over land that's deeply dry and Snip stares at it. Its surface is a hurting scowly red, like a furious sunburn. And her body is still imprinted with the sun's deep stain from her time stranded in the desert, she's branded by tan marks of sandshoes and shorts and bra. She doesn't think they'll ever go.

She'll have to learn a new land, a new way. What keeps nagging her is the fear of some sort of diminishing, a dilution of her talent if the new life she settles into is too distractingly good.

CHAPTER TEN

Wind-bashed and Water-soaked

Dave and Snip and No Food cross water to get to their new place, the ute snug in the belly of a bellowing, ploughing ferry. They've had the car transported by train from Alice Springs to Sydney, because Snip said it was too soon to go back to collect it herself. When the ute arrived they drove down to Melbourne and on to the ferry.

They cross Bass Strait and drive off the ramp under a vast, mushroom-clouded sky. A localized shower in the distance drops to the ground, out of a band of steel grey stretching the width of the sky. They drive through and over water to get to their place. Drive into mist and sleet and rain and hail, over rivers and creeks and brooks. Drive past cheating forests of pine, hidden behind tangles of native growth crowding the roadsides. They stop the car and climb through to the forests that seem scrubbed of the vividness of life, with no birds and no animals and no sound. They leave the trees, hushed, and drive on, learning the politics of this place. They drive past paddocks with clumps of uprooted tree stumps, with jumbles of brown and grey and white tossed together like the carcasses of cows waiting to be torched. And paddocks with just a single dead tree.

'It's as if they've died of loneliness,' Snip says to Dave, and he smiles and nods hmmm and slips his fingers down into the eye of her thighs.

They drive the length and the breadth of Tasmania. A land soaked in blood, Snip had heard once in the Northern Territory, a ghost-land – beware. And the two of them come to rest at a buffeted village on the north-west coast, a town huddled in a crook between the hills and the sea.

A place wind-bashed and water-soaked. Their new home.

TO THIS

A week after Snip came in from the desert Dave had sought out a contract in a place far away from the red sand and far away from his city. He had won one for a year, on the edge of a town neither of them had heard of.

'Neutral territory, that's what we need,' Dave had said. 'A place new to both of us.'

A strange outcrop of rock is at the head of the town. The rock will have a dreaming story but Snip can't track down anyone who knows it. Anything out of the ordinary in this land has a story, that's what she's been told, anything unusual, across Australia, has been sung for at least some time. In the shock of first seeing the immensity of the rock she thought of the Aranda word for land being lonely – meaning land without family or ceremony. She couldn't. All she remembered was that the words for people being lonely and land being lonely are almost the same. And the ground that Snip stood on felt like partly empty ground to her, there was an absence within it, because the people who had sang for it and told stories about it for thousands of years had been mostly erased from it. Almost nothing seemed left of them in this land of smug English place names, but ghosts.

There's an old colonial stone mansion that peers from the top of a high hill behind the village. The house wears slabs of tin across some of its windows and a scumble of graffiti on the base of its walls. It swallows wind and leaves and dirt and rain and derision from the community below it. Dave's job is to save it, to peel back its layers and dig out its history and nurture it back into life.

Their temporary home is the gutted bluestone convict quarters at the back of the house. The building has the dimensions of a cosy barn. Snip's studio is the stable nearby. In the daytime she flings wide the old wooden doors to air that's thickened by the sea. She wants her canvases to eat up paint in this new place but for now, in the first sweetness of settling, the canvases wait.

As can Dave's proposal of marriage. She laughs when he asks. Tells him that she said to a girlfriend once she would never marry. Tells him that one day she might go back on her word, that stranger things have happened, but she's not ready yet to tackle such a question. Tells him it's too soon, they both must see how they go living together, they both must wait.

At night the stone walls around Snip closet her with a stillness. For the first few weeks she sleeps ten or eleven hours in this place, her body greedy, gobbling up sleep. An accumulated exhaustion is being smoothed away. There's a hum of silence deep in the night, it's like she's sleeping insulated by earplugs and an eyepatch. And as she lies sheltered in the thickness of the old stone walls Snip thinks of Dave's room high up in the city where she stayed for a month after flying from Alice. It was a room that vibrated with the noise of the street below it, a space she could never get solidly dark. The night sky at Dave's window was always white-grey from the glow of the skyscraper lights and Snip never, ever saw stars.

On her first night in the city there was a growl from the sky. Snip got up from Dave's bed and lay belly down in the lounge room and she felt the thunder murmuring in the floorboards. It started to rain. She got up to close the windows and stopped herself. Let the sky come in. The rain spat softly at her skin and she took off her T-shirt and went back to lying belly down on the ground. Snip wanted to feel the sky, she wanted to get closer to it. And in the middle of it all Dave padded out to her and stretched his body along hers with his stomach in the dip of her back and he said softly, you don't like this place, do you?

They moved. From the watery night-dark of the inner-city to this dark they have now of deep earth.

At night in this place Snip turns to Dave's sleeping back and holds her belly to his breathing. It's the first time in her life she's been able to sleep comfortably beside a lover, to surrender and relax. She's learnt it, finally, with Dave, as she lies next to him listening to the rhythm of his breathing – the changing, the deepening and the twitching of a dream until she follows him into sleep. One day she half woke in the early morning to find Dave curled around her back, with his arm threaded under hers and his hand balled softly in her groin. And she smiled sleepily and wrapped her arms over his in the vast sweetness of it, and fell back to sleep.

Snip wants to bottle forever this time of her life. A life shared, a spare existence, in a scrap of a place with a mattress on the floor and a shower that's just a piece of iron pipe stuck from the wall, but the water is endless and free and hot. It's a place where the lemon sun pushes its way shyly inside in the morning, licking at the scatter of books and newspapers beside them. A place where the rabbit sex between them has relaxed and settled into something rarer and sweeter and richer.

The secret, Snip knows, is to keep life simple. And to stop.

She wants to stay for a while in this state, in this place. She strides out often into midnight, into the pull of the night. Its presence in this place thickly soaks the air. She never noticed that in Sydney. The night there was shot through with noise and light and movement and colour and cars but here, in Tasmania, she wants to be still for a while with the nights, she wants to preserve the grace of her newly found settling.

But she knows the one certainty in life is that nothing ever lasts.

CRASHING BACK

Moments, perhaps four or five in a lifetime, are soldered in a very white light on the consciousness. For Snip: her father's hands snipping off her hair; the words 'I'll never contain you'; the gift of a dog; a rock through a fuel tank; a landscape torched. And a moment on a late-summer Tuesday when there was a knock on the door, and Bud came back.

He found her in a place that was water-soaked. He found her changed.

The texture of the day of Bud's return is ingrained into Snip, as surely as lines on her hand.

The knock.

Opening the door.

Stepping back.

Saying nothing for a moment with the shock of it.

Looking him over, keen as a doctor. Reading the scars of his journey. Sharp cliffs of skin under the cheekbones. A scalp fragile and pink through shorn hair. A strange yellow wash through the face and the neck. Both sets of eyelashes now completely grey. And something missing from him.

The light gone from the eyes.

'Look at me. Belsen.' His shrug and his grin, his whisper.

The voice is sucked away and she snaps from the staring and takes him by both hands and draws him inside, like a lover. Still saying nothing, not able to: the shock like a knot jammed in her throat. Snip holds her face to Bud's chest, breathing in hungrily the familiar smell that's been with her since childhood. Old singlets and sweat and fuel from cars and the sky and the earth never far from it. But there's something tart and new oddly flavouring it: antispetic and hospitals and swabs.

Bud senses her realization and steps from it.

He walks from his daughter to the kitchen table with the gait of a man who's come to the end of a long journey and can walk no more. His body falls heavily into the wooden chair. Both hands move to his forehead and prop it up. No Food nudges his knees and he doesn't respond. Snip's brimming with questions and she doesn't know where to begin, she wants to hit Bud and hug him but she kneels down beside him, touches his face, springs her fingers back, laughs, tells him he'll have to shave off his straggly bit of beard so she can recognize him before she can actually talk to him and he looks sharply at her, as if woken suddenly from a deep sleep. He tells her he can't shave his beard, that he's a prisoner now in his face.

His trembling hands. His voice sliding into silence. His eyes slipping from her, too tired to talk and not wanting the close looking, she can tell.

Snip says come on.

She takes Bud by the hand and leads him to her bed and he lies down docile, without any more words, his body falling into the mattress like a sigh. She unties his laces and takes off his shoes and his socks. Her fingers skim the deep furrows slicing the hardness of his heels.

The nails of each big toe have grown into his skin, like wisdom teeth into bone. Dried blood is in his socks.

The questions can wait.

TOUCHING LIGHTLY

Bud sleeps and wakes and sleeps and wakes throughout the cycles of twenty-four hours, not following the patterns of darkness and light. He touches the place lightly. He asks Snip questions now and then about where she's been and how she got here and about Dave and painting and the place that they're in and then hours later he'll ask the same questions again. Things are falling out of his brain.

'You're not painting in this place, are you Snippy? That's your job,' he says softly. 'You're not doing it properly, I can tell. Whenever you've visited me you've got all colours in the webs of your fingers and up your arms and in your hair. You're all clean now. What's happened?'

'Painting can wait.'

Bud asks for nothing. Is content to lie on the mattress, or stare, or look at the television without seeming to register it. He tells Snip at one point he doesn't read anymore, because the print is too small, he says, his voice failing as he speaks, yeah, no more books, his voice trailing.

There's something deeply wrong. Something beyond tired. There's an extraordinary mildness floating through him that Snip would never have imagined could be in him. Bud was always a vivid presence, a spectacular failure, a fierce silence. And now, this shell. Snip sits before him, trying to diagnose the chaos he won't speak of that's cut him loose from his mooring. She'll turn for a moment and when she looks back he'll have slipped away into slumber again. His body is like a child's, feeding ferociously on sleep.

When the daylight is strongest Snip sits before him, painting to please him, her canvas flat on the ground, the bush way. Pushing herself into the working mode that's slipped from her in the serenity of this place. But her canvases won't take off, they won't soar, the distractions are too great. She tries again and again to rattle the old Bud out of him with talk and reminiscence and stirring and laughing but he doesn't take the bait. It's as if he's disappeared into himself. The light that was in him, the will to go on, is gone. It's been knocked from him by something he won't speak of.

Snip won't let him get away with it. She has a need to know what happened after he left her, lying belly down on the ground with her cheek on the butt of his rifle. She has to find a way of oiling his memory. To find out how he got here, how he got out of the desert, why he didn't contact her until now. And why he's a remnant of his former self, gutted and missing and limp.

Bud speaks in scraps, evading and wondering and rambling. He says he's been sleeping most recently at a place called the Starlight Hotel. 'You know, Snippy, under the stars. The best bloody hotel in the world.' Chuckling in his whisper of a voice.

The sudden dryness and warmth and humour of it make Snip want to curl up in it but the blanket of his talk is too often mean and small and has too many holes. His words keep dribbling away.

In the cleanness following sleep Snip tries to pluck names and places and incidents out of Bud. He sits propped on her swag and she comes at him with tea and biscuits and concern and questions. All she gets is scraps, bits about ending up at a mate's place, Lajamanu way, someone who's suffered, he says. He likes people who've suffered, he tells her, because they're kinder, because their edges are softened by sorrow. He tells her he tried prospecting with his equipment in a wheelbarrow, every day trundling away into the sand. And then he's off talking about kindness and selfishness and suffering and God, with churches that wouldn't warm him and people who wouldn't feed him and Snip steers him firmly back.

'How did you get out from the desert, Bud? Who got you out of it?' Speaking loud and slow, on the edge of impatience, as if she's speaking to a child.

'Out? Out?'

'Who saved you?'

'Ah, salvation. Bloody hell, salvation. No-one'll save me. I'm beyond it, Snippy.'

'Who got you away from the ute? In the desert. Bud? *Listen. Answer me.*'

'The car? Helicopter, the bastard, the bloody bastard, he got me.'

'Helicopter?'

'Yeah.'

'He didn't say anything to me.'

The shock of it. Bud chuckles.

'He came back for me after he got you, dragged me by the ankles. Helped me disappear, kept me secret. I was in big trouble. Good fella that Helicopter, bloody good. By the ankles he had me, then over his back. Staring at his jeans, long time.'

Snip's throat tightens.

'He didn't let me know. He should've told me.'

'I asked him not to.'

'*What? Why?*'

Bud pauses. Snip thinks he's forgotten the question. She snatches up her paintbrush, exasperated at both of them, Helicopter and Bud.

'It's men's business, Snippy. I wanted to disappear, to walk away from everything. I wanted him to help me disappear. It was like an honour code between us. I trusted him not to tell you and he didn't. And then in the end he was the one who persuaded me to come back to you. She's in your blood, he said, she's in your blood.'

Bud chuckles, and in the silence that follows Snip thinks of the enormity of what Helicopter did for them both. She never properly said thank you for it and is deeply shamed by it. He should have had her ute. Shelly-Anne had told her that Helicopter was an Aboriginal man who couldn't connect well with his own wife and children, like some other community leaders she had known. He was one of the stolen generation, she had said. And perhaps that was why.

And now this. Bud here before her, because of him.

'You could've let me know all of this a bit sooner, you bastard,' Snip says, cross, and Bud replies hey, you know what I'm like, full of bad habits. And in the smile he flashes to her Snip recognizes, absolutely, bits of her own face in his and is startled by it.

Bud's smile fades. Something fragile and vulnerable and old washes through him.

'I didn't tell you sooner because I'm weak, Snippy.'

Snip blinks slowly at him, as still as a cat.

A bustle of noise comes from outside, it's Dave

arriving home from his day on the worksite. Bud rolls away from Snip, shutting his weakness away in sleep.

A BLOOD WHISPER

Bud's shy with Dave. All the sudden leakings of Bud's old humour and warmth and bluster are shut firmly away when Dave returns, with hands and his hair dusty from sifting through history. Snip kisses Dave's eyelashes in a ritualized homecoming, her lips softly cleaning away dust. And as she does it Bud shuts down. Snip remembers then his fear of people with university learning, with good schooling. She remembers his old sneer: city slickers. He doesn't know how to be with them or how to talk to them, he's afraid of them. Dave looks at him, perplexed, and tries to find ways in. Snip tells him Bud won't change. 'It's a shyness.'

He crashes, jaggedly, into the rhythm of their life. He talks to Snip but not Dave at the table, mouth crammed and spitting food. He leaves wet towels in his wake on the floor while shuffling from the bathroom to the swag, he belches and burps, changes the TV without asking and makes cups of tea for himself and no-one else. The selfishness of the lone existence is rotten right through him.

And he doesn't tell them why he's here, or how long he's staying, or what he wants.

Deep in the stillness of Bud's fourth night with them Snip's eyes snap awake. She can sense Bud's not in the building. She rises from the bed and snuggles the blanket around Dave, wraps a crochet rug about her shoulders and steps into the night. There's the immense calming stillness of a high full moon. Bud's sitting on a bench, leaning against the wall, smoking. He's staring at a row of trees by the gate whose seeds were transported from England on convict ships. The trees lean their trunks dramatically into the push of the wind from the sea, battling it and butting it. But tonight the air is warm and still.

Snip can see by the moonlight that Bud's pyjama legs are poking out from his trousers. She smiles. So many vulnerabilities now. She moves to him and sits quietly by him. He takes her hand. He says nothing for a while, then he asks is it raining and she says no. He tells her it's always raining now, he's always hearing rain and he doesn't know why and he rattles his head on its side as if he's trying to rattle the rain out. Snip looks out at the star-crammed night and tells him that perhaps God's talking to him and Bud chuckles and says he's given up on churches. She turns to him, shocked.

'Because, Snip, they're places that have no reverence for the land.'

He flicks away the stub of the cigarette and she closely examines his moonlit face, the new lines etched deeply on it. The furrows have accelerated and bite savagely. Bud tells her that God is in his heart and in the land but not, for him, within the walls of a building. He tells her Helicopter taught him that and as he talks he holds her hand, still, as if he's reluctant to abandon contact now it's been made. Or maybe he's forgotten. His hand is light in hers, it's old and dry and fragile and heartbreaking.

'Bu-ud. Why are you going on about all this?'

Snip runs her hand over his hair like a mother or a lover. He takes out a packet of Drum and rolls another cigarette. He hasn't smoked for years. The smell plunges Snip back to her childhood and Bud lights the cigarette like a movie star, he snaps his new Zippo lighter as if it's the last flourish left in him. He drags savagely on the cigarette and says without looking at her that something's got him well and good, and the doctors can't find out what it is. It could be something from the coalmines, from years back. He says that Helicopter forced him out of the desert and into a hospital. Then they wanted to do more bloodtaking and urine sampling and X-rays and he walked out on it all, he walked from the doctors and forms and air-conditioning and needles and he walked all the way to his daughter in Tasmania. He couldn't believe it when Shelly-Anne told him where Snip had ended up. He swore her to secrecy. Said he wanted his visit to be a surprise.

'Why did you have to pick somewhere so cold, you bugger? I need more heat on me, wrapping me up.'

Snip apologizes. They laugh.

He tells her he's got something whispering through his blood, not letting him go.

'You know, I love my daughter to distraction. I'm not very good at showing it. I just wanted you to know that.'

A shiver of a sob runs through Snip's body and she holds his arm to her cheek, his skin a warm handkerchief for her tears. Bud tells her his fear of an utterly empty church, that at least there's spectacle in the death of the young. He tells her the wisest thing the Walpiri have taught him is that the family, not the individual, is society's basic unit and that for him it's too late. He tells her people in undeveloped worlds are never as lonely as those in developed worlds and he looks at Snip and asks her, very low, if she'll come back to the desert with him. Too cold here, he says, too cold, three days in this place has been enough for me to see it.

He says he's come to Tasmania to bring her back home, that he needs her there now.

She turns her head from him. Stares out at the night. Thinking furiously.

'You can stay here, Bud.'

He's quiet for a while. Then he tells her the story of an old man whose family took him out of the Territory and back with them to their big home in Queensland. And one day, the old man disappeared. He was found walking along the highway, heading due west and still in his pyjamas because the Territory was his home and he wasn't happy anywhere else.

'Bud, I can't, I can't go back there to live. Dave's only here on a one-year contract. And, and I don't want to go back. I want to stay here with him. This is my home now, it's my new life. I want to give it a proper go.'

'Yeah. I know, Snippy, I know. I've been hearing it in your voice. It's like happiness is just sort of zooming out of you.'

He looks at her. He lights another cigarette. He draws strongly on it. 'Well, that's it then,' he says.

Snip sits beside him in the darkness, not letting go of his hand, until the dawn comes. It's a weak watery grey, hardly announcing the end of night. The clouds have come in and there's a light spattering of rain.

BUD'S WAY

Dirty, dishwater light. Snip rises from the bench stiff – the night's coolness has curled up in her bones. Dave brings out to them both a clean smile and two mugs of fresh tea, No Food at his heels. Bud gleefully holds his cup to him with both hands and tells them he wants to go down to the beach.

'I grew up with the surf.' Answering their eyes.

Snip looks at him sceptically. She looks at her watch. Dave says he'll come too, finding a way in.

Snip laughs in resignation. 'Bugger it, all right. You're both mad. You do realize it's raining, don't you? And I suppose we'll have to show you our top-secret place, Bud.'

It's a long walk. To get to it they have to trespass on private land. Bud drops back, his breath rasping loudly. He snags his shorts on the barbed wire of a paddock fence, can't disentangle them, finally rips them free and brushes away Snip's concern. They climb the sharp rise of a dune to the beach. Snip holds her hand out to Bud and hauls his weight up. The three of them catch their breath in a line at the top. The ocean is trapped in a small bay before them and Snip's heart lifts as it always does at the sight of the wide sea. She folds down her umbrella and lets the rain's softness kiss her skin. She breathes deep and the cleanness of the air pushes through her. Bud betrays nothing. Says he loves the sea. Strides forward. Is forced into a run down the sand. Snip looks at his back.

Selfish old bugger, she thinks, dragging them off at six in the morning.

She sees clearly who he is. A man who exists for himself alone. He interacts with other people but doesn't care for them or bother to know them or understand them and he'll never change. There are bits of his life he'll never tell her, there are too many gaps, it's his way. Snip realizes as she stares at her father that she knows almost as little about her immediate family as she does about the Aboriginal people she's occasionally lived among. It's all half-truths and speculation and misunderstanding, fumblings and blunders.

When Dave and Snip catch up with Bud he takes off his shoes and socks and rolls up his trouser legs. Snip asks him what he's doing. He brushes her cheek with a dry whisper of a kiss. Let me go, he says to her, and walks away from her. Leave me be, get on home.

An energy and a resolution stirring in him. The palm of his hand held in front of them. In salute and dismissal.

'But Bud, the rain.'

'It's always warmer in the water when it's raining.'

'But—'

'Snip.'

She knows the tone. She steps back. It's what he wants. She stops herself calling out to him. She watches, a dryness like cotton in her mouth. She's never been able to stop him. Bud walks without hesitating into the water. Its heave has been flattened by the rain. He dives his bulk at a small wave, as if his body is falling into it. He surfaces and flips on to his back, ruffles his fingers across the water as if feeling it for the first time, waves them away and then flips again and swims slowly out, strongly and steadily oceanward. No Food zips and barks along the water's edge. Bud waves again. Dave shouts a warning. Snip stills him with the back of her hand, gently and firmly across his chest.

'Let him go.'

'What?'

'Let's go home.'

Cotton in her mouth. Knowing this could be a terrible thing and there's a horror singing through her and a lifting, a great weightlessness that she cannot explain.

'We can't just leave him here, Snip.'

'It's what he wants.'

'There could be a rip out there and God knows what else.'

Bud shouts at them from the water to go home. Snip turns from Dave and walks away.

'Come *on*, Dave. Please.'

Without looking at him, walking steadily from the beach, whistling urgently to No Food.

'But—'

'Dave, this is the first time in my life I've asked you to do something for me. Leave Bud alone. Please. *Please*. He knows what he wants.'

They climb the dune without speaking and stop at the top and look back at Bud, just a speck now in the vastness of the ocean. And then a swell rises above him and he's gone for a moment but then bobs back. Snip feels an icy calm in it all, she's removed, floating, all-seeing, she's flying above Bud in the eye of the sky because she knows, now, that he can't be held and never has been. He's always acted exactly in the way he's wanted to, and most people haven't. And because he's always done exactly what he's wanted, other people have paid for his actions. People aren't meant to exist solely for themselves.

Her face curves into the softness of Dave's neck.

SNIP'S WAY

The next morning, Snip is gone from the house on the hill by the sea. There is no note. Her swag, sketchpad and latest journal have been taken. No Food is left behind.

Dave ranges the barn and the stables and the house and then the district. No-one has seen her, she's vanished. And underneath all the frustration and despair and anger and pain of not knowing, there's something about her running that doesn't surprise him.

At three p.m. he gets a call on his mobile.

An apology.

Snip will meet him in four days' time. At seven o'clock in the morning, on their beach. Before that, there's something she has to do. Dave tells her, with relief, that he's surprised she rang so soon. She says she is too. That it's something Bud wouldn't do, and that, in the end, is why she did it.

'I'm learning.'

WHO WOULD HAVE THOUGHT

In the church of plastic flowers on graves, in the coalmining district that's dying, Helen and Snip come together.

The memorial service is brief. It's an almost-empty church. There's just the priest, Bud's daughter and his ex-wife, his old schoolteacher who still lives in the district and his best mate from the pit who's now a millionaire. As they walk to the grave of Snip's grandmother after the service, Snip asks Helen why on earth she funded the desert search. It's simple, she replies.

'I know how much Bud meant to you, Snip,' there's a pause, 'and when it comes to the crunch, I hate to see you hurt. Coralie, my secretary in the Sydney office, read about the whole thing in the paper and faxed it to me. I had the money to do it.' Helen enfolds Snip in her arms. 'And I knew what you'd be going through. Because you see, I know what it's like to live with the agony of not knowing, with always wondering what could possibly have happened. I've been through that. It's hell on earth.'

Snip weeps with her mother's words. She weeps over the complexity of love, the fact that it's not always shouted. And in the loosening between them she asks Helen about what Bud had done to her long ago. Helen explains that of course Bud's attack was horrific, it derailed her, she'd had to fight hard to get over it. But years, years later she'd begun to realize it had freed her in a way, propelled her into a new life. Perversely it had given her strength. She was eventually able to heal and walk away from it all, but Bud never was. She says she learnt long ago the power in forgiveness, in losing the anger. She had to.

'Angry women are imprisoned women, Snip.'

Helen tells her that each person has in them the capacity for forgetting, it's a survival instinct that allows them to move on. She says it's why she had shut her hand over Snip's mouth long ago, stopping up the nag of her questions – so that she wouldn't scratch at the scab of her wounds. She tells Snip there can be something so brutal in absolute honesty, and she was never sure how she might have reacted.

'For a long while there I was consumed by this bitterness and hatred and a deep, deep anger. It was killing me, it was affecting everything that I did. In the end I had to find a way to let it go. And I didn't want to have to deal with your trauma on top of mine. One person's was more than enough to cope with!'

They laugh. There's a morning tea at the school-teacher's cottage and the two of them walk arm in arm to Helen's hire car.

'Are you going up to the desert, Snip? Shelly-Anne's organizing some sort of service, isn't she?'

'Yeah, but I can't be there. I've got to get back to Dave.'

'Well, well, well. Snip Freeman. Who would have thought?'

THE BEACH

On the night before Snip is to meet Dave she goes back to the beach of Bud's disappearance. The dark is sharp-ened by wind, it tugs at her, flipping away her blanket and sheet. She zips up her swag, cocooning herself in canvas. The wind blows away sleep and Snip lies, restless, on her back, looking up at the clouds racing and the moon watching. It's as if the sky is fleeing.

Snip rises with the sun and looks once again for Bud's clothes, knowing in her heart that she'll never find them. She walks to the water's edge and the remnants of waves rush over her toes and the bay sings with Bud's spirit, she can hear it, and in the thump and hiss of the beautiful waves she feels an immense calmness and clearness coming into her. She feels free and scrubbed, as if a great weight has been lifted from her.

She knows now that some parents' hold over their children can be a curse.

Snip turns from the water and watches Dave walk towards her with his arms outstretched. She smiles, and as she stands very still thinking of her love for him tremors flutter in her stomach and bowels, small tremblings shooting upwards like the beginning signals of an orgasm, and she laughs at the depth of her body's response.

She tells him, in that morning they spend on the beach, that she can't marry him.

Tells him she ran five days ago, not only because of everything that had happened with Bud, but because of a soft panic that had begun to stain the sweet settling they had in Tasmania. It was a fear that she was blunting the flint that sparks her painting. Her new life was warm and glowing and golden but achieved little in terms of creating, and she felt she had to haul herself out of its silkiness to somehow get back into work. Snip tells Dave she was in a strange and exciting new landscape but for the first time in her life she was distracted, she didn't see things as sharply or as clearly as her painting eyes usually do. How could she paint in the thick of such happiness?

She says an old Greek woman told her once that a wedding is just a funeral where you can smell your own flowers. She says, starting to stumble, that she needs her own life too fiercely. That Helen told her after Bud's service she wished she'd had the courage through her marriage to show her husband the woman she really was. And Snip feels she can more clearly show Dave who she is outside the boundaries of a wedding vow.

She tells him that what she needs, now and then, is the savageness of being absolutely alone, the freedom to go off every four or six or ten months to experience again the unknown. She says that's the odd pattern of her life, coming and going and coming. That she's like a merchant seaman, uncomfortable with stillness and settling solidly in one place. She says her way as a woman is demanding and strange and she doesn't want to inflict it on anyone. And that's why she says no to all the trappings of a marriage.

She tells Dave she wants to be with him very much, that she wants, absolutely, to try a life by his side, but with the freedom to come and go. And she doesn't know if her request for that freedom is too selfish. That's why she's giving him the option to choose.

Dave replies that he needs time to think. He strides down to the water and squats near its edge, gets up, throws some stones, squats again. After twenty minutes or so he walks to Snip's swag. Starts rolling it up. Looks across at her.

'Well, come on,' he says. 'Let's get home. We'll work something out.'